I0637099

# THE LAST ORPHAN

## CARLY SCHABOWSKI

Boldwood

First published in Great Britain in 2025 by Boldwood Books Ltd.

Copyright © Carly Schabowski, 2025

Cover Design by JD Smith Design Ltd

Cover Images: Shutterstock

The moral right of Carly Schabowski to be identified as the author of this work has been asserted in accordance with the Copyright, Designs and Patents Act 1988.

All rights reserved. No part of this book may be reproduced in any form or by any electronic or mechanical means, including information storage and retrieval systems, without written permission from the author, except for the use of brief quotations in a book review. This book is a work of fiction and, except in the case of historical fact, any resemblance to actual persons, living or dead, is purely coincidental.

Every effort has been made to obtain the necessary permissions with reference to copyright material, both illustrative and quoted. We apologise for any omissions in this respect and will be pleased to make the appropriate acknowledgements in any future edition.

A CIP catalogue record for this book is available from the British Library.

Paperback ISBN 978-1-83603-509-1

Large Print ISBN 978-1-83603-510-7

Hardback ISBN 978-1-83603-508-4

Trade Paperback ISBN 978-1-80656-131-5

Ebook ISBN 978-1-83603-511-4

Kindle ISBN 978-1-83603-512-1

Audio CD ISBN 978-1-83603-503-9

MP3 CD ISBN 978-1-83603-504-6

Digital audio download ISBN 978-1-83603-507-7

This book is printed on certified sustainable paper. Boldwood Books is dedicated to putting sustainability at the heart of our business. For more information please visit https://www.boldwoodbooks.com/about-us/sustainability/

Boldwood Books Ltd, 23 Bowerdean Street, London, SW6 3TN

www.boldwoodbooks.com

*This book is dedicated to my father, Leon. Although he will not be able to read this book, I wanted to make sure he was never forgotten. I will forever miss you, Dad.*

# 1

## MARCIN, 1982

*Alpine Lakes Wilderness, Washington State*

Marcin Piotrowski woke to the sound of the telephone. It was a shrill cry that made Moll, his yellow lab, bark.

He rubbed his eyes.

"It's okay, Moll," he said, then stumbled to the living room, the floorboards of the log cabin creaking under his weight.

"Hello," he said.

For a moment, there was nothing. Then a squeak.

"Hello," he tried again.

"Marcin?" The voice cracked.

"Jane?" he said.

"It's Clara. It's happening again."

"She didn't—?" he asked, yet he knew the answer and rubbed at his beard.

"Could you come this time? I think—" Her voice broke. "I think I need your help. I can't do it on my own this time, Marcin!" She wailed down the receiver, so he had to pull it a few inches from his ear.

"I'll be there," he said. "Tell me the address. Which hospital?"

He scribbled on a pad as Moll tip-tapped next to his feet. Now she was awake, she wanted to go out.

"I've got it," he told Jane.

She ended the call for him, and he was glad she had done it first.

"Need the toilet?" He turned to Moll. She wagged her tail.

He opened the door for her, letting her pad out into the still blackness where only the moon's reflection on the lake gave any semblance of light.

He stood at the door and waited for Moll, wondering what he was being dragged back into.

A photograph in a silver frame sitting on the console table near the door caught his eye. He knew the image, but could not remember the last time he had really looked at it. Now, as he waited for Moll, he took the frame in his liver-spotted hands and studied the faces. There was Adam—a young man, his baby daughter, Clara, in his arms; next to him, Jane, his wife. And standing behind them, as if protecting them, Marcin. A clean-shaven Marcin, with slick hair, a pressed shirt, and a proud smile, as if the baby coming into this world had been all his doing.

He looked outside into the darkness then up at the sky where stars pricked their light. Was Adam up there? he wondered. Was Adam still here in a way, part of the world but just beyond reach?

Suddenly angry with such maudlin thoughts, he slammed the frame down onto the table, laying it flat so that he did not have to look at that stupid grin on his face—that naive smile, that happiness shining from him, not knowing that soon it would be taken away and it was all his fault.

Before his thoughts could return to that moment where everything around him, and others, began to crumble, Moll barked.

He knew that particular bark. She had found something and wanted to play with it—a racoon, a squirrel. It didn't matter to Moll; everything to her was a potential playmate.

"Moll! Here!" he yelled.

Moll did not take long to heed her master's call. She returned, paws muddied with a scent of cold stuck to her fur.

He patted her, then headed to the bedroom, took out a brown duffle bag, and filled it with a few bits of clothing and a chewed-up tennis ball of Moll's.

Before the sun rose, he and Moll were sitting in his pick-up. A battered blue, rusting car that would have been on the scrap heap years ago if it had not been for Marcin's deft hand at mechanics.

He turned the key in the ignition and looked at Moll, who was already settling into the passenger seat, and wondered if he should be bringing her. He then thought about leaving her at home for a second, but he was unsure how long this would take. And besides, Moll had gone everywhere with him for the past five years, so he just hoped she would be welcome at their new destination.

As he pulled away from his home, hidden among thick pines, the lake shimmering, calling to him, he wondered once more what he was getting himself into.

Moll barked as they drove away, then stopped and looked at him.

"You scared?" he asked her. "Or just wondering where we are going?"

Her tail thumped at the seat.

"We're going into the past," he said. "I don't know how far. But far enough."

Moll turned to look out of the window.

He turned on the radio, first Queen's "Under Pressure", then turned the dial again where it picked up a random station he did not know. A talk radio station where someone had called in to complain about the garbage trucks coming too early and waking them up.

He shook his head as he pressed down on the gas pedal. Some people, he thought, had nothing to really worry about. No real problems. Then he realized, he was jealous of the caller, jealous that all day long they would worry about the garbage man when he, Marcin, thought of nothing more than what he had done and whose lives he had ruined just by being alive.

Moll barked again.

"You scared?" he asked her one more time.

"Me too," he said as the truck rumbled over the deadened ground, the light on the lake disappearing behind them.

# 2

## CLARA, 1982

*Seattle, Washington*

When Clara Abramowicz first tried to wake, it was past midnight, but the hospital was just as alive as it was during the day. Shoes squeaked on linoleum floors, sirens from the ambulance bay below her room waxed and waned, and fluorescent strip lights flickered every now and then as their tubes wore out.

There was a scent of disinfectant in the room, along with something sweet that did not belong. She wanted to open her eyes, but the lids were too heavy, and she was sure someone must have taped them shut. She wondered about the time of day and whether she had been there for days, perhaps weeks.

Clara tried again, and her eyes opened for a second, then slammed shut. She could hear the nurse, who seemed to bump into things, and Clara desperately wanted to know what she was hitting in to.

The nurse, who had been on duty for ten hours, did not care about Clara. Nor did she care for the wailing and lamenting that this patient had done when she was first admitted. She was just another young woman looking for attention. That was why, when Clara tried to shout for help, she left her alone in the room with only the pitter-patter of rain on the window for comfort.

The second time Clara tried to open her eyes was because she heard the voice of her mother and wanted desperately to wake up and tell her that this was just an accident. Just like the last time. That she shouldn't worry. That she should stop crying.

"I do think that she needs to go to the psychiatric ward," a male voice said.

Clara opened her mouth, but her gums and tongue were dry, and all she could manage was a strange gargle that reminded her of the time she'd visited her grandmother in a nursing home, how her lips were crusted, split open, how her tongue seemed too big for her mouth. Her grandmother died an hour after that visit, and Clara wondered, not for the first time, if she, too, was dying.

"The insurance won't cover it." Her mother's voice was high, too high, and Clara knew that this meant she was near to tears.

"There's the State Hospital," the man said.

"No. She's been there before. It made her worse."

"Mom," Clara finally managed to croak. "Mom."

"Clara! Oh, Clara!"

She felt her mother embrace her, the scent of Anaïs Anaïs perfume on her skin, a perfume her mother always sprayed on too liberally. It made Clara nauseous.

"Open your eyes, sweetheart. She can, can't she, open her eyes?"

"She can. It is just an after-effect," the man said. "We pumped most of it out."

"See, Clara, listen to the doctor. Open your eyes. There you go. Keep trying."

Clara's eyes finally flickered open, and her mother's face loomed over her. Her lipstick was smudged below the thick red pencil line, and her mascara had been coated too many times and had stuck her lashes together. This was her fault, Clara thought; this was Clara's doing, making her mother worry so much that she couldn't put her makeup on properly.

"It was just an accident," Clara managed. "Just an accident."

Her mother smiled, and the lines under her eyes creased. "Hush. No need to talk about that now."

"We can't let her go unless she has somewhere safe to go. Will she be staying with you, Mrs."—the doctor paused—"Mrs. Abramowicz?" He stumbled over the pronunciation, and her mother immediately corrected him.

"She'll be safe," her mother said, and that seemed enough for the doctor, who had been on duty for twelve hours and wanted to get home to a warm bed and a warmer body that had been waiting for him.

"Good, good," he said and left the room.

Over the next hour or so, Clara started to come around, and she could see the IV drip in her arm, a purple bruise underneath the needle that she knew wouldn't go away for a few weeks.

She itched to yank it out, to get out of bed, leave the hospital this minute, and go back to her tiny room, which she shared with two med students who were rarely there. She itched to get back to that room, that bed, and the things on her nightstand.

"So," her mother started, then stopped. Coughed and tried again. "So. What happened?"

Clara smiled at her mother. "It was an accident, like I said.

I'd been working long hours and just took too many sleeping pills."

"But the doctor said they found some other things too—"

Clara laughed. "Weed, Mom. Just weed. Everyone does it."

She saw her mother purse her lips together. Weed was the devil's drug to her, and no matter how much Clara tried to downplay it, it was a gateway to other things. The other things that had been found in her bloodwork, too, that did not belong.

"Look, Mom." Clara reached out and took her mother's hand in hers. "For the final time, it was just an accident."

"There were other things," her mother said, but Clara could tell she wasn't sure she should say them aloud. So there was silence until her mother broke it with another cough, kissed her on top of her head, and said she needed to make a call and would be back.

An hour went by, and Clara swam in and out of sleep, images of the past few days scuttling over her eyelids, making her wonder which parts were real. She saw herself in her room, sitting in bed, the pale blue comforter with yellow flowers wrapped around her legs, her hand reaching for a sleeping pill. Then there had been something else—another pill, orange and too large. She'd had to bite it in half before attempting to swallow it. Her head had hurt, so she'd taken aspirin, shaking out five white rounds into her palm before tipping them into her mouth.

She still could not sleep. Her head still ached. Memories had threatened to overcome her—her father, his face gray, his lips open, his eyes wide. She'd taken more sleeping tablets. Another orange pill. More aspirin until she'd sunk deep into nothingness. And now she was here.

She snapped open her eyes and looked about the room for her mother. Clara sat; her legs felt too heavy, and her arms were a dead weight. She managed to maneuver to the edge of the bed and let her feet touch the cold gray linoleum floor. She winced with the change in temperature but forced herself to place her feet flat. With a heave, she stood and shuffled to the window, feeling as if she were in a dream, as if her body was not her own. Outside, the rain still fell, blurring the car park below where a beaten-up blue pick-up sat, parked awkwardly over two bays.

"Clara," her mother said, and Clara turned quickly and almost fell as her head spun. There was someone behind her mother, a bear of a man with a heavy beard that was speckled gray. His scraggly eyebrows, almost pure white, seemed as though they were trying to hide the eyes below them.

But she could see the eyes, the ruddy cheeks. She knew the man who was hidden underneath all the hair.

"Uncle Marcin," she said, then looked to her mother, who was fussing with a red canvas duffle bag. Clara's red canvas bag, the one that was meant to be under her bed on Jackson St., had no right to be in this room with her.

"Clara," Marcin said. "You are fine."

"Is that a question?" Clara asked.

He shrugged.

"Marcin has been very kind to me," her mother said, now bringing out a pair of jeans from the canvas bag. "Very kind. I've been speaking with him and he knows about it all, about... well"—her mother looked at her—"you know?"

Clara nodded.

"So, he says you can stay with him a while. Get better. Get away from all this." Clara's head was still dreamlike and fuzzy. She tried to think about Marcin—a man she had not seen for eleven years, since she was just twelve years old—who had disappeared into the wilderness of Alpine Lakes, more than two hours away. Who had not even come to her father's funeral when she turned fourteen. A man she called uncle, though he was not a blood relation. A man who'd raised her father despite not being much older than him. A man she suddenly realized she did not know anymore.

"How long?" Clara asked her mother.

"How long what?"

"How long have you been talking to him? Papa didn't talk to him before he died. So, why are you still talking to him?"

"Because," her mother said.

\* \* \*

Marcin was not offended that Clara was talking about him as if he were not in the room. To be honest, he expected her to say more than she had, but he could see how pale she was, how thin, how the veins on her hands were too blue and too pronounced.

"Because what?" Clara was still asking her mother while Marcin's eyes roved about the room—the IV drip, the plastic cup on the side that was half full of water, the machine that was bleeping. Marcin realized he had not been in a hospital like this before. The last time he was in a hospital, it had been a makeshift affair in the bowels of an abbey in Budapest.

"Marcin." Jane snapped him away from his thoughts. "Can you give us a minute?"

He saw that she was holding up Clara's jeans and a green knitted sweater.

"Yes," he said and left the room.

\* \* \*

She wanted to laugh. It seemed so absurd. Her mother picking clothes out of her bag, her uncle Marcin waiting outside the door. It was a joke, surely? Her mother continued to pack things in the red bag. A bag that used to be her father's.

"The zipper is broken," her mother said, tugging at it against the teeth as she shoved the rest of the unneeded clothes back in. "I should have brought a different one." She sighed and pushed a stray hair away from her head.

Clara saw the bruise on her mother's hand. The veins below thick and pushing against her thin skin. She turned away. She had done this to her mother; it was all Clara's fault.

"You know I would have you stay with me," her mother said. "You know I want to, but you know—"

"I know," Clara cut her off. "I understand. But I don't need to stay with Marcin. I'll be fine on my own."

Clara waited a beat, expecting, as usual, for her mom to start arguing with her, Clara coming back stronger, until eventually her mother would relent, and Clara would be free. This time, though, her mother started to cry.

"Mom." She turned to look at her. Her mother sat on the chair, one hand loosely clutching the red knapsack, the bruised hand wiping away tears that fell too quickly.

"Mom," she tried again, then started to maneuver herself off the bed.

"Mom." She got close to her mother, close enough to hug her, to whisper that everything was going to be all right. That the past few months were just a blip. That she could manage, and this wouldn't happen again, that this time she would be there for her as she should have been from the start.

But Clara did not bridge the inched gap between them. Afraid, almost, to say what she needed to in case other unsaid things came out of her mouth.

"Please do this for me, Clara." Her mom sniffed and looked at her with a mascara-streaked face. "Marcin loves you, and you loved him once. I know it has been a long time, and I know you have all sorts of questions, and I know memories too will come up. I know it all, and I know it will be painful. But I can't do it this time, Clara. I can't see you do this to yourself and take care of myself."

"I should be taking care of you," Clara stressed, her eyes landing on her mother's bruised hand again.

"You can't. You need to take care of yourself first and then we'll see."

Her tone reminded Clara of a small child, still hoping and clinging on to something even though they were so unsure whether what they wanted would appear.

"I'll be fine, Mom."

"With Marcin?"

"Yes, with Marcin. I'll go. And you'll see, in just a few days I'll be fine and then I'll come stay with you."

Her mom sniffed again then rummaged around in her sleeve and brought out a used tissue. She blew her nose, then wiped her face. "You'll need some toiletries," she said, looking at the bag. "I'll just go downstairs to the store and see if there's anything suitable."

Her mom stood, then kissed the top of Clara's head. "You get changed now. I'll be back in a minute."

As soon as her mother left, the room felt too big and too quiet. Her mind roved over the years, grasping at snippets of memories that she wanted to forget, then landed on one of Marcin, of a happy time.

It had been a Thanksgiving pageant at school. She was six, maybe seven, she wasn't sure, but she could remember the scent of the auditorium—musty curtains and floor wax. Clara had stood in the wings dressed as a pilgrim, her hat too tight, her legs scratchy from the tights she had to wear. Together with two other girls, she'd peeked out into the audience to find her parents as those with speaking and singing parts moved about the stage under bright lights and the scent of burning dust as it hit the bulbs.

Clara could not find her parents. She'd scanned and scanned the crowd, her chest tightening. They weren't coming. Why weren't they coming? Her mommy had promised they would be there.

Poking her head out a little more, she had seen a hand raise up and wave. Uncle Marcin! She'd waved back and seen that the seats next to him were empty. Her parents hadn't made it. Something to do with Daddy being ill again. She'd seen it that morning, how his face was white, but Mommy had still said they would be there.

She'd felt the tears welling in her eyes as her hands pulled and stretched the hem of the black coat she'd worn. She'd wanted to go home. She'd wanted her mommy and daddy.

A teacher had told her to stop crying; a boy from her class had called her a baby. She'd been moved away from the wings, toward the rear of the stage, and told she would go on in a minute with everyone else and sing the final song, and how wonderful it would be and how brave she would be.

Clara had cried and shaken her head. She hadn't wanted to be brave. She wanted to go home.

She remembered how the teacher's hand had gripped her arm a little too tightly, how she had told Clara to stop crying again, which only made her cry more.

Then, she'd heard him.

"Come, Clara."

She'd turned to see Uncle Marcin. He'd picked her up

swiftly and said something to the teacher as she nuzzled into his neck.

As they'd walked out of the school, he told her that they were going to get ice cream and then go home and see her parents, that her dad was ill, but it would be okay.

Now, he stood outside her room, and even though there were years that had separated them, she clung onto the memory of how safe she had felt that day, of how she'd believed him when he had said everything would be okay, even though it had been a lie.

\* \* \*

In the corridor, a light flickered above Marcin, and he yearned to stand on one of the plastic orange chairs that lined the waiting room across from him and fix it. Instead, he stood, leaning against the wall, and imagined what they were talking about inside, how Clara was confused, tired, and wondering why this man from her childhood had come to rescue both her and her mother, even though he had removed himself from their lives. Not that he had wanted to, of course. It was just the manner in which the falling out between him and Clara's father had occurred that had sealed Marcin's fate to disappear to the log cabin he owned upstate, sell the house in the city, and live without a family. It was his burden to bear. And bear it he did.

Jane had kept in touch though—letters and calls to talk to him about Adam, about how he was changing. She kept him abreast of it all even though there was nothing that Marcin could have done to save him—Adam would not let him. But now. Now, perhaps he could right that wrong. Save Clara. Save her before it was too late and not let the past obstruct the present.

He did not think for one moment about what it was going to be like to care for Clara in this state. He did not wonder who she was now, nor that he had only known her as a child and that this Clara was someone new and might not like him the way she had back then.

He remembered how Adam had always welcomed him at Christmas, merging the Jewish tradition of Hanukkah with Marcin's Catholicism. A merging of two people, of two separate existences, and saying that they were one. Marcin had wanted to believe that was true, but he'd never felt truly comfortable, as though at any moment, that tentative thread that connected them would be pulled too tight and snap, leaving him adrift, which eventually it had. Leaving him without Clara in her pajamas on Christmas morning, her hair a ratty jumble, her face still pink and creased from sleep. He remembered the years that he'd sit and watch her open gifts, and marvel at how happy she would be from a simple gift of crayons and a coloring book, and how that smile of hers would last days and even weeks.

Stupidly, he thought about going to the gift shop and buying crayons for her now. Maybe they would cheer her up.

The paperwork was going to take over two hours, Jane said, so Marcin went out to his car to get Moll and take her for a walk. He took her to a patch of damp grass underneath the bright hospital sign. As he looked down at her, she was bathed in a warm glow, and he chuckled to himself. An angel dog.

"She might not like me," he admitted to Moll, who had found a discarded burger wrapper to sniff. Marcin knew better than to try and drag her away from it—she needed a moment to make sure that it contained nothing to eat. So, he continued.

"She's changed, you know. Not a child now. In my head, always in my head, I had thought of her as a child. The last time I saw her, she was at the top of the stairs as Adam yelled at me and then slammed the door in my face. But I saw the look in her eyes as that door slammed; I saw how scared she was."

He stopped and rubbed at his beard. "I've left it too long, Moll. I should have tried. But what could I do? How could I show my face again?" he asked her. "But these are just excuses, yes? Just excuses."

Moll finished and looked up at him sadly. But he knew it was because there was no burger in the wrapper. She wasn't sad for him.

"I get you one," he said. Then he corrected his grammar. "I will get you one."

# 3

## CLARA, 1982

*Alpine Lakes Wilderness*

The weekend before, she had been at home in the apartment she shared with roommates in Chinatown, her head resting against the chest of a man she did not know that well. And now she was in a car with Marcin, a man she hadn't seen in years, with a dog on her lap called Moll. Funny how things changed so quickly, she thought.

The radio was on and ghostlike voices of a talk show filled the cabin. Someone was saying Reagan should do more for the economy. That things were bad again. She wasn't sure about the economy, nor Reagan. She wasn't sure about much really. Was it the drugs still in her system?

She stroked Moll's fur and felt the softness under her fingertips. She was alive. She smiled and then saw Marcin look at her. She stopped smiling.

Headlights glowed in the dark as cars rushed off in the opposite direction. She watched the lights and decided that she wasn't fully back yet—wasn't fully clear headed—the lights were too blurry, moved too quickly. She felt sick.

"You all right?" Marcin asked her.

She nodded then placed her head against the cool glass.

"We can call your mother when we get home."

"Home?" she said.

"You know. My home. The cabin."

The cabin. She had been once, maybe twice, when she was younger, and from memory it was a ramshackle affair in the middle of nowhere, next to a lake. Marcin and her dad had talked about how they would fix it up, a new roof, and a workshop for Marcin. But she hadn't seen either of them work on it. Instead, they'd sat by the edge of the lake and cracked open beers from a blue cooler while she and her mom walked through the woods and looked for fairies.

Fairies. God. She must have been young.

"You all right?" he asked again.

"Mom said I had to come here," she said, her voice syrupy with sleep and tinged with the sedatives. "She said you were still family. But I'm not sure, you know. Not sure about anything."

"Get some sleep," he told her.

"Sure," she said, and closed her eyes.

* * *

Marcin glanced at her now and then as she slept, her head resting on the window, Moll almost covering her entire body. She had come easily—Jane had said that she had expected a fight, an argument at least. But after getting dressed, it was as though any energy that she might have had left her, and she'd slumped into the wheelchair that the orderly had brought and barely acknowledged her mother's goodbye.

He had seen this before. How a person gives in. Gives up. They have nothing left. It wasn't the drugs. The tiredness. It was as though Clara was letting go. He had seen it on faces now long gone, people who had fought so hard against the relentless tide of bombs, of soldiers, of fear. He had seen how, bit by bit, parts of them fell away, leaving little else than a shell.

He looked again at Clara, her fingers fidgeting in her sleep, as her dreams—or nightmares—refused to let her rest completely. He hoped it was not too late for her. He hoped that he had time to show her how to fight again.

Marcin caught his reflection in the windscreen and saw an old, tired man, and he wondered whether he actually had any fight left in him either. He had given up a few years ago, hadn't he? Or had he given up before then—way before, as a twenty-two-year-old who had no real way of being himself, and had no family? Was that when he had given up?

* * *

The jolts of the wheels as they dipped in and out of potholes woke Clara. She slammed her head on the cold glass as the car slowed to a stop. It was 7 p.m., and night had settled itself around them. She climbed out of the car and saw the light of a plane slicing through the sky, leaving a white trail in its wake. Its nose light flashed red, warning others that it was there. She thought for a moment about the passengers on the plane—whether at that moment a woman like herself was peering out onto the darkening world below, catching a glimpse of pine trees, a cabin, and her, Clara, standing there looking back, a red duffle bag in her hand with clothes inside that her mother had chosen for her.

She shivered then licked her lips.

"Do you want to stay outside?" Marcin asked, then laughed. "I have a tent."

She turned to look at him, perhaps to volley back with a weak joke of her own, but he was already retreating into the cabin, Moll at his heels.

Marcin opened the door and did not look back to make sure Clara was following. Moll did, though. She was interested in, if a bit wary of, this new guest but sensed that she could not leave her outside in the cold.

Clara saw Moll stop in the doorway and then heard a soft bark.

"Coming," she told the dog, carrying the red bag in one hand, letting it trail behind her like a petulant child.

Inside, Marcin had been enveloped by the house. A large living room was in front of her, the ceiling reaching up to the roof, and a flight of stairs to her left leading onto a mezzanine. It was nicer than she remembered. Watercolor paintings adorned walls— mostly of lakes and mountains that she imagined he'd bought from a thrift shop, painted by the kinds of pensioners with knobbled arthritic hands.

A boar's head, whether real or not, she did not know, proudly hung over the gray stone fireplace. Red scatter cushions with gold tasseled trims sat on the worn but comfortable-looking brown sofa—oddly (posh) for such a room, and it made Clara wonder whether a woman might have chosen them. It certainly looked like the type of thing her mother would have chosen. "Adds some class!" she would have said, then looked to her husband, to Clara's father, and waited for him to roll his eyes and say that they were too poor, too unrefined, to pull off cushions like that.

Moll liked the cushions and had already jumped on the couch, snuggling into one of them, yawning and making that little squeak of a noise that dogs did. She sat down next to her.

"Long day." She patted the dog's head.

"You know how to start a fire?" Marcin had appeared from a room to the right, his big arms holding a stack of logs. He dumped them next to the fireplace and dusted his hands on his trousers. "Matches on the mantel, kindling and paper in those baskets there. You think you can do it, so I can be started on dinner?"

There it was. "Be started"—a small grammatical error that Clara remembered she'd once loved so much, reminding her of when Marcin used to speak more, and when he did, with humor, love, and affection, and as the words fell out of his mouth, the errors came aplenty.

She smiled at him, wanting him to return it.

Marcin did not. "Is that a yes?"

She nodded.

"Good. Quickly. It was being very cold that night."

Again, an error, but this time it did not have the same effect on her.

The fire's heat could not fill that room, let alone the whole house. Icy whispers seeped through the cracks in the window frames and under the doors. Clara saw that the windows were mismatched, like he had made them fit, stuffing the edging with putty. He had spent a lot of time changing it from the dilapidated state it had once been in. She wondered if her father had ever seen it like this before he died. Had he patted Marcin on the back for a job well done, and then handed him a cold beer?

She patted Moll again, this time a little too forcefully, making her edge away.

"You are all right?" Marcin was now in the doorway, watching her.

She nodded that she was and suddenly felt like she wanted to laugh. What was going on? Why had she agreed to this? Had she even agreed to it?

She thought back to the hospital room, how it had all just happened. She had asked her mother why he was here, why now, after all these years, but couldn't remember the answer her mother had given her, or whether she had given a response.

"Marcin," Clara said. "Why did you bring me here?"

"You are all right." He gave a half smile. "Not so sleepy now. Light the fire and I make dinner."

\* \* \*

That evening, she watched Marcin as he cooked, and when everything was chopped, boiled, and placed into the oven, she saw that he became lost in the stillness and immediately picked up an already clean pot and wiped at it hard. Those hands of his—those hands—large, with black hair sprouting from his knuckles, would not sit still, and she realized that she had not yet seen him relax, had not seen those hands of his take some respite.

"Give me that." She stood and went to him, reaching out for the pot.

He hesitated for a moment and handed it to her, then his eyes roved about for the next thing to place in those meaty hands of his.

"Sit," she told him.

"You're a guest," he grumbled.

"And I'm showing my appreciation. You've done enough. Let me finish up. Sit down, have a drink, and I'll do something."

He went to the kitchen table and sat, and for a moment, Clara was glad for the stillness of his hulking frame. Then she saw that his hands were exploring the knots and flaws of the wooden tabletop, then exploring his beard, tugging at it, scratching at the skin hidden beneath.

If it had been her father doing this, she would have yelled at him and told him to please stop. That it was too much. To take a drink and just, for God's sake, stop it!

But Marcin wasn't her father. Marcin wasn't even that uncle she remembered from her childhood anymore. This man was a stranger—a stranger who was trying to help her even though she knew she did not want his help.

"Clara," he said. "Why did you do it? Why did you do it again?"

The question threw her. She wondered why he was asking it now, as the pot on the stove boiled and the chicken in the oven spat fat, as its skin took on a golden hue.

"It was an accident," she said to him, as she had to her mother, then turned away and walked into the living room, flopping back down onto the couch next to Moll.

He followed her and stood in the doorway, leaning against the doorframe. She thought the whole cabin would give way under his weight if he leaned harder.

"There are no accidents," he said.

"Why didn't you come to Dad's funeral?" she asked.

He rubbed at his beard. "It wasn't right."

"Why had you and Dad fallen out? Why had you stopped coming to see us? I mean, one minute there you were, Uncle

Marcin with the smiles and the cuddles, and the next, poof! Gone. Living in the wilderness."

"I can see you are back to normal now," he said.

She was fine now. The drugs, the tiredness, had left her and she could feel herself warming up now, needing the fight, needing the argument as it would give her the excuse she needed to go and disappear into something.

"You want a fight," he said. "I see it. I'm not stupid. Old but not stupid."

"So what if I do?" she huffed at him and stroked Moll too hard, who, under pressure, leaped off the sofa and ran into the kitchen.

"You want to be angry at me so you could take drugs," he said simply. "You think I am stupid. That I can't see things. I see many things, Clara, I just don't feel the need to tell everyone everything."

"So just tell me one thing. Tell me why you and Dad fell out. Tell me why you didn't come to the funeral. Tell me why you want me here now. To be honest, I don't even need to be here. I could go, right now. Go home."

"Home?" he asked.

Clara nodded. Home. Her bedroom and the pills and the roommates that were never there, and the pizza box under her bed that had been there a week, and the towel on the back of her door that she hadn't washed in a month. And the diary. And the loneliness. And the fear.

Suddenly, she was tired again.

"After dinner," he said. "Maybe after dinner we talk."

"Sure," she said and slumped against the tasseled cushions.

Marcin turned and headed into the kitchen, mumbling something.

"What did you say?" she called after him.

She heard plates being placed on the table with too much force; one broke.

"What did you say?" she tried again.

"Some things that are broken… they can never be fixed," he said, louder now, and she wasn't sure whether he was talking about the plate or about her.

\* \* \*

That night, Marcin went to bed and could not find sleep. He sat on the edge of the mattress and listened to Clara, who was bumbling about from room to room, her mind wanting to find some relief, but both she and Marcin knew there was nothing in the house to dull the pain. Marcin did not keep alcohol at home, and his only tablets were in his bathroom cabinet.

Moll nudged at his hands, which were clasped as if in prayer.

"If I tell her," he said to the dog, "if I tell her, it's a risk. She might understand. It might help her. But it might make her worse."

Moll's wet black nose nudged him again, and Marcin picked up his journal and began to write.

# 4

## MARCIN, DECEMBER 1939

*Poznań, Poland*

Stary Rynek bustled with life despite the changes in the city. Indeed, it was no longer Poznań, but Posen, a now-German city, annexed only a few months before, leaving Poles bewildered with their sudden nationality change. Shoppers shopped, harried mothers ushered their children toward the bakery, the ice cream parlor—just one treat, they said. Closer to Pijalnia Wódki i Piwa bar, older men huddled to talk—serious talk. The Germans were there, and they questioned what that meant for them. Two Jewish men passed by the huddle of Poles, and looks were exchanged. Someone said that it wouldn't be long now—wouldn't be long until the Jews were gone. Another man agreed and said that was the way it should be.

"You can't honestly believe that?" said a man with a wire-haired terrier at his feet. He smoked hard on his cigarette, then flicked it and ground it out under his boot. "You can't honestly really believe that?" He walked away from the huddle and told himself not to go there again.

Soldiers walked with purpose through the cobbled streets, their shiny boots glinting in the weak winter sunlight. They looked at people as they passed, noting the fear on each face, and looked now and then at the prettier Poles, the young girls who gave a quick smile that told them to come and visit this bar, or that café, when they were free.

Above the noise—the chiming of the clock that signaled 10 a.m. from the town hall watchtower, the rumble of tires that came from Germany, the heavy boot fall of soldiers as they walked among the natives and eyed each one with suspicion— above all that, in an apartment above the square, Marcin Piotrowski slept and dreamed of water.

In this dream, he walked barefoot in a field of rape. The yellow flowers emitted their dusty aroma, so strong, so visceral in the dream that the sleeping Marcin rubbed at his nose. The sun was high, beating down on him, and behind him, he could hear his father calling to him. He wanted to go home, back to his father, drink water to loosen his dry mouth, talk it all through with him, and try to make him understand that what happened was a joke, a misunderstanding, that their neighbor thought they saw something that really didn't happen.

But every time he tried to walk toward his father's voice, his feet refused to move, his legs were too heavy, and he could not lift them. The sun was hotter. The yellow flowers curled and died in front of his eyes. He heard his father's voice call again, but this time he told Marcin not to return, that he was no longer a son of his. Marcin opened his mouth, but sand poured out of it. He tried to spit it all onto the ground, but more and more of it came.

Then there was a bang. A bang that would not cease. He wanted the noise to stop. He wanted to get rid of the sand in his mouth. He wanted water. Where for the love of God was the water?

His father shouted over the banging, "Stay away! Don't ever show your face here again!"

Marcin woke to a simultaneous pounding on the door and in his head. Outside, the clock chimed quarter past the hour. On the balcony below, a dog barked and was then told to come inside. The dog did not listen and continued to yap.

Marcin wished the dog would stop. He wished the pounding at the door would stop. It was quieter now, less insistent than before, but he knew that the visitor would not be dissuaded and would continue until his small knuckles were bloody. He sat and told the visitor to stop knocking at the door, that he was coming, and was relieved to find that there was no sand in his mouth, just a dryness from the amount of alcohol he had imbibed the night before. He swigged from a glass of water on his nightstand and finally went to the door to let his morning visitor inside.

The boy, Adam, raced inside, sat on the wooden chair by the window, and rummaged around in his trouser pockets. "I have a new trick," he told Marcin.

Marcin yawned. "You do?"

"I do. It's a good one. It's one with a knot in the middle of a piece of string, and then I make it disappear."

Marcin yawned again and fumbled around in the tiny kitchen, trying to find a coffee urn and coffee. He placed it all on the stove and then drank back a glass of water.

"You're thirsty," Adam said.

He nodded, gulping down the last bit.

"I get thirsty sometimes, like when I go out and play in the square with my friends. We play all sorts of games. I liked the one when we played pirates. Do you know pirates? I read about them in a book, in school. Do you know about them?"

Marcin did not answer, and Adam continued to fuss with the piece of rough twine that he had managed to pull out from his left trouser pocket.

"I ran and ran, and then I got thirsty and had to come home for Matka to give me water, and she put a cold cloth on my head and told me to slow down. Do you need to slow down, Marcin? Have you been playing pirates too much? I could fetch Matka if you have. She would know what to do," he rambled, making him seem much younger than the nine years old that he was.

"I haven't been playing pirates."

"Oh. Well. I am sure that if you drink water, it would all be fine, whatever it is. Anyway. My trick?"

"Your trick," Marcin said.

"Right. So..."

Marcin watched as the coffee urn bubbled away on the stove and ended up pouring a cup while Adam was still fiddling about with the twine, trying to make the very hard knot that he had made in the middle disappear. He could not help but smile as he watched Adam's face get redder and redder, how he bit his bottom lip in frustration, how he kept trying and did not give up—not once—even though Marcin knew that the knot was not going anywhere.

Marcin sat opposite the boy and sipped at his coffee, the headache not quite subsiding yet.

"I give up!" Adam threw the twine onto the floor and sat with his arms crossed tightly. His face was rounder and redder, as if he was holding in not only his anger but his breath.

Marcin bent down and picked up the twine.

"This is a boring trick," Marcin told him. "Once, when I was young, I went to the fair and I met a man who could breathe fire, who could make coins disappear into thin air. Some even said that this man could make it rain and make rainbows appear."

Adam leaned forward. "Did you see him make rainbows appear?"

"No. I didn't. But others said they had."

"I want to do that. How did he do it? Do you know how to do those tricks?"

"Sadly not, Adam," Marcin said.

"Why?"

"Because they aren't tricks, they're magic."

Adam screwed up his face. "Tata says there is no magic."

Marcin shrugged. "Believe what you want."

"Do you believe in magic?"

"I do."

"Like God?" Adam asked.

"Not so much God," Marcin said. "But maybe. Who knows. All I know is that we don't know everything. None of us do."

Marcin handed Adam the twine.

"It's gone!" Adam exclaimed. "The knot, you did it, how? I didn't see how you did it."

"Maybe I'm magic!" Marcin said.

Adam grinned, and Marcin realized that his headache had lessened.

"Show me," Adam demanded.

"Why don't you go outside and play with your friends instead of sitting here with me?" Marcin asked.

Adam looked at his shoes.

"What is it?"

"They don't want to play with me anymore," Adam mumbled.

"Why's that?"

"They told me their parents say they can't play with a Jew."

Marcin clenched his fists. "They are stupid. Just stupid. Don't listen to a word they say."

"But you don't mind, do you?" Adam looked up at him.

"No, I don't mind at all." Marcin smiled at him. "Tell you what, I'll show you some magic tricks and if your mother says it's all right, we'll go to the *piekarnia* and get *pączki*. As many as you want."

Adam grinned. "The ones with strawberry jam and the ones with lemon?"

"As many as you want," Marcin said.

* * *

That evening, Marcin, still with a heavy head, made his way to Filip's bar, hoping that a shot of the vodka that Filip, the owner and his friend, brewed in barrels in the courtyard would wash away some of the haziness. As he walked, he passed Nowak's Book-keepers, and his head began to swim with the thought that tomorrow, Monday, he would have to be back there again, behind his little desk, calculating income versus outcome for business he knew little about. His boss, Mr. Nowak, a staunch Catholic, would no doubt ask if Marcin had spent his Sunday in prayer, and Marcin would have to lie as he always did.

He did wonder why his boss still clung to his faith in such a time. A number of Catholic priests had been arrested, academics, doctors, anyone it seemed with any influence or education. If he were Nowak, with the money he had, he would be worried that he could be next and perhaps leave as so many had already done. But Nowak, perhaps like Marcin, was hiding from the truth of the situation. Where Nowak hid at church,

Marcin for the past four months had been hiding in a fog of alcohol.

A small voice in his head told him to think about turning home—it was not worth the risk to be seen in the bar, nor was it worth the vodka seeping from his pores at work the following day. To lose his job now would mean he had nothing left, and the bar would be his only friend.

But the pull to see Filip was too much. It wasn't just the vodka he needed right now, he told himself; he needed to seek counsel from Filip, about what Adam had said about being bullied, to talk about how things were changing too quickly. How even though they were all supposed to be part of Germany now, no one felt safe and he was not sure what to do with that feeling. He wanted to feel, he supposed, normal—like perhaps all of this wasn't really happening, and that twisted feeling in his gut that was trying to warn him that things were going to get much worse would finally go away.

"Ah, here he is, I knew you would come!" Filip greeted Marcin as he entered the dimly lit bar, expecting—as always on a Sunday—the blinds to be drawn and the drinkers quiet at their tables.

But there was something off. The gramophone, usually silent on a Sunday, played Zarah Leander, an unusual choice for Filip, Marcin thought. Filip stood behind the bar as always, but not in his usual attire of a flamboyant bright red or green shirt that he had made specially, but in a white shirt and black trousers.

The tables, too, were unusually empty, with just a few men drinking quietly, their eyes flicking toward the door every so often.

Marcin sat on a bar stool and, dutifully, Filip poured vodka into a glass.

"I knew you'd come but I also hoped you wouldn't," Filip said.

"What's going on?" Marcin looked about the bar again.

"I made a deal," he said. "Someone I know knows someone high up. Says our German friends like to drink, so here we are, open for them from now on."

Marcin almost choked on his drink. "That's like inviting a pack of lions to dinner. You'll know they'll know!"

"I've toned it down." Filip gestured to his shirt and trousers.

"And your usual clientele?" Marcin nodded to a table with two men who were getting up to leave.

"I told them. They won't come back in here again."

"Filip, you're mad!" Marcin leaned over the bar and took the bottle of vodka and poured himself another. "My brain is not working right, and I want to shout at you, to tell you how stupid you are, but there are no sufficient words in my head yet to express this foolishness."

"You expressed it just fine with that!" Filip gave a laugh then placed his hand over Marcin's. "Better they are here where I can keep an eye on them," he said quietly. "Better I give them what they want, so that I can keep my friends safe. And besides, some of the Germans are like you and me, you know. Perhaps they found this bar for a reason. They know what used to be legal here?"

"It isn't safe," Marcin persisted. "That's why I came to talk to you. To get your advice. It's all getting worse, Filip, it's all getting too much—"

"Much better to hide in plain sight then, eh?" Filip refilled his glass.

"No, no." Marcin tried to make sense of his earlier thoughts. Of the priests being taken, of what Adam had said, of the bubble of fear that would simply not go completely away. But his mind was becoming numb again. The warmth of the vodka spread through his face, touched his lips, and made his muscles loosen.

"Don't get overwrought," Filip said. "You need to stay calm. This will keep you calm." He refilled the glass again.

"I should be clear-headed right now," Marcin slurred. "Just in case."

"Last time you were clear-headed, you panicked, remember? Remember how you panicked and what it could have meant?" Filip gripped his hand tightly. "We can't have that again, Marcin."

Marcin nodded. He knew what Filip was talking about but did not wish to revisit the memory of a few months ago. He did not wish to remember what he had witnessed. Filip thought he knew about the memory, about all of it, but Marcin had held back with the complete truth—there was no need to tell Filip what he had agreed to that night, as the promise had yet to be fulfilled and Marcin desperately clung on to hope that it would never happen.

"Like I said, better to be in plain sight. It is too dangerous otherwise for you, and for others. This way, at least, we have some form of control."

Marcin nodded again.

"I think you should go home now, Marcin," Filip said.

"I can't," he slurred as he fell off his stool.

He heard Filip sigh, then felt his friend's hands under his armpits as he was half-carried to the rear stairs and taken to Filip's apartment, where he was deposited on a couch and covered with a blanket.

"I'll be up soon," Filip said as he walked away.

Marcin smiled, watching him go. "Thank you," he said and

closed his eyes, feeling, finally, at peace, knowing that he was always safe with Filip.

* * *

The next time Marcin then remembered someone knocking at his door, it was not Adam. The knock came a month or so later, January, he thought. At night. Too late for Adam.

As Marcin headed to the door, he thought this was the end. That his past, his life, had finally caught up with him.

He opened the door to see Cyla, Adam's mother, standing in front of him. Her husband, Abraham, was two steps behind. Both had red eyes and neither knew how to look him in the face.

"They're coming," she said. "Tonight, they're coming."

# 5

## CLARA, 1982

### *Alpine Lakes Wilderness*

The following day, Clara woke early. Too early, and she found Moll in the living room, a blue leather book between her paws, her nose trying to open it and tear away the pages held inside.

Clara took the book away from her and patted her on the head, then realized it was not a book but a journal.

The first page bore yesterday's date. It described the drive from the hospital. Then Clara saw a name she recognized. Adam. Her father.

She read as much as she could, some of it in Polish, which her father had taught her as a child, and some in English, as if the author could not decide what his voice should be.

She knew, of course, that this was Marcin's work. That, for some reason, her being here had prompted him to write down something about his past. But the story was different, perhaps more detailed than the one she had been told. Her father had told her that Marcin had rescued him in the war after he was orphaned. That he had saved other children too—that Marcin was his family, if not his savior.

Yet this narrative was distinct. It portrayed Marcin as a young man, someone who had only recently left boyhood himself. He was following a path that she knew of herself—hiding inside a liquor bottle to avoid the reality of the situation. He was also a man with a nine-year-old friend, whose mother had stood at his front door, telling him that someone was coming for her.

She read quickly then started it again, but heard footsteps and hurriedly gave the journal back to Moll, who was surprised to receive her toy back, then scurried into the kitchen.

"Ah, Moll. That's not for you," she heard Marcin say.

Then, to her, "You are sleeping good?"

"I did," she said. "I was thinking that you could probably take me home today. I'm fine now. Mind clear, body intact." She tried a laugh, but it came out wrong.

"I cannot," he said. "You stay with me and Moll for a while. That's what your mother wanted."

Clara felt a bubble of rage in her stomach. She was not a child and he and her mother could not decide what was good for her. She knew what she needed. And it wasn't going to be found here.

"I'll make my own way," she said, pouring coffee into two mugs.

"Ha! If you like. It's a walk. And you are not well enough to make it."

She was about to turn and argue with him when she caught sight of her hand holding the mug. It trembled, growing ever more noticeable until the coffee sloshed over the rim and burned her hand.

"Shit!" She placed the mug down and turned on the tap, holding her hand under the cool stream.

"See," he said.

Without warning, a ball of sadness appeared in her throat. Her eyes burned with tears that threatened to spill over. She sniffed hard and looked out of the window at the lake beyond her reflection. A reflection that she could not really bear to look at as she knew that the face would be pale, the cheeks hollow, dark circles under her eyes, hair split-ended and dull. She would see herself as she really was, and she needed to cling to her belief that it wasn't that bad—not yet. She was still fine.

"If you want to go," Marcin was saying behind her, "you should head out now in the light."

She looked to the mug on the side, a cream chipped mug, and beside it the spill of brown liquid.

"Maybe tomorrow," she said.

"Maybe."

\* \* \*

As Marcin fed Moll, Clara took her coffee, carefully in both hands, and went out onto the deck. She stood, staring at the lake, spotlessly clear, reflecting the mountains, the trees, creating a dual image. It was perfect. Too perfect, though. She wished some sort of algae covered the lake, or at least for there to be an unforgiving gray sky. But the winter-blue sky reflected in such a way that she had to turn away from it, resting her lower back against the wooden railing, drinking her coffee and hoping that she would not spill it again.

"What do you do all day?" she asked Marcin as he ventured onto the deck.

He stuffed his hands into his pockets and shrugged.

"What am I meant to do all day?" she asked.

He shrugged again, then said, "Don't take any drugs."

His deadpan delivery made her laugh, but then she saw that he wasn't laughing. He took his hands out of his pockets and tugged at his beard, as if he thought it might come loose.

"I..." she started, ready to defend herself.

"Just don't," he replied.

"So?"

"So. What?"

"So, what can I do all day?" she asked again.

"I don't know, Clara. I don't know." He turned from her into the cabin, with Moll following at his heels.

She stood there for a moment irritated with Marcin's reticence. He had not spoken to her after dinner last night about her father, nor about why he had suddenly shown up back in their lives—but then again, she had not talked much either. She could feel the tug of something deep inside and she knew she had to stay quiet, swallow it down, otherwise she would run to find the nearest road, the nearest shop, the nearest something to make the feeling go away.

She wanted more from him now though and he wasn't going to give it to her easily.

She listened to the trees around her, whispering to each other as they shed the last of their leafy costumes, and she wondered what secrets they spoke of. Then she thought of Marcin and wondered about his secrets too—about why he and her father had fallen out.

Then, from inside the cabin, she heard Marcin's voice. "You coming?" he yelled. "I find something for you to do."

She set the mug on the balustrade and followed the voice. "I'm coming," she said.

* * *

All morning, she watched Marcin in his workshop—there he trimmed down a piece of wood, slice by rhythmic slice, the shavings falling on Moll's head, who lay underneath the rotting workbench and seemed unperturbed by the coils.

She asked him more than once what he was making. "I don't know yet," he told her. "I'll see it and then I will know." She remembered a teacher saying that once to her in high school, how when she wrote stories, sometimes she did not know what she was writing until she could see it—as if the characters unfurled themselves on the paper and made their stories known and begged her to continue writing. She supposed that woodworking might be the same thing.

At first, Clara found the rhythmic noise of the hand plane comforting. It was the only noise other than the gentle patter of water that now and then fell from half-dead leaves to the ground. Then, the noise became too much—too repetitive— and she found herself looking to the dog for some comfort.

Moll came to her, almost reluctantly, and Clara wondered if the dog could sense that there was something wrong with her —perhaps something that the dog would not like to witness. She tried her best to reassure her, whispering that she was a friend, not a threat. Although Moll let her pat her, her docile eyes were always trained on Marcin and his large hands, which never seemed to stop moving.

"I'm going to take her for a walk," Clara said. "You'd like that, wouldn't you?" she asked Moll, who suddenly became her best friend, tail wagging with such fury that Clara was sure it was going to come loose.

"Okay, but you take her leash and take the whistle I have in the house, as she likes to think that squirrels and things are her friends, and they are not. She is not very smart." Marcin smiled.

"I'll be back soon," Clara said and followed Moll outside.

\* \* \*

Marcin worked alone for the next hour. He planed a piece of oak, and with each stroke, curls of wood cascaded to the floor. He tried not to think about what he had written the night before; he tried not to remember. But the simple act of putting pen to paper had released the past like the scent of mothballs on old clothes. The memories clung and stuck like the scent, and he knew there was no way to rid himself of it now.

He started to mumble to himself as he worked, recalling that night when Adam's parents had come to him. He remembered standing there, listening to them as they begged him for help—begged him to do something that would change his life forever. He had wanted to say that he was not the right person to do this, that they should look elsewhere. But he didn't. He couldn't.

He did not hear Clara approach as he worked. The leaves had become sodden, losing that crunch that usually alerted him to someone nearby. So he did not know that she stood there, listening as he talked to himself, as the wood shavings became tight coils littering the floor like petals at a wedding. She listened to what he said, how on the day that he'd helped Adam, that was when his penance began.

# 6

## MARCIN, JANUARY 1940

*Poznań, Poland*

They came at midnight as if some tenet stated this was the best time to take people from their homes. Perhaps it was because most would be in bed, and the banging on the doors would confuse them, as they dragged themselves from their half-sleep, never fully waking. They stood in their nightshirts, robes hurriedly thrown on and the cords around their waists untied. They rubbed at their eyes as the men in uniforms yelled at them to pack a bag, to do it now, to do it quickly. They woke then, full of fear and, in their discombobulated state, complied with the requests that were being made of them.

Across the hall, as this happened, Marcin sat on the edge of his bed and waited. He knew a knock would come. That it was time. That it was over.

He clasped his hands together so tightly that he felt pain between each finger. The pain was welcome; it stopped him from thinking about what was happening. The apartment block was filled with the shouting of soldiers, the police, children crying and things being knocked about upstairs, to the left of him, to the right and down below. A man's voice traveled upwards. "Please stop!" he yelled, and then there was a thud and a woman's scream.

Still, though, there was no knock on the door for him.

He heard Cyla and Abraham shouting at the police officer, who told them they were packing too much. He heard them tell the officer that their son was dead, that he had died a month ago and that they had the wrong records.

The officer responded that he didn't care. That if they were lying, it didn't matter, that all Jews, even nine-year-old boys, would be found.

Marcin clasped his hands even tighter and told himself to breathe. In. Out. In. Out.

More shouting erupted—voices one on top of the other, some afraid, some angry.

*Breathe, Marcin, breathe*, he told himself.

Soon, there was the clatter of footsteps on the stairs and the gentlest of knocks on his door. He knew that knock. He knew who it was from and why.

Heavy treads descended and soon filtered outside, where a dog barked, police yelled for those they had brought outside to hurry, to walk in pairs, to follow and not try to run.

Marcin waited five minutes, then ten, to see whether they would return, but there was only the unnerving silence that an empty building brings.

"Can I come out now?"

Marcin bent down and lifted the edge of the sheet that draped down. "Come out."

The back of Adam's head appeared as he squirmed out from under the bed. Then he stood in front of Marcin and smiled.

"I did good, didn't I?" he asked.

"You did."

"I didn't make a sound," he said as he brushed down his jumper, where dust clung in small clumps. "We can go and tell Matka and Tata that I did well."

Marcin tried to swallow and found that his mouth was dry.

"We can, can't we?"

"Adam," Marcin managed to force out. "Adam. Your parents are gone."

* * *

Marcin waited until late afternoon to leave the apartment. Adam had spent the day sitting next to the window, staring out onto Stary Rynek, watching as life continued while his own was forever changed.

Marcin had explained to him that his mother and father had asked for him to hide Adam, and, if what they'd heard was true, that the police were coming to take all the Jews from the building, then Marcin was to take care of him.

"Why didn't they take you?" Adam had asked.

"Because I'm not Jewish."

"But Zygmunt downstairs is not Jewish, and he is gone. I heard him yell at the police. Why did they not take you too?"

"I don't know," Marcin had said.

He'd wanted to reach out and hug Adam, to give him some words of comfort, but he had none to give. What could he say to him that would make him feel better? Would he ever be better—could either of them?

At a loss, Marcin allowed Adam to sit quietly at the window. He did not push him to talk or ask him how he felt; he just let him be while he, Marcin, tried to think of what to do next. He hadn't really planned for this. He had dreamed that none of it was ever going to happen, but it had, and it had transpired in such a way that Marcin was now left with a child.

His first thought was to have a drink, to wash away some of the fear and dread. But he wasn't going to do that in front of Adam. Then, he remembered what Filip had said a while back—how Marcin had panicked before and that had left a stain behind on his heart. Suddenly, Marcin was in the memory and could hear himself begging and crying while painful screams came from other people. Then words came out of his mouth, making a promise that he should never have made.

He shuddered and tried to force the memory away. Then the next memory came of Adam's parents standing in his doorway, confusion etched on their faces—they had been so close to leaving; they had papers, they told him, but now it was too late and Marcin was the only one who could help them by hiding Adam.

His heart raced. What was he going to do? How could this have happened? He wanted to cry, to scream, to do something, anything, but Adam was looking at him, waiting for him to take charge to make him feel safe.

Marcin swallowed, his mouth dry—too dry. "We have to go somewhere," Marcin told Adam as the town hall clock chimed 3 p.m.

"Are we going to find Tata and Matka?" Adam asked in a small voice.

"No. But we are going to go and see someone who might be able to help us understand what we should do next."

"I don't want to," Adam said.

"I know. But we have to. Adam, please. Come on," Marcin begged.

Adam stood and let Marcin button up his coat. Then, Adam held out his hand.

"You want me to hold your hand?" Marcin asked, surprised. Adam was nine. Adam had never asked before.

Adam went to drop his hand by his side, but Marcin quickly took it in his own. "We'll sort this out. It will all be fine," he said, the words hollow even in Marcin's ears.

"No, it won't," Adam said as Marcin closed the door behind them.

Outside, the world was still in motion, without a hint of what had happened just hours before. Women shopped, young children on their hips; men who had finished work early sat in the bars and cafés, tumblers of vodka on the table as they smoked and talked.

Marcin hurried Adam out of the square, away from normality to the backstreets and narrow alleyways that he was sure he had been warned about playing in.

Here, the noise of the day subsided. They skirted down Ulica Franciszkańska where a leaking gutter dripped water onto the pavement below. Most doors that they passed were entrances to apartments, but now and again, a small sign indicated that inside there was something else to be found— whether it be women, late-night alcohol, or gambling dens, these were the streets that Marcin found comforting.

Adam tugged on Marcin's hand a few times, indicating that they should stop, his cheeks red from keeping up with Marcin. But Marcin could not stop—he had to see Filip. Filip was the only one who would know what to do.

"Did I do something wrong?" Adam suddenly asked as they rounded the corner, passing a tobacconist and what Marcin knew to be a front for *konopie indyjskie*, cannabis, which Marcin had tried once and immediately hated.

"What do you mean?" Marcin asked, trying to hurry Adam on, not wanting to stand outside this shop for too long.

"I mean"—he sniffed—"did I do something to make my parents leave, or make those men come and take them? Did they not want to stay?"

"It wasn't your fault," Marcin said, not looking at the boy.

"It was just because we are Jewish?" he implored.

"Yes. Just that."

"Are you sure, Marcin?"

Marcin then stopped. He swallowed and bent down to look Adam in the eye. "I promise, Adam. There was no other reason that your parents were taken. I promise."

Adam nodded. "But you're not Jewish, so that means I'm safe with you."

"Yes," Marcin said. He stood, held out his hand for Adam to take and continued on, realizing that he had just told Adam a lie.

# 7

## MARCIN, JANUARY 1940

### *Poznań, Poland*

The bar was closed, but Marcin would not give up. He went to the rear of the building and stomped on the wooden cellar doors, wanting Filip to finally wake. It took a few more minutes until the bleary-eyed face of Filip appeared at the rear window. He mouthed something to Marcin, then shook his head.

"Let me in," Marcin yelled.

A bolt was drawn, and Filip stood in front of the pair, wearing creased trousers and a white T-shirt that had an orange stain just under his left nipple.

"Bit early, Marcin. You know I don't wake until six," Filip said, yawning, then looked to Adam. "Who's the boy?"

Marcin pushed Filip into the darkened bar, ignoring him as he asked more questions, and told him to shut the door and bolt it again.

"Are you going to tell me what this is about?" Filip asked, placing a hand on Marcin's shoulder and taking a step too close.

Marcin shrugged him away, then looked to Adam. Filip raised his eyebrows, then nodded and went behind the bar, uncorking a half bottle of red wine.

"Too early?" he asked Marcin, then poured himself a glass.

"Adam, can you go and sit over there?" Marcin asked the boy. "Just over there." He pointed to the one comfortable chair in the bar, a green-covered armchair that Filip often referred to as his throne when he had had too many and liked to sit on it and recite poetry to the drunk crowd. Not that he had sat there now in weeks, not since his clientele had changed to mostly men in uniforms.

"Don't tell me," Filip said once the boy had left them a few yards of speaking distance. "He's your son and you only just found out?" Filip let out a laugh, then belched and wiped a hand across his mouth.

"My neighbors," Marcin said, "they were taken last night. Along with the whole apartment block, it looks like."

"I told you, Marcin. I told you about living there with the Jews, that it wasn't safe."

"Don't start that again. Just don't."

"Have it your way." Filip belched again. "So, this is one left behind?"

Marcin nodded. "The Abramowiczes' son."

"So, your landlord's son is with you. And you are here. And no one took you?" Filip raised an eyebrow.

"I hid him," Marcin said.

"Did you hide yourself too?"

"No one knocked on the door," Marcin said.

"Lucky," Filip said and raised his eyebrow again. "So now what? You have to keep him hidden, yes?"

Marcin sat heavily on a bar stool. "There's no way they are coming back, is there?"

"Gone to the east," Filip said. "They won't be back for some time. If ever. Looks like our Führer will get his way—he said no more Jews in Poznań. Right on track, I'd say."

"How can you be so flippant?"

"Because it's happening. Because there is no way to stop it. I have made my peace with it. They will take the Jews, take the academics, anyone they like. They'll come for me soon enough. You too." Filip took two clean glasses and poured each of them a shot of his strongest vodka.

"You said we were safe. You said that you were hiding in plain sight, that as long as you kept them drunk, here, that you were safe and I would then be safe," Marcin whispered.

"I did. But now I am not so sure. Karol and Eliasz haven't been seen in a week. Didn't turn up to work, just disappeared. It seems we are no longer Polish at all. Now we abide by their laws and what we do is illegal."

"You think?" Marcin asked.

"I know." Filip knocked the rest of his vodka back in one go.

"What am I going to do?" Marcin asked.

"I'd suggest drinking through it," Filip said.

"About Adam."

"Drink first, and then we'll discuss," Filip ordered. "Adam! Come here, boy."

Marcin was mid-swallow and couldn't tell Adam to stay put. He did not need to hear this conversation.

"How old are you, Adam?" Filip asked.

"Nine," Adam said in a small voice, his hands pulling at the edge of his coat. "Nearly ten."

"When I was nine, I loved to read. Do you like to read, Adam?"

Adam nodded.

"Say. Up those stairs behind me is my apartment. And in the living room, you'll find rows and rows of books. Books from all over the world. Books that let you travel through time and space and meet new people. Would you like to go and take a look?"

Adam looked at Marcin.

"It's all right, you can go and look if you like," Marcin told him.

Adam nodded and removed one hand from worrying at his jacket and started to chew on a thumb nail.

"I'll be down here. I won't go anywhere," Marcin said.

Adam nodded again and went behind the bar and up the narrow staircase, twice turning round to make sure that Marcin was still there.

Marcin smiled at him, hoping that his face displayed trust, comfort or confidence, but then he caught a glimpse of himself in the mirror behind the bar and all he saw was a pale, frightened man whose face was not so dissimilar to Adam's.

"Now then." Filip leaned his forearms on the bar, removed them, wiped the wood down, and then took his place once more. "Now then. What are we going to do?"

"I don't know. You know that. That's why I'm here."

"Because I'm a genius?" Filip gave a quick smile.

Marcin felt the tug at his own lips to respond but didn't.

"Is it possible to go to your parents?" Filip asked. Then, "How long has it been though? Five years? Maybe your father has—"

"My father said never to come back, and he meant it," Marcin said, cutting him off.

Filip shrugged, then licked his lips.

"Maybe," Marcin said, "maybe we could stay here?"

Filip shook his head. "You know that won't work, Marcin. You know that being here is just as dangerous as staying in your own apartment. Nowhere is safe. No one is safe and especially not now, with a Jewish boy in tow."

Marcin nodded.

"What about your uncle?"

"No," Marcin said.

"You're not still holding on to that, are you? What he tried to do for you—"

"No!" Marcin shouted.

Filip stood straight, placed his hands on his hips, and stared at his green chair. "What I wouldn't have done for an uncle like that when I was young," he said softly.

"He made it worse. He made it all happen."

"It was happening anyway, Marcin. You can't honestly hold it against him?"

"You're right. I know. I know it was. I just wasn't ready. But besides, he's in Hungary. It's not like he's right here."

"You know his address?" Filip looked at him.

Marcin shrugged.

"You have papers? Passport?"

"Maybe. But Adam doesn't."

"Ah, that's just a small issue. I'll get him one. I'll give him your surname. You'll be his father."

"Father?"

"All right, older brother then!" Filip laughed. "Look, Marcin, this is the best way. Go to your uncle. He will help you. It's safer there—others have been going that way the past few months so why shouldn't you? Just go. Make amends. I mean, really, you have no choice."

"But I'll be leaving," Marcin said. "I don't know if I'll come back."

Filip smiled. "You'll be back. We'll be friends again. You'll see—this is just something you need to do now, but it will all be fine. Trust me."

Marcin's head swirled with the vodka, with tiredness, and with the thought that he was now in charge of Adam. "I trust you," he said. "I always have."

**8**

---

## MARCIN, JANUARY 1940

*Poznań, Poland*

Two days later, Marcin stood in his apartment, looking at the papers Filip had given him. There it was in black and white: Marcin Piotrowski and Adam Piotrowski. Marcin listed as Adam's brother.

"What are those?" Adam asked.

"Papers."

"For our trip?"

Marcin nodded.

"Do you think Matka and Tata might be at the end of our trip? We'll get there and see your uncle and then we'll find them too?"

"Maybe," Marcin said.

"I don't think we will," Adam said. He stared at his hands, tightening his hands, making the knuckles shine white under his skin. "I think they will never come back."

"You never know," Marcin said.

"I know." Adam looked at him. "I know, Marcin."

For a second, Marcin thought he was talking about something else. He opened his mouth to say something, then closed it again—what could he possibly say to the boy?

"I know because I know what is happening. Matka and Tata told me. They told me that people could be taken, could be made to disappear. I'm nine but I'm not stupid."

Marcin wondered if he had been wrong about Adam—perhaps he was not as childish as he seemed. "So why did you ask me then?"

Adam shrugged. "I just wanted to see if you were going to lie to me. And you did."

Marcin sat across from Adam and placed a hand on his arm and gave it a gentle squeeze. "I'm sorry that you think I lied, Adam, but I honestly don't know. I don't know where your parents are, or if they are all right or if they will one day come back. I just don't know. But that means something when you don't know everything—it means that there is room for hope. That there is still a chance that things will be fine. I just want you to think about that—keep hope with you at all times."

Adam nodded but then went back to staring at his hands, flexing them, tensing them, staring at the whiteness underneath his skin.

"Don't lie to me," Adam said quietly. "Please promise you won't lie. If you know something, promise you will tell me the truth."

Marcin swallowed. "I promise," he said, noting how the words sounded hollow to his ears and was sure Adam would hear it too. Instead, Adam gave a small smile.

\* \* \*

In the early hours of the following morning, when the world was still lost to sleep, dreams, and nightmares, Marcin woke Adam.

"It's time," he told the boy.

Adam moved slowly, the right side of his face pink and creased with sleep. "Are you sure we have to leave?"

"I'm sure, Adam."

He helped the boy get dressed, and tried not to get too irritated with his sluggishness, reminding himself that he was nine, half asleep, and probably afraid.

As soon as Adam finished tying his shoelaces, he sat down on the edge of the bed, rubbed at his eyes, and let out a loud yawn.

"Adam." Marcin nodded toward the door, his hands full with one small bag for him, another for Adam.

"I'm coming," Adam said and moved so slowly that Marcin felt his teeth grind.

"Adam, hurry," he said.

"I'm coming," Adam whined and shot a look at Marcin that made him see he did not know Adam that well. Of course, he knew the Adam that knocked on his door, the Adam that wanted to tell him about his friends, or lack thereof, but he didn't really know what Adam was like in all those other hours of the day. Did he get angry, did he whine, did he argue?

"Marcin." Adam had the door open.

"Good. Good boy," Marcin said, then realized it sounded as though he were praising a dog.

Marcin walked quickly, Adam taking three steps to every one of his own. He knew that he was tired, that he wanted to stop, and that the blisters on the back of his heels were causing him pain. But Adam did not lament to Marcin about any of it;

he just kept a tight grip on his hand and continued to walk with him.

The train station was only a few kilometers away, and he wanted to get there before the world woke up. The train would stop briefly in Katowice, and then continue out of Poland, through the Slovak Republic and into Hungary. It seemed a fool's errand to leave Poland for Hungary—a place he had never been to—but staying was not an option, and his uncle in Budapest was the only person he thought would help him.

They reached the station as dawn crept over the horizon, painting the sky with shades of pink and orange. It was busier than he thought it would be, people bustled about, suitcases in hand, shouting at an overwhelmed ticket officer, scurrying off to the platform to find their train. Was it always like this, at this time in the morning? Marcin did not know, but it seemed to him at least that half of Poznań was in this station, all wanting to get away.

German guards stood watching and chatted to each other, seemingly bored with the daily business of travel and perhaps glad that people were leaving of their own accord—it made their job easier.

As he waited in line to get their tickets, he shifted his weight from one foot to the other, glancing at a drowsy Adam, who rubbed at his eyes and yawned.

"Stay close to me, Adam," Marcin murmured, scanning the line in front, wondering how long it would be until it was their turn.

He reached into his pocket, feeling the weight of the papers, and glanced down at Adam again, scared he would suddenly disappear.

Finally, it was their turn. Marcin asked for the tickets, and the ticket officer huffed out a response that he was lucky—

there were hardly any seats left. "Four changes," the officer said as he handed over the tickets.

"I thought there was just one stop?" Marcin asked.

"You thought wrong. Four changes. Make sure you have your papers ready," he said, giving him a small nod then waving at the next customer to step forward.

Marcin checked the departure board—platform two. He maneuvered both him and Adam through the crowd, trying not to think of changing trains four times—four times to show papers, four times that it could be discovered that Adam's were not real.

The train sat waiting for them. Adam suddenly let go of his hand and raced excitedly toward it. "Look, Marcin! Look how long it is."

"Adam!" Marcin raced after him and grabbed his hand. "Never, ever let go of my hand—not until we get to Hungary. You understand? Stay right by my side."

Adam looked up at him, shocked, and gave a little nod.

"Sorry, I didn't mean to scare you," Marcin started as the whistle from the conductor sliced through his words.

They scrambled aboard and found their seats in a third-class carriage, the wooden benches underneath sure to cause aches and pains within minutes.

Adam scooted up to the window, watching as they pulled away from the station.

"Marcin, look." Adam pointed out of the window. But Marcin did not want to look, to see his home disappear, to see his country as it sped by.

Adam soon became bored with watching the outside world and wriggled so much in his seat that Marcin took off his coat and made a cushion for him.

"Better?" Marcin asked.

Adam nodded. "What's it like, in Hungary?"

"I don't know."

"You've never been?"

"No."

"What's your uncle like?"

"He's nice. He's old. He likes books," Marcin said, trying to think of anything else he could offer.

"But I heard you and Filip talking and you said that he was angry with you, or you were angry with him?"

"We were angry at each other," Marcin said.

"Why?"

"It was something silly. It doesn't matter."

"Will he still be mad at you?" Adam asked.

"I don't think so."

Adam fell silent for a moment, and Marcin was glad of it. He didn't want the endless questions; he didn't want to think about "what ifs"; he just wanted to stay alert and get through the journey.

"Marcin?" Adam asked.

"Yes," Marcin said tiredly.

"Are you scared?"

"Why would you ask that?"

"Because I am. I wanted to know if you were too."

"I'm not scared." Marcin forced a smile. "It will all be okay."

Adam nodded, then rested his head against Marcin's arm.

"Try and sleep now, okay?" Marcin said.

"Okay."

Within minutes, the rocking of the train, the repetitive tack tack of the wheels against the rails, soon lulled Adam to sleep. Marcin found it hard not to close his own eyes for a moment, but he knew it would be foolish to do so—he had to stay alert.

He tried to imagine that one day soon, he would be on a

train returning home. He would go to Filip's bar, he would resume his own life, and Adam's parents would return. The Germans would be gone; everything would be as it was. But as hard as he tried to imagine it, he couldn't see it. Life had changed in such a way that there would be no going back, no returning to normal.

He felt a bubble of fear rise in his chest. He tried to swallow it away. He looked out of the window, at people's heads in the rows in front, anything to try to take his mind off the fear. He couldn't do this. What was he thinking?

He started to sweat and wanted to jump up, run down the carriage, and get off the train. This was madness. He couldn't take care of a child. He couldn't do this!

Suddenly, his father's face came into his mind. His father, who he no longer spoke to. A man who had gone to war and come back broken, then who had found a way to mend himself. He wanted his father's face to disappear—he didn't want to think about the pain of his family now—but it would not abate. It was then that Marcin saw not just the face, but the face firmly within a memory from when Marcin was just eight years old, riding on top of the cart, the horse, named Falbanka, plodding along, now and again stopping to chew grass on the verges. It was summer, but the sun had yet to fully rise and burn away the mist over the fields; the crows, pigeons, sparrows, and magpies had only just left their nests to screech into the morning, searching for food.

Both Marcin and his father were quiet. There was only the birdsong and the clomp of hooves on the ground to fill the void.

Then, his father turned to him, looked at him, and said, "Do you remember when I came home?"

Marcin shook his head at first, then nodded. It was only four years ago.

"You remember how I was?"

Marcin nodded again, and his father stopped talking.

Marcin remembered the days his father came back from war. How he, Marcin, watched as his mother tended to him as if he were a newborn. For he was like a newborn. He cried and wailed into the night, and nothing would soothe him. He remembered the priest who came and chanted things in Latin, then again in Polish, but nothing would calm his father.

During the day, his father would work, would act normal, if a little quiet. But as soon as it was time to sleep, the nightmares for his father would return, and the house would be filled with regretful recriminations, guilty pleas to the dead, and eventually sobbing.

He had asked his mother about it. He had asked his father, too. Yet neither one would speak of where this all came from, and Marcin had imagined that his father, while in the army, had witnessed something so frightening, like Baba Yaga or the Strzygoń, and now his father dreamed of them.

"You started to have nightmares too," his father had said. "Just after I came home. You started to scream and cry at night."

Marcin nodded once more. His father's nightmares had eventually seeped into his, and it was as though the more Marcin screamed in his sleep, the better rest his father had.

"What did you see, Tata?" Marcin asked him. "Was it Baba Yaga or the Strzygoń?"

His father shook his head. "Worse, son. Much worse."

"But you are fine now?" Marcin asked.

"I am. Sometimes. Perhaps I am weaker but maybe I am stronger too."

"I don't understand," Marcin said.

His father had looked at him and given a small smile. "Neither do I, Marcin. Some things break and then mend. Some parts are weak. Some stronger now mended. I don't know which are which. But you see, don't you, that you can be strong, you can be brave. Those nightmares you have. The times you cry when someone hits you at school, or how you sometimes panic over the smallest of things—like when you ripped your trousers that you wear for church and thought I would whip you for it—you see that you can come to the other side. That you don't need to be weak anymore?"

Marcin had not understood his father's speech, and now, looking back, he wasn't sure his father really knew what he was trying to say.

He looked now to Adam, who had curled up into a ball, as the train rocked them, and tried to understand what his father had been attempting to say. It was true that Marcin, as a child, had perhaps not been like the other boys. He cried a lot, at the simplest of things; he would not climb a tree for fear of falling. He was constantly scared of being shouted at or whipped for doing something wrong. And he knew that his father had disliked that about him.

Either, that summer day, his father had simply been trying to tell him to act more like a boy, and to stop his blubbering, or, in his odd, roundabout way, he had been trying to show Marcin how anyone, even his big strong father, could be broken sometimes, but could always mend themselves.

Marcin decided upon the latter. He let himself think of his father, of his hands like plates, how he could swing an ax, how he went off to war and came back a child, but rebuilt himself again. He thought of it all and told himself to be like his father

—to be strong, to take care of his family, to cast his weakness aside, to be someone else. Surely that was all he had to do, to take care of Adam. Just stop being Marcin—a coward.

# 9

## MARCIN, JANUARY 1940

*Budapest, Hungary*

Toward late afternoon the following day, Marcin and Adam crossed the bridge over the Danube, the river sluggish beneath them, dappled with icy rain. Their journey had been unremarkable, which had surprised Marcin. The border guards glanced at their papers and handed them back so quickly that Marcin was sure they hadn't bothered to read them. Now they were tired, wet, and cold as they navigated the alien streets, speaking into foreign ears that did not understand him when he asked for directions. Only one man, his hair slapped to his head from the rain, who was trying to sell sodden newspapers on the Chain Bridge leading from Pest toward Buda, where his uncle lived, gave them some form of directions upon seeing the address written down. A mixture of hand gestures to go toward the castle that loomed over them as if from a fairy tale, then a grunt, another hand gesture to turn right, then another left, another right.

The January dampness clung to their skin as they walked

over rain-slicked cobblestoned streets, every now and then a careless foot slipping and rolling an ankle.

Marcin pulled his coat tight against the chill, though it offered little protection from the cold. He felt Adam shiver as the rain picked up its pace.

"We're nearly there," he told the boy, his eyes scouring the street names attached to buildings for the one he was after.

"Ah-ha!" Marcin saw it. Dárda, a narrow street wedged between three-story houses, away from the main street where restaurants, cafés, and bars sat with their steamed-up windows.

Number three was the door he was looking for. He found it, lacquered royal blue without a fleck of paint missing, the brass knocker and number both polished to a high shine.

Marcin knocked softly on the door, his fingers cold against the wood. As soon as Marcin knocked, Adam took a step backwards and hid behind his legs.

"It's all right," Marcin said.

"But you said he was angry with you. Or that you were angry at him. Or maybe both?"

"That was a long time ago," Marcin replied. "I told you he's not going to be angry now."

Marcin knocked again, coughed, then smoothed down his wrinkled shirt, feeling each button under his fingertips. He coughed once more and then heard footsteps.

His uncle opened the door, his face deeply lined, his eyebrows raised in question. The door was open only a fraction, as if he was expecting an unwanted visitor, as if, perhaps, Marcin thought, he was expecting him.

"Marcin?" his uncle asked, then his eyes went to Adam.

"Czeslaw," Marcin said.

"You're old," Czeslaw said, and inched the door open a little more.

"It's nice to see you too."

"And this?"

"Adam," Marcin said.

"Nice to meet you, Adam," Czeslaw said, holding out a hand for Adam to take.

Marcin watched as the boy gently shook the old man's hand, then quickly pocketed his own.

"Shy one, eh? Not yours, I don't suppose?" his uncle asked.

Marcin knew better than to answer, knew where that line of conversation would eventually get to.

"Please can we come in?" Marcin nodded toward the hallway.

"Ah, yes, come in," his uncle said, stepping aside, allowing them entry.

Czeslaw led them down a narrow hallway, past a staircase that was littered with books on each step, and turned to the right into a high-ceilinged living room, crammed with a too-large pea-green sofa that seeped horsehair from the armrests. Books lined shelves up to the ceiling, sat lazily on an armrest of a chair, and lounged on the windowsills, scattered like petals at a wedding.

Czeslaw told them to sit, that he would get them a hot drink each, and disappeared from the warm, yet claustrophobic, room.

Marcin removed his coat before sitting, loosening his collar.

"I like this room," Adam whispered, sitting down next to him. "Look at all the books!"

Marcin nodded. "He was always a reader. An intellectual—that's what my father said. A man who thought his sister should never have married my father, a farmer."

"Is that why you were angry with him, or he you? Because your mother married your father?"

"Maybe." Marcin leaned back.

"I don't believe you."

"I don't know, Adam. I'm tired. It started a long time ago. He made my father angry too by paying for my education, getting me a job in the city. Anger sometimes takes years to build."

"But you said you were angry with him, and he you, not your father," Adam stressed.

Marcin sighed. "It's complicated," he said.

Before Adam could ask more questions, Czeslaw came into the room, carrying a tray with cups of hot coffee, the steam curling toward the ceiling.

"I thought you might be hungry too," Czeslaw said, knocking over a stack of books on the coffee table and setting down the tray to reveal pastries stuffed with walnuts and apple.

"Thank you," Marcin said.

Adam tucked in furiously and it made Marcin feel somewhat proud. For days the boy had not eaten much, barely said anything other than repeating questions of where his parents might be, or whether Czeslaw would still be mad at Marcin, but here in this room he had come back to life a little.

"So," Czeslaw said, reclining back into the armchair, knocking more errant books onto the floor. "What's all this about?"

"His parents were taken."

"Jews?" Czeslaw asked.

"Yes. But I hid him."

His uncle tilted his head to the side, considering what Marcin had said.

"What? You didn't think I would?" Marcin asked.

"It never occurred to me, dear boy, to even examine what you would or would not do. I believe the last time we spoke, you said that you would make your own decisions from now on, and that I was not to have an opinion. And I stayed away, didn't I? Other than putting in a good word for you with Nowak to get you that job, I kept schtum."

Marcin felt his face flush.

"Where's your wife?" Adam suddenly asked, and Marcin wanted to pat the boy on his head for getting him out of what was sure to become an argument.

"I don't have one," Czeslaw said.

"Marcin doesn't either," Adam mumbled as he chewed. "But he's not as old as you."

Czeslaw let out a bark of laughter. "Indeed, he isn't. Now, don't be embarrassed, Adam, I see your face flushing. Say what you mean, dear boy, say what comes into your head all the time. I fear as we age, we somewhat censor ourselves, which is never a good thing, is it, Marcin?"

Marcin ignored his uncle and asked him if Adam could go and look about the house while they talked.

"I can leave after a few days," Marcin said as soon as Adam left the room, a pastry in each hand.

"And where would you go?"

"France. England."

"You'll need a lot of help to get there," his uncle said, leaning forward to take a cup of coffee for himself.

"I assume that means you won't help?"

"I never said that, did I?" Czeslaw relaxed back into the chair, stirring the coffee with a silver spoon that clinked against the porcelain and set Marcin's teeth on edge.

"So you will?"

"I will. Of course I will. I still care for you, Marcin, even though it seems to me that you do not care for yourself very much."

"What is that supposed to mean?"

"It means, Marcin, that you will stay here. That I will help, and maybe we can put the past to rest, eh?"

Marcin did not answer, just nodded.

"There's no rush, though. No rush at all. Going further west is not wise right now. Our dear leader, Horthy, is strengthening his ties to Germany, so there will be no war, just yet, so staying here for now, I must say, is preferable for you."

"And what will I do here with a small boy in tow?"

"Well, what would you have done in France or England? Live a life. Find a way. At least staying here means I can help you, as I assume you have little to no idea what a young boy needs."

"I was young once," Marcin argued.

"You were. But you still had parents. That boy"—Czeslaw nodded toward the closed door—"does not."

"Am I not enough?" Marcin asked.

"Oh, Marcin, always one who is quick to argue! You tire me, you really do. That is not what I am saying. I am saying I can help you. Isn't that why you came?"

Marcin nodded. He wanted to try to explain how he felt. Relief at seeing his uncle, resentment over their falling out, fear that he wouldn't be able to take care of Adam. Instead, though, he stood and picked up a pastry.

"I'm going to find Adam," Marcin said.

"Make yourself at home," his uncle called after him.

Marcin was not sure if his uncle was being sarcastic or genuinely meant for him to feel at home here. Home. Could this really, ever be home?

Marcin pushed thoughts of Poznań to the back of his mind and climbed the stairs in search of Adam. He had to try to make this a home, if not for himself, then for the boy who had no family.

# 10

## CLARA, 1982

*Alpine Lakes Wilderness*

Clara stood until her toes became numb, listening to Marcin talk to himself about a man called Filip, about memories fragmented and strange that made little sense to her. He spoke of his uncle of that first day of arriving in Hungary with a scared Adam in tow and she tried to imagine it for herself.

It was Moll who stopped Marcin in his storytelling, barking at Clara for not taking her for the promised walk, and instead making her stand in the cold.

Marcin turned, and she walked in, pretending that they had just returned.

"It's getting late," he said, surprised at the darkening sky outside.

"It is," she replied, trying to ignore Moll, who danced about in an energetic frenzy. Someone would take her for a walk, surely?

"She had a nice time," he said, placing his tools back on his workbench and dusting his palms on his trousers.

"She didn't really want to walk much," she tried. "She wanted to come home."

"Is that so?" he asked. "Well"—he bent down and ruffled Moll's head—"she'll want dinner then I suppose?"

Clara followed Marcin back to the house, Moll nudging her leg. "Hush. I'll take you out later, I promise. Don't give me away," she whispered to the dog.

As Marcin made dinner, Clara sat in her room thinking about what Marcin had said. She thought of Filip, of his bar, and the strange things Marcin had said about himself. Filip sounded as if he had been gay, she was sure of that, but Marcin?

She thought back over the years and realized she had never seen him with a woman, and it had oddly never occurred to her to think that was strange. Her parents had never said anything —never insinuated that Marcin might be gay.

Clara chewed on a fingernail. If he was gay, then why hadn't he said so she wondered. And why had Marcin been so angry with his uncle? The bits Clara had heard him say in the shed had made little sense:

"We went to my uncle's. It was cold, wet. I was angry with him still, and he still said he had only been trying to make me comfortable with who I was—who said it was his place to do that? Pah!"

She wanted to know more, to fill in the blanks that he had left out. She thought of the journal and jumped off the bed and went to her bag that her mother had packed. She knew it would be in there, her own notebook, given to her by her thera-pist, who'd told her she should write down her feelings.

Her fingers found the wire-bound notebook. She flicked through the pages where she had rambled on about grief, about her life, drawn pictures and then given up around halfway through. She found a clean page and jotted down everything she could remember from the journal and from Marcin's ramblings, piecing together a picture that she knew only Marcin could complete.

When Marcin called her for dinner, she closed the notebook and felt a flutter of satisfaction. She had done something —something productive in its own way. She also felt a little excited, like she had a mission, or at least something to do that wasn't thinking about why she was there, her past or her future. All that mattered was completing the picture, she decided, and she left the notebook on her bed, adamant that she would find a way to get Marcin to paint a more vivid image for her.

* * *

As they ate, Clara tried to think of a way to ask Marcin about the things she had read in the journal and for him to expand upon the disjointed narrative of his spoken thoughts from earlier that day. But whenever she opened her mouth, the words would not come. She was frightened that he would feel she had invaded his privacy. And God knew, she hated how people had done that to her lately, so she sincerely did not want to be that person.

"She didn't want to walk, eh?" Marcin suddenly asked.

Clara looked at Moll, who was in the process of tearing up an old stuffed toy, spilling its innards all over the kitchen floor.

"Not really," she said.

"You heard, yes?" Marcin said.

"Heard what?"

"Me. Talking to myself."

She flushed crimson. "I'm sorry. I didn't mean to pry."

"I knew you were there after a while. I saw you this morning with the journal too."

"You knew? Why didn't you say anything?"

Marcin smiled. "You're interested, aren't you? You have questions now that you want me to answer. Did you think about drinking today? About drugs?"

Clara thought back. "No. Not really."

"So it worked, then." He sat back in his seat, a smug smile on his lips.

"You wanted me to know. You wanted to distract me."

"And what if I did? It worked, no?"

She smiled back at him and could see the old Marcin for a moment. The man who played games with her as a child who taught her the trick with the knot in the twine, who made up fantastical stories, who took her for ice cream and sweet treats whenever he visited.

"I'm glad you did. Thank you," she said. "But a lot of it didn't make sense."

"I tell you what." He placed a hand either side of his now empty plate. "I say let's keep playing the game. You want to know more, and I will tell you more."

"Sounds good," she said, and added, eagerly, "Tell me about Filip, about those memories you spoke about. What did you mean about a promise you made? And what about my father— what happened in those days in Hungary and why did you say you weren't strong? You said things like you were weak as a child; I would never have imagined that—and what about—"

Marcin raised his hand to cut her off. "It's a game, Clara, and it has rules. I will tell you more, but you have to give me something in return. Remember last night, I said I would tell you things but you had to tell me why you did what you did. Last night you did not want to play, but now that your appetite is whetted, I can insist that you now play by the rules."

She wanted to say no, to scrape back her chair and sit alone in her bedroom. She did not want to revisit those days, years even, that had brought her to this moment in time. She was not sure what she would do when it all came spilling out of her.

"There's nowhere to go. No harm you can do to yourself," Marcin said as if reading her mind. "Just one small question, then I will answer your questions, tell you about Filip, tell you about your father."

Clara weighed her options. She did want to know more, and she was scared that if he said nothing more, then yes, her mind would return to a darker place, making her palms itch for things she wanted, making her mouth dry, and her head ache until she wouldn't be able to take it.

"Tell me," he urged. "Just tell me why this time, why the relapse. Your mother said you had been doing so well."

She didn't know when she began to talk. Perhaps after a minute or so of sitting in Marcin's kitchen, the silence weighing on them both made her want to fill it with something, with one thing that she thought she could talk about.

*They told me grief came in steps. Predictable ones. Ones I could count on. What no one told me was that the steps weren't linear. Anger could come first. Then denial. Then back to anger. Then a plunge into the kind of depression where life didn't matter.*

*There was one step I could never quite reach: acceptance. It was always somewhere out of reach, like a hand waving from the far side of a river I couldn't cross.*

*It was a Tuesday when I relapsed. I hadn't planned it—it just happened, the way it always did.*

*This time it was because I thought I saw my father in the store.*

*Khaki trousers, tied and ruffled across the waist, a brown belt pulling them together. His shoes—the same kind he always wore—scuffed running shoes he refused to replace.*

*He was chatting with the cashier, handing over a twenty. I took a step closer—too close—because I wanted to smell him, just to make sure. Even though I knew it couldn't be him.*

*The scent hit me. Woody aftershave. A slight musk from the day's heat. My eyes closed and, for a moment, I imagined he'd turn around and say,* Clara, have I forgotten anything? Your mom told me what to get, but I'm sure I've missed something!

*I'd smile, toss a candy bar onto the counter—the joke we'd kept going since I was four.*

*But when had it stopped? Had he stopped buying them, or had I stopped going to the store with him? The memory shifted, warped.*

*No—it was me. I had stopped. Teenage pride, embarrassment at being seen with my father. But he still brought the candy home, trying to coax a smile from his moody daughter.*

*My chest tightened. I felt sick. Was that why? Was that why he'd done what he'd done? Did he think I didn't love him anymore?*

*"You okay?" the cashier asked, her blonde hair dark at the roots, snapping her gum like she'd done it a thousand times.*

*I realized I was crying. Silent tears. Bread and laundry detergent in my hands.*

*The man—not my father—turned to look at me. "You wanna go ahead?" he asked.*

*I shook my head, dropped the bread and detergent onto the floor, and ran.*

*It's my fault. The words looped, relentless, as I pushed past strangers on the street. I didn't know where I was going until my lungs burned and my legs ached.*

*When I finally stopped, I recognized the neighborhood. The one I'd sworn I'd never come back to.*

*"Clara," a familiar voice sang out—Thomas, his accent warm*

and teasing. He was outside his parents' deli, cigarette in hand, trying to sell a few pills and things to help him save enough for college. My heartbeat slowed. My breathing steadied.

"Thomas," I breathed, my voice filled with relief.

"I knew you'd come back," he said, grinning.

"So that was it," she said to Marcin. "I thought I saw him, saw Dad, and I just felt like I was going insane and there was only one thing to stop it."

She looked at Marcin, who gently stroked Moll's head, as she had come to the table to listen to Clara's tale of woe. She suddenly felt embarrassed, stupid even, and the look that both Marcin and the dog were giving her was one of pity—one she could not bear.

"I'm going to actually take Moll out now," she said, scraping back her chair and hurriedly trying to find her boots, her coat.

She expected Marcin to stop her, but he simply handed her a leash and a flashlight and said, "Don't go too far."

As soon as she was outside, she gulped the cold air in, letting the iciness burn her lungs.

Moll raced off, toward the lake, the moonlight dancing on its surface. She did not switch the flashlight on, instead following the light on the lake and the scuffle of Moll's paws on the now-frosted ground.

She followed Moll, trying to ignore the hunger that was gnawing on her stomach. A hunger not for food and one she knew she would not be able to satisfy—not out here. Her mind started to spin. She wondered if she could find her way to the highway, to flag down a car, get to some town and then—then what?

"What are you going to do then, Clara?" Suddenly, she could hear her father's voice.

"No," she said, loudly. Moll stopped snuffling in a pile of leaves and looked at her.

"I know he's not here, but he's here!" she cried at the dog.

"Hush, Clara. Quiet now. Deep breaths. Second by second, minute by minute," her father's voice said.

"You never said that!" she screamed into the night. "That's what the therapist said. People at AA. You never said it, because you weren't there! And you're not here!"

Her voice carried over the stillness of the lake, echoing back at her. Tears streamed down her face. Moll nuzzled at her shin and whined. She felt like she was going insane. Her father's voice that had come back now she was sober—his voice clear as crystal—but always spoke words someone else had said, telling her not to do it, not to drink, not to take drugs.

She knew that if she were in the city, she would be halfway to the store now, or to see Thomas, knowing that he would help drown out her father's voice and satiate the hunger. But she was here, in the middle of nowhere. What was she going to do?

Moll nudged at her again. Clara was about to yell at her, to tell her to stop, but then she saw her face, those eyes, the way her paws danced on the cold ground with worry, and stopped herself.

"I'm okay, I'll be okay," she reassured the dog.

Moll did not believe her and nudged again and then sat on her feet so she could no longer do anything. Clara gave in. Gave in to Moll. Gave in to the tears, the hunger, the everything. She managed to get Moll off her feet for a moment so she could lie down on the cold ground. Moll seemed more perturbed by this and lay on her torso, licking her hand.

"I'm okay," she kept telling the dog. "I'll be okay."

As she lay there, the soil both cold and damp underneath her, she looked to the stars.

"Speak then," she told them, told her father. "Speak then," she whispered as her breath curled above her.

\* \* \*

Marcin sat in front of the fire and waited for Clara. He stared at his hands, at the door, back at his hands. He had made a mistake—it was too much for her. He should not have pushed so hard.

He thought about what she had said, how the pain on seeing a man that looked so much like her father had sent her spiraling once more. And then, here Marcin was, thinking that telling her stories from the past would, what, amuse her? Keep her occupied? Cure her?

"You're a stupid old man!" he told himself. "You know nothing. Never have. Never will. Stupid. Always making mistakes."

As he said the words to himself, he realized that he had heard that word before—mistake—from his father, who took every opportunity to remind Marcin how he was such a disappointment.

A noise from outside made him think that Clara had returned. He stood and went to the door and caught sight of his reflection in the mirror. An old, bearded, graying man stared back at him. An old man, he told himself. Yet the words from the past had made him feel like that scared, naive twenty-something-year-old all over again. He had been ready, or so he'd thought, to tell her about Filip, about his uncle, about it all, but now felt his confidence slipping away. The years might have aged his appearance but inside, he was still as frightened as he had always been.

He turned from the mirror and placed his hand on the doorknob, ready to go and search for Clara, to bring her home, to try again and this time not mention anything about either of their pasts. No good could come from it.

As he opened the door, he felt the knob turn from outside. He found Clara, her cheeks stung red by the cold, with Moll at her side.

"We didn't go far," she said.

She came into the living room, removed her coat and sat by the fire, the dog looking to Marcin and then to Clara, wondering who needed her the most. Not being able to decide, she sat on the rug, her back against the flames, her eyes flickering between the two, waiting to see who called her first.

"Moll." Clara reached out a hand and the dog went to her, nudged at her palm then licked it. Marcin saw Clara smile. She looked at him with watery eyes. "She's a good girl."

"She is," Marcin agreed.

"I get you something?" he asked, unsure exactly what he should get her.

"I'm fine."

"You no look so fine to me," he said.

She gave a wider grin. "I love it when you do that."

"What?"

"When your grammar isn't quite right."

He blushed.

"No. No. It's fine. I like it. Reminds me of when I was little and you would say things wrong on purpose to make me laugh."

"Well, what you want to do then? Read?" Marcin said.

She smiled at him. "Sure. I will to read," she said, seeing him chuckle.

"Okay, I get you to the book!"

Their game of grammatical incorrectness continued until Marcin became absorbed in a book he had chosen.

\* \* \*

She watched Marcin as he read, his glasses slipping now and then off his nose so that he would have to push them up with his thumb.

"Stop staring," he said.

"I don't know what else to do," she replied.

"Read the book I was to give you." He grinned.

Clara shrugged. "I'm not really a reader."

"Apart from my journal, eh?" he asked, still smiling.

"I'm not going to say I'm sorry for reading it. Nor listening to you talk to yourself. It was nice, you know, to hear about Dad when he was young. He never said much. Other than you had saved him, he never elaborated."

"Wise man," Marcin said.

"How so?"

"Oh, Clara." He dropped the book on his lap and removed his glasses then rubbed at his eyes with a thumb and forefinger. "You're just the same as you were when you were a child—you never stopped talking!"

All at once she felt embarrassed then sad. She couldn't quite understand the emotions but it was as though she had lost the child she'd once been. The one that talked. The one that brought a frustrated smile to someone's lips. She had become a shadow of herself, feeling embarrassed at the thought of being a chatterbox. Why should she feel embarrassed? Why shouldn't she talk? But she still felt uneasy, like she was completely unsure of who she was meant to be.

"What do you want to know?" Marcin asked.

"You said you would tell me about Filip. He was your friend, wasn't he?"

"He was."

"What happened with Filip? Why did he tell you not to panic?"

"I did something—something stupid. Something weak. It made him nervous."

She waited a beat to see if Marcin would elaborate, but he sat in silence. "What about your uncle?" she tried. "You said you would tell me why you were angry with him."

Marcin sighed, then gave a little laugh. "It's not so easy to talk about them. I shouldn't have agreed to that. I see I was too quick to think I could put those things into words for you."

Clara smiled at him. She knew what it was like to not have the words at the ready. "It's okay. Keep reading."

Marcin placed his glasses back on but did not pick up the book; instead, he stared at the flames as they leaped their dance over the wood.

"Your father loved to read. All the time. At my uncle's, that's all he did in the first year—just read and read and read."

"What was he like, you know, after knowing what happened to his parents?" she asked quietly. "Knowing they had died."

"He didn't know then. Not in that first year. None of us really knew much of anything. We knew many had been sent to Warsaw. We heard about the ghettos, and then the camps. It wasn't until perhaps the summer of 1942 that we knew the enormity of what could be happening."

"And that's when you went back?" she asked. "To Poland."

Marcin nodded. "That year before going back was like a dream in a way. Like being normal. Working, your father going to a school, my uncle and I having some form of friendship, I suppose. But it was like..." He shook his head. "What is the word, when you are in the water but not going under? Like you are still there but it is hard work?"

"Treading," she said. "Treading water."

"Yes. Treading water," he said. "That's what it was. Really we were all pretending."

"But you didn't pretend forever."

"No. We couldn't."

He fell silent and reached out a hand to stroke at Moll, who lifted her head and licked his hand.

"Dad said you rescued so many children."

Marcin nodded.

"He never said much more, though. Why is that?"

"Because he was there too."

"In Hungary," she affirmed.

Marcin shook his head. "No, Clara. He was with me. With me the whole time. He saw things no child should see. Did things no child should do. With time, it was easy to simply say I had rescued children. That was true. But to put into words all that went with it was too much for me, too much for him, I expect."

"Would you tell me a little about it?" Clara asked.

"I don't think that is a good idea," Marcin said.

"I think it will help," she tried.

"Really?" Marcin looked at her.

"To know more about the past, about Dad. I dunno. I feel like... like it will heal something. Does that sound stupid?"

Marcin did not answer so she continued on, letting the thoughts tumble out. "I—I don't know," she said. "I feel like I knew him, like he was a good father, but then when he did what he did, I felt like I didn't know him at all. And I know it's done something to me. Like I was supposed to be one person, but after that, I became someone else. And now I don't know who I am. I know this doesn't make sense. I know it all sounds" —she waved her hands in the air—"crazy. A term by the way that my therapist told me not to use. But that's how I feel. Like I am going mad with it all. Like I find one answer for myself, or I stay sober for one day, and I think I have that thread, you know, like I have a good hold on it. And then it just slips through my fingers."

She saw Marcin had leaned forward in his seat, a look of worry on his face. Or was it fear? She did not know. But she ploughed on. "Then, outside just now, I realized I had been grasping onto the wrong thread. No." She shook her head. "Not the wrong thread, but the wrong one at the wrong time. I need to go back to the beginning and get the right thread. It's my dad. I need that thread first. Do you see?"

"I think so," Marcin said. "But his childhood, my life, that doesn't really matter now."

"It does!" she cried. "Can't you see? What Dad did, who he became and why he did it, I mean, it's all there hidden in stories and shadows and that's the damned start of it all!"

"This might not give you the answers you are looking for," he said. "This might not do anything at all but make things worse for you. You might never know why he did what he did."

"But it's worth a chance," she said. "Please. Maybe if I knew more, maybe if I could see all the parts that form the whole— like the whole of who he was—then it would make sense to me."

"Like a jigsaw," Marcin mumbled.

"Yes," she said, "like a jigsaw."

"I always hated them," he said. "It takes so long to fit the pieces together and then you see the picture and you wonder if it was worth all that effort."

"Let's try," Clara said, sitting back and sounding like her doctor. This was her only chance. Marcin was on the edge of jumping off or stepping back onto safer land. "It might not be the picture I want at the end, but at least it will be finished. At least it's a start. Isn't that why I'm here, to get better? It might help and it might not. But it can't make things any worse." She rolled up her right sleeve to make her point. Blue and purple bruises littered her arm. Some courtesy of the needles at the hospital, some she had no memory of getting.

He stared at her arm, then looked to Moll, who looked back at him with her chocolate eyes. "She's a good dog, eh," he said.

Confused, Clara simply nodded.

"Always a good dog. Always by my side. Loyal. Helps me, you know."

"Sure."

"But that's not enough, is it? Just having her to make you feel better, me feel better. It's not enough. God knows I wish it was." He sighed, then slouched down on the couch and closed his eyes.

Clara felt that it was over. He wasn't going to talk, wasn't going to give her what she wanted.

Then, quietly, he said, "It was the summer of 1942, I forget the month. I forget the day, but I know it was hot..."

# 11

## MARCIN, SUMMER 1942

### *Budapest, Hungary*

From the balcony at No.3 Dárda, Marcin looked out over the city. From his vantage point, he could just make out the copper-green of the castle's dome as the sun rose behind it. Church spires, orange-tiled roofs, and the green tips of oaks and firs completed his morning vista. He sighed. A happy sigh? Perhaps, he thought; he was somewhat happy now. He had come to appreciate the beauty of the city, its winding streets, open parks and, of course, the castle that dominated the land-scape, promising stories of long-forgotten kings and queens.

The language, he was less than happy with. Although he knew what people said, and replied in such a way that no one questioned his accent, he missed his native tongue dearly. His uncle had forbidden him to speak anything but Hungarian, even at home, so that he would sound just like everyone else.

As he looked out at the city, he thought of how he was now living in a country that had allied itself with Germany—with the very oppressors who had taken Adam's parents and so many others too.

He had thought that he and Adam should leave, yet his uncle had told him to remain here. For now, at least; although some restrictions were placed on Jews, and rationing had been introduced, Germany had left her quite alone.

"They'll tolerate Jews and us, as long as we keep our heads down. The Gestapo doesn't operate here the way it does in Poland," his uncle had told him.

Despite his fears, Marcin had listened to his uncle, his uncle who disappeared at odd times of the day and said he had gone to meetings. Meetings which Marcin had asked him about—what were they; who was he meeting? But his uncle always told him that it was better he didn't know, and Marcin was happy to stay in the dark.

Adam had seemingly thrived in the past year and a half, delighting in the language, the new corners of the city to explore, and his daily lessons with Czeslaw, while Marcin worked for a friend of his uncle as a bookkeeper once more, tallying numbers that he had little care for.

Adam had grown too. No longer a little mite of a nine-year-old, he was now twelve, and almost as tall as Marcin. His face had lost that childish roundness and was becoming longer, more defined, reminding Marcin of Adam's father, Abraham. Although—he never told Adam this—he was growing up to look like his father, scared as he was that this would open up a new wound.

As he sat and watched the world wake up, he could hear Adam bustling about downstairs, talking loudly with his uncle about what they would learn that day and whether Adam would soon be able to go to school. He wished he had the same relationship with Adam that Czeslaw had. He had tried in those first few months to be the friend that he had always been to Adam, that neighbor who knew a few magic tricks, who would buy him ice cream, but Czeslaw had been right. Adam had lost his parents and he desperately needed guidance, love, care—things that Marcin was unsure how, or was unwilling, to provide.

It was Czeslaw whom Adam cried for in the middle of the night, plagued by nightmares of his parents, as Marcin stood awkwardly in the boy's bedroom doorway, chewing on his bottom lip, wondering what he should do or say. Czeslaw always knew what to do. He would hold Adam, whisper words of comfort, tell him stories that made him smile, laugh even, before he would fall back to sleep again.

That wasn't to say that Adam and Marcin did not spend time together. They both found the city's cobbled streets intriguing, and would set out on the weekend with no place in mind and see where they ended up. They went to the old spa, to the botanical gardens, wandered around the castle and found tiny bookshops, delighting when they were able to get cheap books.

But on those days, no matter how hard Marcin tried to get Adam to open up, just like he did with Czeslaw, Adam would change the subject, instead asking for sweet treats or insisting they visit a bookstore again.

"Marcin!" Adam's voice sang now. "Breakfast!"

Marcin reluctantly left his view and meandered downstairs, making his way out into the scrap of a garden that Czeslaw insisted was where one ate during the summer months.

Although a small garden, his uncle obviously had green thumbs, for pink roses roamed on trellises, placed against the red brick walls that encircled the patch of green lawn, which itself was perfectly cut and watered each day, but was never to be trodden on. And terracotta pots holding blue, white, yellow, and red flowers dotted the small space. Marcin had asked what the flowers were but could never remember their names. To him, they all looked the same, and his uncle told him he was stupid for saying that.

Adam and Czeslaw sat at the small wrought-iron table. Marcin pulled out a chair and sat, hating how the metal felt on his backside.

"You need to get cushions," he said grumpily.

"You have been saying that for months. You want them, you buy them," his uncle said between a mouthful of bread and sausage.

Marcin ignored him and asked how Adam had slept, if any more nightmares had appeared.

"No. I'm fine," Adam said. "Czeslaw says I can stay home alone this evening when you both go out."

"Go out? Where?" Marcin looked at his uncle.

"Somewhere we both need to be," he said.

"Care to elaborate?"

Czeslaw waved a hand dismissively. "You'll see. It's a surprise."

"I don't like surprises," Marcin said.

"Ha! You sound like a child when you say that."

Marcin did not want to argue with his uncle in front of Adam, and had for the past year tried to swallow down any irritation with the man, instead trying to talk with him as a friend. But there was always an undercurrent of the argument from years ago that tainted their interactions, each of them looking to the other to bring it up so that perhaps they could move past it once and for all.

They were both as stubborn as each other, and even though

both wanted the same, neither would budge in this strange game they had concocted.

"Marcin, I think I am ready for school. Czeslaw agrees. But he said that you have to agree too." Adam cut into the silence.

"I don't know," Marcin said.

"It's safe, it's a Catholic school," Czeslaw said.

"What if he slips up?" Marcin asked. "It's getting worse here. Even though you say it is safe, it's getting worse, and you know it."

"It is. Indeed, it is. But the restrictions are still relatively few. Jews are still safe here. In fact, it will be a part of our excursion this evening. A hint that will now ruin your surprise," his uncle said.

"I don't know," Marcin said again. The thought of Adam being at home with his uncle while he was at work made him feel as though he was doing his duty to keep him safe. If Adam were to go to school, and if what had happened in Poland were to eventually happen here, there was always a chance that Adam would be outed as a Jew, even with Marcin's surname.

"Please, Marcin," Adam pleaded. "I need some friends. I mean, you're both fine." He grinned. "But I'm young and—"

"Yes, we're old," Czeslaw interrupted. "We know."

"I'll think about it. See how you go on your own this evening first," Marcin said.

Adam's smile dropped a little, but he agreed that he would show Marcin that he was fine and could be trusted.

"It's not really you I worry about," Marcin said as he stood and went to the kitchen for more coffee.

When he returned, Adam was mumbling something to Czeslaw and stopped when Marcin sat.

"What are you talking about?" Marcin asked.

"He was just telling me about resistance fighters," Czeslaw said.

"In all of the wars," Adam said, "there were always people resisting the enemy."

"Is that so?" Marcin said.

"It is. I read it."

"And?" Marcin said.

"And, Adam was asking whether there were resistance fighters in Poland. Trying to stop the Germans," Czeslaw said.

"I don't see why you need to know that." Marcin sipped at his coffee, wondering how he could change the conversation. He did not want to think about Poland, about Adam's parents, about what was happening.

"Aren't you angry?" Adam suddenly stood up, his thigh knocking the table, rattling the coffee cups and plates.

"Adam," Marcin said.

"No! I'm angry. Czeslaw tells me about what is happening and I can't believe it—I can't stop thinking about it. But you pretend like nothing is wrong!"

Marcin did not know what to say. Adam had never shown a temper before, never shouted at him.

"Adam," Marcin tried again.

But Adam ignored him and stormed off into the house.

"What brought that on?" Marcin asked. "What have you been saying to him?"

"He asks questions and I answer, that's all. It's normal that he would feel anger. Most of it comes from the feeling of helplessness," his uncle said. "Don't you feel like that sometimes, Marcin?"

His uncle did not wait for an answer, simply picked up his coffee cup and went into the house, leaving Marcin alone, wondering what on earth had just happened.

* * *

That evening, Marcin returned from work, and before he could even get into the house, his uncle ushered him back out. "You're late," his uncle reprimanded, slamming the door behind him.

"The heat," Marcin said, his voice laced with tiredness.

"Pah! A young man like you shouldn't be tired from the heat!"

"I need to check on Adam," Marcin said in Polish and made to push past his uncle to reopen the door.

"Ah, Hungarian please! And no, you don't. He's fine. I told him not to open the door to anyone. He's in the living room reading. Leave him be."

Marcin was too hot to argue. The office where he worked was stuffy at the best of times, but in this summer heat it baffled his brain, like the flies that bounced against windows trying to find the slit to get out.

Then, the walk home, usually something which he enjoyed, walking over the bridge from the hustle and bustle of Pest toward Buda, the castle on the hill guiding his way home, and with each step the city became quieter, the streets narrower, bringing with it a sense of peace. But today it seemed as though the business of Pest had overcome Buda. He was sure that was not the case, but people moved slower, tempers were fraying in the summer fever and everyone seemed to be unable to walk without bumping shoulders, irritating each other.

As the bells of Matthias Church tolled seven, Marcin and Czeslaw made their way toward the castle, the Danube to their left, sunken from the heat, bringing with it a heady scent of mud and sewage.

For a moment, Marcin thought they were going to walk up

the hill to the castle, but then his uncle turned right, up a narrow alley, and then stopped outside a wine merchant's. Marcin's heart sang. They were going to sit and drink wine— that was the surprise! Thank God. He could already taste a crisp white on his tongue, or perhaps a thick red that would numb his thoughts.

But his uncle did not open that door. Instead he turned to the side alley where another smaller door sat.

"It's open," Marcin said, waving his hand at the wine merchant's main door.

"This way."

"But..."

"Marcin, come." Czeslaw knocked four times—two quick, one slow, then one more—and the door creaked open. A priest in a black cassock nodded at Czeslaw and then gave Marcin a quick glance.

"This him?" the priest asked Czeslaw.

"It is."

The priest raised his eyebrows, then stood aside. "Come, both of you. The others are here."

As soon as the door closed, Marcin thought they were in complete darkness. It was only when his eyes adjusted that he could see a small flickering light below them.

"Watch your step," his uncle told him as he descended toward the light.

Marcin followed, placing his hand on a cold stone wall for guidance. The further they went, the air shifted, becoming cooler and damper with each step. Marcin welcomed the air and wanted to stand for a moment, his head pressed against the stone, and just have a minute to himself, to readjust, to try and think what his uncle was up to now. Were these the meetings his uncle had mentioned?

What kind of meetings were they? One where wine was drunk, and what else?

Soon they reached the end of the staircase and Marcin found himself in a cavernous room where dusty bottles of wine stored on racks covered each wall. In the center sat a table and chairs and sitting on these chairs were five men, two dressed in the same black cassocks as the priest who had opened the door, one man with a large mustache and three-day-old stubble on his cheeks whose red spider-veined face, illuminated by the candles on the table, hinted that he might be the wine merchant.

The other two men were as unremarkable as Marcin. Dark brown hair, slim, with faces that you would see once and never remember again.

Czeslaw pulled out a chair and nodded to Marcin. "Sit," he said.

Marcin sat and looked at the men who seemed uninterested in him and spoke to each other about the weather, the fact that prices had gone up again and how rain might come soon.

"Now then." The priest who had opened the door for them took a seat at the head of the table. "Introductions, I believe, are necessary. Everyone, you know Czeslaw, and this is his nephew, whom you have heard about, Marcin."

"Speaks Hungarian now, eh? Took you long enough!" the bushy-mustached man said.

"Please ignore him," the priest said. "That is László. He drinks too much and says too much but it is his cellar so we must put up with him!" The others laughed and László stubbed out his cigarette on the stone floor. "I am Father Aldony, that is Father Banjok and Father Elek," he continued, as he pointed to the two other priests, one short and rotund, the other thin with a crop of white hair and bushy white eyebrows. "And these two"—Father Aldony pointed to the last two men—"are Piotr and Witold, compatriots of yours. From Warsaw."

"From the ghetto," one of the men said. "Piotr." He nodded at Marcin. "Witold here is my cousin. He does not speak, almost completely deaf."

Marcin nodded hello at Witold, who smiled back, displaying two missing front teeth.

"And of course, Janos. Or should I say, Professor Janos?" Father Aldony said.

Marcin looked about him but could not see anyone else in the room. Then, there was someone, half swathed in shadows. A red glow from his cigarette illuminated his face, allowing Marcin to make out a thin face, a long nose, and narrow lips.

"*Jó estét*," the shadowed Janos said.

Marcin returned the greeting, expecting the man to say more, or at least come closer to the candlelight on the table, but he stayed hidden.

"Now. Marcin, your uncle has insisted we invite you here, and we were more than happy to upon hearing about you saving that young boy, and how you have so seamlessly integrated yourself into Hungarian life."

He paused, waiting for Marcin to respond.

"I don't understand," he answered.

"Your uncle hasn't told you about his activities?" Father Aldony asked.

"He said he went to meetings."

Father Aldony laughed. "Meetings, eh? Well, we do have meetings. Mostly to do with helping others. People stuck in Poland, people and children who need our help to escape."

"Resistance?" Marcin said. "This is a resistance group?"

"You sound disappointed," Janos said from the shadows. "What were you expecting? An army?"

"No, no, you misunderstand," Marcin tried to explain, embarrassment making his Hungarian accent wobble. "I didn't know what to expect. I didn't know we were coming here."

"He's not very good at reading between the lines," Czeslaw said with a half laugh. "I thought you would have figured it out yourself when I told you we were going somewhere this evening and it was about our current situation that we find ourselves in."

"I—well, I was working today. I didn't have too much time to think." He stumbled over the words, embarrassment slowly being replaced by anger at his uncle for making him sound and look foolish.

"No matter," Father Aldony said. "We are part of a wider network, you understand. A network of sympathetic souls, some Hungarian, some Polish, some Jewish, some priests, but all of us with a common goal. And that goal is to aid as many people as we can that find themselves in the hands of the enemy. Piotr and Witold here came to us a few months ago and told us of the conditions many find themselves in the ghettos dotted about Poland. They have described to us the horror, the starvation and then the deportations."

"Deportations? To where?" Marcin asked.

"To camps," Piotr said, his Hungarian still stilted. "On trains. No food, no water. All in cars made for animals. Crates. Like animals. Witold and I escaped. Jumped from the train. Many others did too. Many died."

"And children too," Father Aldony added. "Children thrown from the trains by their parents, trying to save them from whatever awaits them at these work camps."

"Death," Piotr said. "They will work them to the death."

A general hum of agreement came from all the men, with the rotund priest crossing himself.

"Here in Hungary, Jews and non-Jews have been relatively safe. Through the efforts of Polish refugee committees, many have crossed the border to this country. But we must do more. It is not refugees who we must help now, but those unable to reach the safety of our borders. And for us, for this group, we are tasked with aiding orphans, or children who have been sent by their parents to safety. There are others who are assisting adults to escape, but we, primarily, with the grace of God, are here to help those who cannot help themselves—the children."

Marcin took a moment to digest what the priest said. Children, just like Adam, being thrown from trains, being rounded up and kept in ghettos. Children with no parents, or those with parents who wanted to save them, just like Adam's parents. He swallowed.

"I don't know how I can help," he said, feeling inadequate and afraid, as he so often did.

"Your uncle seems to think you would be a good fit," László said, tucking a cigarette underneath his large mustache and lighting it. "He says"—he let out a stream of smoke—"that you could go back, help Janos, Piotr, and Witold here get those children from the tracks. From the ghettos, maybe, and bring them here. And then me and these robed men will get them to orphanages, get them papers, keep them safe."

Marcin looked to his uncle, who stared at the tabletop.

"I don't think I'm the right man for this," Marcin said, still staring at his uncle, waiting for him to agree. His uncle knew Marcin—really knew him—knew how he wasn't brave, was prone to feeling too much and allowing it to come forth. God, that was why they had fallen out in the first place!

"I disagree," Father Aldony said. "You rescued one boy, why not rescue another, and maybe another?"

"I didn't rescue him." Marcin could feel the creep of shame coming from his gut.

"Then what did you do, Marcin?" His uncle finally spoke.

Marcin tried to think. How could he explain it all to them? How could he really tell them what happened—that he had had no choice, that it had just happened to him. Then a thought came to him. It hadn't just happened to him; he had been a cog in the wheel, he had been a part of the beginning and the end, he had...

"I think you will be fine." Father Aldony interrupted his whirring thoughts.

Marcin wanted to argue, but his mouth was dry, the cold cellar suddenly warm and claustrophobic.

"Do we have an update, Janos?" Father Aldony asked the shadow, who took a step forward and placed a map on the table.

"We have managed to get twenty children this month," Janos began. "Railways from Warsaw and Radom. We have a corridor." He pointed at a line on the map. "We have people all over sympathetic to our cause. They move them on trains from Przemyśl, Košice. They bring them to us in Eger, two hours from the city, and then we take the children to Buda, get them papers and get them into orphanages, or find families willing to take them.

"But there are not enough people on the ground still. I have been into the Slovak Republic twice, Poland five times, to help with getting the children and bringing them here. We need more men. More help."

The rotund priest—what was his name again?—began to

talk about false baptismal papers, codes involving flour sacks, and train schedules.

He couldn't keep track of it all, just kept looking at Janos's hands as his fingers flicked across the map, pointing to Krakow, to Warsaw again. As the men spoke, his mind went back to the night Adam's parents had come to him, to ask him for his help. He had agreed but deep down inside he knew the real reason why he had agreed, and it had nothing to do with being brave. He should tell them all, get it off his chest once and for all. Explain who he was, how he was nothing and all he had ever done was leave a trail of disappointment in his wake—his parents, his uncle, Filip, and now Adam. He couldn't be trusted, couldn't be the person they sorely wanted him to be.

"So you see," Janos said. "Marcin. Do you see?"

"What?" Marcin shook his head.

"You are from Poznań, yes? You speak German, Polish and now Hungarian. You see the benefit here, how useful that can be as a courier."

"It's dangerous," Marcin argued weakly, sounding like Adam, if not a child much younger who knew they had already lost the fight. "If the Arrow Cross finds out—or the Gestapo—"

"That's why we keep changing our routes," László said, then sighed. "Have you not been listening? I thought Witold here was the only one who was deaf!"

"Come now, László," Czeslaw said. "It's a lot for him to digest."

"Still." László harumphed. "I think my niece who's five could pick it up quicker than him."

"Enough!" Piotr abruptly said, then looked to Marcin and spoke to him now in Polish. "I know you are scared. I was too. Still am. Witold here would tell you he is scared, but he can't. So I need you to understand, Marcin. You left last year, yes? You did not have the enjoyment of spending time in a ghetto, being interrogated, watching your family die from starvation, beatings, and disease? You did not have the pleasure of learning about the deportations to camps, and the rumors about what happens there. You got out. You got out with Adam. Think of all the other children, just like him, younger even, with no one. Not just Jews, if that helps your thinking. Polish children too. Ones with blond hair, taken from their parents and sent deep into the Reich to new, German parents. That could be happening to your family. Your uncle said that neither of you speaks to your parents, but how do you know that things are not happening to them too? Wouldn't you want someone to help them? That's what we are doing. We are helping the most vulnerable. They are children, for God's sake. You can do it, Marcin. And if you don't, it will forever be a stain upon your soul." Piotr stopped and looked to the others. "Apologies. My Hungarian not good enough to say it all, so you can all understand."

The silence that followed was suffocating. Marcin stared at the table, at the flickering candles. Then he looked at the map —so many pins, red and yellow and blue. Each a name. A child.

"How many have you saved?" he asked.

Janos answered. "Since January? Four hundred and twelve. But we've lost one hundred and seventy-nine."

"To the Germans?"

"No," he said softly. "To time. We were too slow. Or not careful enough."

Marcin lowered his head, then took a deep breath and nodded once.

# 12

## MARCIN, SUMMER 1942

### *Budapest, Hungary*

As he left the cellar, the evening air hit Marcin like a warm slap. He gulped in the soupy air, hoping it would somehow clear his thoughts. If anything, the transition from the cold to the warmth made him feel even more discombobulated, but it did not seem to have the same effect on his uncle.

Czeslaw walked ahead, chewing on a piece of long grass he had picked as if he were out for a stroll in the countryside. He did not speak to Marcin until they reached Castle Hill, then he sat on a stone bench underneath a shady lime, its branches full of white flowers, their honeyed scent stuck in the dense evening air.

"Sit," Czeslaw commanded.

Marcin sat, too, and looked to the Danube, to the buildings of Pest beyond, and tried to make sense of what he had agreed to do.

"You're nervous," his uncle said.

"No. Not nervous," Marcin replied.

"What is it then?"

"I feel you should have talked to me before we went. It was an ambush. There was little room for me not to agree."

"I thought you would want to agree. I mean, over a year ago you turn up with a child you rescued, so, tell me, Marcin, what was I to think?"

"I didn't rescue him," Marcin said quietly.

"So what did you do then?"

Marcin shook his head. "Nothing."

"I can see that something is weighing heavily on you," his uncle said, his tone softer than Marcin had heard it for years. "For the past year and a half, we have been dancing around each other, taking care of Adam, speaking to one another, but never really saying anything. I think you need to say something, Marcin. Let it out."

"You've said those words to me about something else before."

"I have?"

"Don't be obtuse," Marcin said.

"All right. No need to get angry."

"I'm not angry." Marcin sighed heavily and leaned back against the stone bench, tipping his head back slightly to look at the canopy of leaves above.

"So what are you? Not nervous. Not angry. Not scared. So what?"

Marcin let the question linger for a moment. Then he closed his eyes and let the words come out. "I was angry at you. For years, for what you did."

"I know, and I said I'm sorry—"

"No, please. Let me talk," Marcin interrupted. "Father

always said I was useless on the farm, always making mistakes. That I was stupid. Said I was worse than a girl. Always telling me to walk differently, straighter, be stronger, stop crying over things. I tried, I did. And I was so grateful to you when you offered to pay for me to leave the farm, to go away to the city. But then... that thing happened."

Marcin stopped. He couldn't speak about this still.

"The thing with the boy." His uncle said it for him. "The thing that sent your father into a rage, hitting you with a belt so many times that you still carry those scars? The thing that happened that made your mother send for me to collect you and take you away, and for your father to stand on the doorstep and scream at you and me never to return..."

"Yes." Marcin swallowed hard. "That thing that happened."

"And then there was the other thing," Czeslaw said. "The thing that you railed at me about. Blamed me. And this time it was you standing on a doorstep, telling me that you never wanted to see me again."

"Yes," Marcin said.

"I didn't make you who you are," Czeslaw said and placed a hand on his arm. "I hope you can see that now."

Marcin did not agree nor disagree but let his uncle keep his hand on him.

"I tried to show you, you could be yourself," his uncle said tiredly. "Education, dinners, music. And I introduced you to Filip, with his bar, so that you would feel more comfortable— so that you would feel as though you could be you and no one would persecute you for it."

"And I believed you," Marcin said. "For a time at least, I did."

"Then you went home and tried to make your parents understand. Tried to bridge a gap. But it didn't work."

Marcin shook his head and felt a tear escape. He swallowed the rest back. No, he would not cry, would not be that Marcin.

He could hear his father's voice as he sat with Czeslaw. "You're just like him! *Homoś!* And you come here and think we will say you are normal? Look at you!" His father had laughed nastily. "All dressed up in a suit, thinking you are better than us. Thinking that your lifestyle and that of your uncle's is acceptable."

Marcin had looked, with tear-filled eyes, to his mother, desperately wanting her to look back at him, to give him some words of comfort. It had been she, after all, who had sent for his uncle, her brother. She must have known, must have thought it was the right thing to do.

But she would not look at him, would not speak to him.

"See what you are doing to your mother? What you have done to all of us? People laugh at us, gossip. There goes Piotrowski, couldn't have a daughter, so made his son into one!"

"I just wanted—" Marcin began.

"Look at you crying," his father railed on. "Like a woman. Always soft, always fucking useless as a man. Your uncle has made you worse, made you what you are. If you had stayed here, maybe you would have been able to grow out of it— grown into a proper man. But no, just like that uncle of yours. So why don't you go back to him and tell him thank you for breaking his sister's heart, for ruining our lives!"

His father pushed him out of the house, so that Marcin skidded and fell backwards. It was then his mother came to his aid. She knelt down beside him and he could see how pale, fragile, she looked.

"Matka—" he started.

"Go now," she said. "Go and don't come back."

She stood and went back inside, his father looming over him once more.

"She's dying. You can see it, eh? The doctor says it can't be cured. Every day she wastes away a little more. Speaks less, can't eat." His father had bent down and placed his face close to Marcin's. "And you did this to her. You and that *homoś* of an uncle. You live with that. You live with the fact that this woman, who brought you into the world, has had her life ruined by you both," he'd spat.

Marcin now tried to come back from that memory, that feeling of being wrong, of guilt, of shame, of hating himself. He fixed his eyes on the river and concentrated on breathing in and out.

"I understand why you were angry at me," his uncle said. "And I shouldn't have left. Shouldn't have let you push me away. But I was hurt by what you said—how you believed your parents to be right, how you thought I had turned you into who you are. I was angry and thought it best I leave, let you find your own way so that you could not blame anyone else for what you became. And for that, I am sorry, Marcin. I should have stayed, should have kept taking care of you."

"I'm sorry too." Marcin let the words out and felt his shoulders sag a little with the relief. "I just wasn't sure who I was. What I wanted. I was angry with everyone."

"But you know who you are now?"

"I still don't know." Marcin looked at his uncle and gave a weak smile. "Some days I am the same angry, confused child who cries and gets too emotional. Some days I am convinced that I am strong and know who I am, what I am. Then some days, I walk about and feel like I don't belong in this world— like I don't know how to exist..." He trailed off.

"I think you'll find that's called the human condition." His uncle chuckled. "We all feel like that from time to time. All of us. But as you get older, as you learn what you are capable of, some of those bad feelings go away."

"And you think I am capable of helping children?" Marcin asked.

"You know the answer to that, Marcin. I need you to think you are capable of it. Now." His uncle stood. "Let's go home, get some dinner, and start a new day tomorrow with all of this mended. Let us start our friendship anew."

\* \* \*

That night, the heat did not abate. Marcin let the balcony doors sit open, wishing for a fresh breeze to rustle the curtains and reach his skin. The heat was not the only reason he could not sleep. His thoughts kept going back to the cellar, to that strange teacher, Janos, to the maps, the talk of children being thrown from trains and then the fact that Marcin had agreed to help.

Although he felt a little more at ease, now he and his uncle had put the past aside, he still felt a weight upon him—like he was a fraud, a liar. His uncle and the others saw him as a brave man who had rescued a child, and were happy to put their faith in him to save others. Yet, Marcin was sure they were not seeing the real him.

He turned and screamed with frustration into his pillow. Why was he so insecure? Why did he still feel this hatred toward himself? Why couldn't he be like his uncle, like any other man who walked about, head high, brave, ready to fight? Why did he constantly deny who he was, and why did he always distrust his own feelings and decisions? What was wrong with him?

He remembered when two of his friends had joined up to

fight years before, both of them so sure that this was their destiny, to bravely fight the enemy, to come home a hero. As soon as he heard what they said, he felt a tremor of nerves; his legs felt weak, and he started to sweat. Would he, Marcin, have to go? Would he have to kill someone? Would he die?

The fears had rattled around in his brain, making his head spin until Filip gave him a drink and he could then remember that he had a medical certificate—his heart was weak, or at least it had been in his childhood years—so he was safe. No one was going to make him fight.

He never admitted any of these feelings to anyone but Filip, ashamed that he wasn't brave, he was just as weak as his heart. Filip had said, just as his uncle had then, that everyone felt that way. Just no one spoke about it. Everyone pretended. "It's all about how you present yourself," Filip had said. "You look at someone, think they are brave, successful, intelligent, but I can guarantee that is not what is going round in their heads!"

"Marcin," his uncle whispered, breaking him out of his thoughts. "Are you asleep?"

"I'm awake. What's wrong? Is it Adam?"

"No. Nothing of the sort. I have an idea—something that will make you feel like you can do this. So you can believe in yourself a little."

"What is it?"

"Get dressed and meet me downstairs. We are going on another little adventure."

He met his uncle outside. The heat wrapped itself around them.

"Will Adam be all right alone?" Marcin asked.

"He's fast asleep. Not to worry."

The pair made their way through the navy-blue, inky streets, the sun never letting the sky turn fully black. They took a similar route to a few hours before, near the castle, and then skirted around its edges, but this time, his uncle was focused on the Church of Saint Mary Magdalene, its cross still a bright white in the summer evening light.

"You'll see what you are meant to do here. You'll see it for yourself," Czeslaw whispered.

The streets were quiet, not even a lone dog strutting about looking for scraps, and they soon came to the church where his uncle skirted round to the rear and knocked three times on a wooden cellar door.

Marcin felt déjà vu as soon as he saw Father Aldony emerge from the cellar. This time, however, he wore no robes, just a shirt and trousers and a silver cross around his neck that glinted in the moonlight.

"Czeslaw?" Aldony asked. "Had we an arrangement for this evening?"

"I just needed Marcin to see. It will help him find his courage, I think."

"And the other one you have brought?" Aldony asked.

"The other?" his uncle asked.

Both Marcin and Czeslaw turned to look where Aldony's eyes were fixed, and there, only half hidden behind a tree, was Adam.

"Adam? What are you doing?" Czeslaw said.

The boy stepped forward, his hands in his pockets, and looked at his shoes rather than making eye contact with any of them.

"What are you doing here?" Marcin asked.

"I heard you leave," he said, talking to his shoes.

"We would have been back soon."

"I heard you talking too. After dinner. You were talking about me. About orphans."

Marcin could not help but smile. He had thought he had heard a creak on the stairs that evening, when he and his uncle discussed more about the children that had been saved, about the news coming from Poland. He thought of himself at Adam's age and knew he probably would have eavesdropped too.

"Go home," Czeslaw said.

"I want to see."

"See what? There's nothing to see."

"I want to see what's inside the church—why you have come out at night to see it."

"Go home!" Czeslaw told him, but Adam didn't shift.

"If the boy wants to stay," Father Aldony said, "you should let him. It may help him too, Czeslaw."

"Please," Adam begged. "Marcin, please."

Adam looked at Marcin.

"Yes, come." Marcin waved him forward.

"Marcin," his uncle hissed.

"The Father is right. It might help him—whatever this is— and you are sure it will help give me courage, so why not Adam too?"

"Boys!" Czeslaw pushed past Aldony, shaking his white wiry head, muttering as he headed downwards, his frustrations echoing back to Adam and Marcin. "No one listens to me, no one thinks I know best!"

Adam grinned at Marcin. "You made him mad," he said.

"He'll be fine. I make him mad at least once a day."

The pair then followed Czeslaw into the dark as Aldony shut the cellar hatches over them with a bang.

Marcin was going to talk to Adam, joke with him about his uncle some more, enjoying that brief closeness, but then the sight in the cellar struck Marcin dumb.

Makeshift beds littered the floor, each with a small child

wrapped in blankets lying on them. Through the dimly lit room, Marcin saw robed figures hunched over them, whispering words of comfort, wrapping wounds, offering drinks of water.

"We got a lot in yesterday," Aldony whispered now beside him. "Usually we take one or two at a time to the infirmary, or if they are well enough, place them with Jewish families. But with this many"—Aldony paused—"it takes time to find them safety, without raising too many eyebrows."

"Come, come." Aldony stepped between the beds, waving a hand at Adam and Marcin to follow.

They walked into a second room, this one holding only two beds.

"These are children from the ghetto," Aldony said. "Piotr brought them a month ago. They are not faring well."

"Injured?" Marcin asked.

"No. Nothing physical, not anymore. They suffer from nightmares, from ailments of the mind. Losing their parents, well..." Aldony splayed his hands.

Adam brushed past Marcin and before he could stop him, he leaned over one of the beds.

"Polish?" Adam asked Aldony, who nodded.

Adam nodded back, then crouched down and began to talk.

"Adam, no," Marcin said.

But Adam did not stop. He spoke to the child in the bed about his parents, about how he had Marcin and Czeslaw to take care of him now, how everything would be okay for them.

"It is good that you try," Aldony said. "But I am afraid she will not talk. She lies there and stares at the ceiling, sleeps and cries. But she will not interact with anyone."

Adam continued to talk. This time, he spoke about how he used to play pirates with his friends on the banks of the Warta

River, how he would get ice cream in the square and play hide and seek in the alleyways.

"Do you like ice cream?" he asked the girl. "There is ice cream here too. I didn't know that other places had ice cream. But they do. Marcin showed me. He takes me there, just as he took me at home, and we eat ice cream, and it all doesn't feel as scary. I miss my parents still, you will miss yours, but they might find us again one day. That's what Marcin says, and he never lies."

Marcin swallowed.

Suddenly, the girl moved to her side. Marcin and Aldony took a step forward. Marcin could see that she was eight, maybe nine.

"When do you get ice cream?" the girl whispered.

Marcin felt Aldony nudge his ribs, then looked to see that the priest was beaming.

"As often as I want to," Adam said.

"Can I come next time you go?"

"Of course," Adam said. "What's your name?"

"Zofia," the girl said.

He dug around in his pocket and pulled out a piece of string. "Well, Zofia, do you want to learn a magic trick?"

The girl nodded and sat up, watching as Adam showed her how to make a knot in a piece of string disappear.

Marcin watched Adam and the girl for some time, not noticing that Father Aldony had left his side until he heard his uncle's voice.

"Absolutely not," Czeslaw hissed.

Marcin turned to see the priest and his uncle, heads together toward the rear of the cellar, Aldony waving his hands about as he tried to explain something.

"What is it?" Marcin went to the pair.

"Nothing, it doesn't matter. Does not warrant discussion," his uncle said.

"But Czeslaw," Aldony pleaded. "You see what he has just achieved. He can be of use too. Other older children are helping. Especially with our couriers—it raises less suspicion if a single man has a child with him than if he travels alone. We have women too, to make it look as though they are a family. You know this, Czeslaw, and you know we must all do what we can right now—we have no choice."

"Not Adam. He's just a boy," Czeslaw said.

"Think on it. Just think, Czeslaw, promise me that at least."

His uncle gave the briefest of nods, then told Adam and Marcin it was time to leave, stomping up the stairs ahead of them.

*** 

Once they arrived home, Czeslaw closed the door with a soft thud, the sound echoing in the quiet of the house. The dim light of a single lamp illuminated the small living room, casting long shadows on the walls.

"Marcin," his uncle began, rubbing his temples as he sank into a chair. "What you did tonight... I don't know if it was wise to let Adam stay."

Marcin leaned against the doorframe, arms crossed. "I think he needed to be there, Czeslaw. After what he said this morning. He wanted to feel that he was still him, still Polish, still fighting in a small way."

Czeslaw looked up sharply. "This is dangerous work we are involved in."

"I realize that," Marcin replied, his voice steady. "But if we can offer hope to someone like that girl—if Adam can connect with her and give her a glimpse of normalcy—then isn't it worth it? These children need to know they're not alone."

"You can and must go," his uncle said. "But not Adam. I mean, seriously, what was Father Aldony thinking even suggesting it?" he puffed. "Ah, yes, take a boy through the Slovak Republic, back into Poland from whence he escaped and put him in danger!" He laughed.

Marcin sat quietly while his uncle pontificated, knowing better than to interrupt until he had tired himself out.

It didn't take long. Czeslaw soon yawned and slapped each side of the armchair, ready to raise himself to bed.

Marcin was not sure what to say. He agreed, yes, it was too dangerous. But at the same time, he had seen how Adam had lifted his head as the priest spoke in not-too-quiet tones, and how he had smiled, a smile Marcin was sure he had not seen on the boy in months.

Then, he thought of all those bundles on the small beds. How they needed someone to help, how they needed Marcin, and maybe, just perhaps, they needed Adam.

Before Marcin could try to express his thoughts again, the door creaked open, revealing Adam.

"Listening at doors again?" his uncle chided.

Adam normally would have shuffled away, an embarrassed grin on his face. This time he stood straight and stared at Czeslaw and Marcin.

"I'm going to help. I'm going to go with you, Marcin," he said.

"Now listen, Adam," Czeslaw began.

"I can decide. You are not my father. Neither of you," he said.

Both fell silent. Marcin felt he had been slapped in the face.

No, he wasn't Adam's father. He knew he wasn't. But still, he had tried to be more, hadn't he?

"Adam." Czeslaw tried a gentle tone. "We know that. And we admire your bravery. But this is too dangerous. It's dangerous for Marcin, let alone a young boy."

"I'm twelve, coming up to thirteen. Do you know if my father were still here, and if the war hadn't happened, I was to go to boarding school at ten. So you see. I would have been alone, I would have had to grow up anyway."

"This is a bit different than going to boarding school!" Czeslaw laughed. "It's just not going to happen."

"You can't stop me," Adam said, his face flinty, his hands balled into fists at his side. "This is what I am meant to do. Marcin rescued me. And seeing those other children, who were not as lucky as me, shows me what I am meant to do now. I can help. And I will. Whether you want me to or not. I'll leave right now, go to Father Aldony, and stay with him. You can't stop me," he said again.

Marcin looked to Czeslaw, expecting him to get angry, to come up with a clever argument that would make Adam understand.

But his uncle simply sat, his head cocked to the side, a finger tapping on the armrest as he looked at the boy. "What say you, Marcin?" Czeslaw asked without looking away from Adam.

He knew he should side with his uncle and say no. But Adam reminding him that he wasn't his father had troubled him, and he found himself desperately wanting to prove some-thing to Adam, that perhaps Adam could trust him, perhaps they could forge a bond in another way. Besides, Marcin real-ized, he owed him this at least.

"He can make up his own mind," Marcin finally said.

"I thought you might say that." Czeslaw broke away from looking at Adam and heaved himself up from his chair.

He walked to Marcin and placed a hand on his head, then went to Adam and hugged him gently. "My brave boys," he said, almost sadly, then trudged up the stairs, leaving Marcin and Adam wondering what on earth had changed the old man's mind.

# 13

## CLARA, 1982

### Alpine Lakes Wilderness

"That is all for now," Marcin said.

"But you and Dad, you went to Poland?"

"We did." Marcin yawned. "No more tonight, Clara."

"But, but—" She had so many questions. He couldn't just stop there!

She could see he was getting ready to stand. No. Not yet.

"Filip!" she blurted. "Filip was gay. And your uncle, and—" She stopped. She was going to say, *And you*, but felt she couldn't be the one to admit it for him.

Marcin's face first registered shock, as if he had forgotten that he had told her that, then it turned to some form of relief. He rested back on the couch and sighed.

"Yes. Yes, he was. But he was also my friend. When I went to Poznań, he became my... close friend. He was older than me, helped me understand things. He owned this bar and was funny and loud and all the things I hadn't seen before. It was my uncle who introduced me to him."

"Wasn't it illegal to be gay back then?" she asked, ignoring the fact that he had overlooked what she had been about to say.

"No, not in Poland. Not until the Germans came. Then it was illegal. I mean, it was okay if people knew if you were gay, but it would cause problems, so you didn't shout about it, you know? You kept it hidden. But not Filip. Filip kept nothing hidden."

"So what was the other thing you said—you said you denied who you were," Clara said. "That you weren't sure you could trust yourself."

Marcin coughed. "It isn't easy for me to tell you this," he stated.

"You're gay," she said for him now.

He nodded. "I still cannot say it out loud. You see, after my uncle left, after our falling out, I was not myself. I wasn't sure who I was. I spent time with Filip and the others at the bar, and when the Germans came, when they were in the streets, in their uniforms, I was careless."

"In what way?"

He gulped. "There was this one day, an afternoon. I was walking to the bar, two other men ahead of me. I knew they were going to Filip's; I had seen them before. I didn't know their names." He stopped, then shook his head.

"You can say it, Marcin," Clara encouraged. "I think you need to."

"You see, I told you it wasn't illegal to be what we were. When the Germans came, we knew that would change, and all of us should have been more careful. I mean, going to a known bar—it was obvious who we were. I was walking, like I said, and two men stopped me. They wore normal clothes, just normal, but there was something about them that made me uneasy. They asked me who I was, where I was going. They spoke Polish but with an accent. I knew then they were German police of some sort, but like I said, in those days I was a bit stupid, not thinking straight. So they asked me questions and then I thought I had gotten away with it, but one of them, this one with blond hair, he pulled out a baton—you know, a stick—and hit me in the stomach. He hit me so hard I screamed in pain and fell.

"The two men in front, they turned and saw me. And I screamed out—not to them but to the police—and told them that the two men ahead of me were gay, not me.

"The confusion on their faces—I still see it, Clara. Confusion and then fear. I had panicked. Said the wrong thing, made it so that they would be arrested."

"But you were in pain, scared," Clara said. "You can't blame yourself."

"I do. I do blame myself. The falling out with my uncle, the start of the war, the Germans, it was like I couldn't control anything, but the one thing I should've been able to control was what came out of my mouth—what I said. But I said the wrong thing."

"So they got arrested, and then what?" she asked.

"They weren't arrested, Clara," he said. "The two policemen went to them, dragged them into an alleyway, and beat them half to death."

Marcin fell silent. Clara tried to imagine the pain inflicted upon those men, and the pain that Marcin had carried all these years. The only way she could even try to understand was the weight of guilt, shame, and pain she carried with her daily for what she had put her mother through all these years.

"It wasn't your fault," she repeated.

Marcin shook his head sadly. "When I told Filip, I was a mess. I was in shock, scared, crying. He gave me a drink to calm my nerves. And then another and another. He said he would find a way to make sure we were all safe. That's why he opened up the bar to Germans and tried to hide in plain sight, thinking that if he kept them drunk, they would be less likely to seek us out one by one, I suppose. I think too that he thought that some of the Germans who would come to the bar would do so exactly because it was a known gay bar—that they wanted to be there, if you see what I mean.

"But I was not right. I could not sleep. Could not eat much. I drank more and more, trying to drown it all out. And in a way, it kept me calm enough when I was walking through the streets and would see uniformed soldiers, police or even hear the German language. I could exist, I suppose, I could make it through the day. The days I didn't drink, I was afraid all the time. I knew what could happen. I knew it was going to get worse, and it did."

Clara nodded. "I felt that too. You know. The drinking, it made everything worse overall, but in the moment, in that exact moment, it made everything okay. It made me think I was coping with life."

"We are not so different then." Marcin smiled.

"Do you think Dad ever felt that way too? I mean, he drank sometimes."

"I honestly don't know, Clara. Men, we don't talk about what we feel. Just like Filip said—we are all just pretending. None of us really know what is going on inside someone's brain."

Clara thought of her father then—really thought about him—how he had quiet moments and would look off into the distance and it would be hard for anyone to reach him. How he would have days, sometimes, of sitting in his study, saying that he was working on some paper, but then she would sneak in and see him staring at his hands, or curled up on the old leather couch, not sleeping but once more staring into nothingness.

"Clara," Marcin said.

"Yes, sorry." She shook her head and smiled. "I was just thinking about Dad."

"I know. Do you want to talk now?" He grinned.

"No. I think I need to sleep," she said, suddenly feeling a crash of tiredness in her muscles that felt as if it were traveling quickly to her bones.

"You sure you are fine?" he asked.

"I am. Really, I am. Thank you for telling me what you did. I needed to know that. I hope you feel better for saying it too."

"A piece of the puzzle," Marcin agreed.

"Soon to be completed." She stood, patted Moll, then gave Marcin a brief hug, smelling the outdoors on his jumper, the scent of wood and smoke.

"Sleep well," he said as she climbed the stairs. "Make sure the bugs are not biting!"

She gave a small laugh at Marcin's version of "Good night, sleep tight, don't let the bedbugs bite," reached her room and lay down fully clothed, expecting sleep to ferry her away within seconds.

But sleep would not come. She thought of Marcin, of how all these years he had hidden who he was, how he had felt shame. She wished she had the right words for him, to make him understand that there was nothing to be ashamed of, that all these years he hadn't fully lived.

He saved all those children, and yet, she realized, he hadn't been able to save himself.

She turned on her side, willing sleep to find her. Then tried changing into pajamas, took them off and had a shower, put the pajamas back on, and tossed and turned in bed until she heard the soft pad of Moll on the stairs, followed by Marcin's heavy footfall.

She waited until he had finished in the bathroom, the old toilet honking when it flushed, heard the click of his door as he retired, heard an owl hoot outside her bedroom window, and finally gave up.

She switched on the bedside lamp and picked up her diary, sure that if she wrote something down, her mind would soon rest. As she flicked through the pages, she came across an entry she had written years before. Jumbled to any other reader, but it made perfect sense to Clara. She inhaled quickly with the shock of it, reliving it all again.

The entry started with lists. Make lists, the therapist had told her. Lists are good. List everything you need to do that day and even if you only cross one thing off, you will at least see that you are making progress.

How old was she then, when the therapist had said that? She considered it for a moment, closed her eyes and tried to imagine which therapist it was.

The candy-floss-white hair, the smell of furniture polish on the too-lacquered side tables, the glasses that slipped off the therapist's nose too often so they had to push them up with their index finger.

Fourteen. Clara had been fourteen, and it was Dr. Michael, a woman in her sixties, who spoke about her grandchildren.

That was the first therapist. The one that the insurance had paid for after Clara went out with Zoe, a sort of friend from school, drank half a bottle of vodka and was found alone, asleep on a park bench.

"It's a miracle you were alive," the doctor had said. "It's surprising that nothing worse happened to you. All alone like that. I couldn't imagine. Your poor mother. If that had been my child, or my grandchildren. Well!"

Clara was sure that the therapist shouldn't have said those things to her. Shouldn't have tried to make her feel guilt over her behavior. She had felt guilt, shame, and more. She didn't need the therapist with the fluffy hair making it worse.

"Grief does funny things to us all," that therapist had said. "Makes us do strange things."

"It isn't grief," Clara had told her. "It's not grief."

"What is it then?"

Clara had shrugged—there was no word for it.

\* \* \*

She'd found him on a Tuesday afternoon. It was autumn and one of those days where the sky streaked blue, the sun shone, but the air was crisp and stung at your cheeks. She had been at school that day and walked back kicking leaves of red and yellow like she was small again.

She was home early. Debate class had been cancelled because Mr. Lomax had broken his leg and was off sick for a few weeks.

She got home, opened the door, and threw her bag on the floor, kicked off her shoes and told herself she needed to put them away properly, before her parents got home from work.

There was nothing different about the house. The grandfather clock in the hallway ticked loudly, perhaps too loudly, and made Clara turn on the radio, changing the station from KING

FM to a rock station where singers, who her parents disapproved of, would scream and yell and call it singing. She wasn't much partial to it herself, but everyone at school was obsessed with the likes of The Rolling Stones and Elton John, and she didn't want to be left out.

Her foray into finding snacks in the refrigerator yielded little but two cold slices of bread. She placed them on the counter and stared at them, thinking about reaching up into the cupboard to get the peanut butter, but then she decided she couldn't be bothered.

It was then that she noticed a half-eaten piece of toast on a blue chipped plate on the side. She drew it toward her and pressed her finger down into the bread. Finding it still soft, she realized it wasn't from that morning and that someone else must be home.

"Mom? Dad?"

She turned the dial and the radio fell silent.

"Mom? Dad?" she shouted again.

Perhaps one of them had come home and had a snack. Perhaps it was from that morning. The grandfather clock ticked the seconds by.

She didn't know why, but she suddenly did not want to be in the house anymore.

"Mom?" she asked the hallway as she walked toward the front door.

"Dad?" she asked the staircase.

"Mom?" she asked the closed study door to her left.

Her hand hovered over the brass knob of the door.

"Don't be stupid, Clara," she said.

"Dad?" she asked as she opened the door.

There was no answer.

But she found her father.

* * *

She stood for a moment and looked up at him. The autumnal sunlight lit dust motes as they danced around her father's face. His eyes were open, too open, his face pale, too pale. His mouth open, as if ready to scream, but the rope around his neck would not let him.

She stood there and watched the dust motes. She watched them and watched them and wished they would go away.

Outside, a car horn screeched in the air and made her jump, made her come to. Made her realize that she was standing, looking up at her father, who swung ever so slightly from a rope around his neck.

She opened her mouth to scream, to yell.

"Oh my good God!" Her mother was behind her.

"Mom," Clara said, her words thick as her eyes began to swim about the room. "He ate toast first."

Then, blackness.

* * *

So after this, after the vodka with Zoe in the park, and after Dr. Michael, Clara made lists. Long ones, short ones, never really crossing much off them.

Shower, dress self. Some days neither of those were done.

Homework.

Tidy room.

Help Mom.

Help Mom. She wished she could. She wished she could have helped her in some way, tried to be a good daughter, tried to make the lists and cross things off them, tried to make her smile.

But then it would come back. The toast on the kitchen counter. She would imagine her father, thinking about taking his life, knowing what he was going to do next, but first, for his last meal, he would eat buttered toast.

Was that how it went? Or did he not plan it?

Had he instead come home early, tired perhaps, eaten the toast and then halfway through decided that that was the moment when he would change everyone's lives.

She'd tried to say this to the second therapist, when she was fifteen and got suspended for smoking pot in the girls' bathroom at school. Not with Zoe this time. She couldn't remember what happened to Zoe. This time it was with a boy called Greg who had long, greasy hair and whose eyes were always red and half closed. But she'd liked Greg. He didn't ask questions, didn't say much really. Just offered her a joint now and then and they would sit in silence together.

This therapist, this second one, had a name but Clara could not remember it now. It was a man. She knew that. And young (ish), with a gold wedding band that he constantly fiddled with, which made Clara want to scream at him to leave it alone.

"The toast is not important." That's what he had told her. "Tell me about seeing your father like that."

She had told him that the toast was very much important. That how could she talk about what she'd seen without understanding what had happened just minutes before she had got home? How could she make sense of it?

"Grief affects us all differently," he had told her. "Stages of it vary. I see you are not on any medication. I think your mother and I need to have a conversation about you taking something now."

"It was just weed," she had told him. "What medication would stop me smoking weed?"

"It's not for the weed," he'd said. "It's for the depression. The grief."

"It's not grief!" she had screamed at him.

"Then what is it, Clara?"

\* \* \*

The third therapist was based in the state mental hospital, and Clara had turned sixteen during her stay. This therapist gave her pills, so many pills. Orange, pink, blue. All after Clara had drunk more vodka, snorted cocaine with Greg, smoked weed, and then run out into traffic wearing only a T-shirt with Led Zeppelin emblazoned on the front and got knocked down by a taxi carrying an old couple who were visiting from Wisconsin to see their new granddaughter. Instead, they saw Clara fly over the bonnet of the cab and land in the gutter, her T-shirt hitched up, displaying pink polka-dotted underwear.

This therapist tried with Clara. Tried to get her to talk about the day she'd found her father. Tried to get her to discuss her feelings. But Clara wanted to talk about the toast.

"The toast is irrelevant," the therapist had said.

But Clara had known it wasn't. Clara had known that if she could piece together those moments before her father dying, she could form some understanding of them and then perhaps continue on into the memory of finding him. She had to see it all, she told the doctors; she had to see that whole day play out in her head and see her father do it. Then it would make sense.

They'd kept her in for three months and sent her home with more pills. A regimen—make your lists, do one thing per day, see a therapist, get back to normality.

For the next two years, in a fugue of drugs, she'd navigated life to a degree. She'd felt little to nothing. Had no likes or dislikes. Didn't drink or smoke. Just ticked off things on her list and kept moving.

Orange pill in the morning with food.

Yellow one, one hour after eating breakfast.

Orange-and-blue pill at lunchtime.

No more pills till bedtime. That was when she'd got the pink one. The pink one that sent her into a dreamless sleep for thirteen hours a night.

Then, about five years ago, when she turned eighteen, she'd left home. Got a job at a library where she stacked books in cold, dusty silent rooms and found that it gave her some peace.

There were no more therapists after that. She took her pills, moved in with two roommates in the city, away from the suburbia of Greenlake and her mother, started to go out, to have fun. Found that she could drink and take her pills. Found that they didn't make her too sick.

But then, she'd ruined it all. That one night. Went out too late—actually it had been her third day in a row of partying too hard with Thomas after seeing a man who looked like her father in the store. Came home. Cried in bed. Roommates had asked her to keep it down. She said she would.

Wrote a list for the next day, closed her eyes and saw the damned toast. Then saw her father.

Pink pill. It was time for the pink pill.

She took it with a swig of vodka, but nothing happened.

She got the others. Orange, yellow, blue; found some aspirin.

This would work. This would drown it all out. She'd sleep and then go and stack books and make a list of nice things to do for her mother and her roommates, because they had put up with so much. She'd be a better daughter. Better friend.

As her eyes closed, she had smiled. She remembered that.

Smiling. She'd been happy. Warm. Safe. Then a voice: *It's grief, Clara. It's drowning you.*

Her mother's voice? Therapist one, two or three?

"It's not grief!" she'd mumbled.

"Then what is it?" the voice had asked her.

# 14

## CLARA, 1982

*Alpine Lakes Wilderness*

"I heard you bashing around last night," Marcin said as Clara came into the kitchen, bleary eyed. "You find what you were looking for?"

She plonked herself down at the table and mussed Moll's head, who had come to greet her.

"You find nothing, yes?" Marcin said as he stirred eggs in a frying pan. "There is nothing here. No alcohol. No pills."

"I know," Clara replied.

"You want the eggs?"

"No. Just coffee."

He poured her a cup and she drank as quickly as she could, wanting some sort of hit.

"It was too much, all of that, yesterday. I think we should talk no more about it," Marcin said.

"I'm fine. It wasn't that, not what you said. I just couldn't sleep and I needed to."

"So you went looking for things to help?"

She nodded. She had scoured the house and found only a medicine cabinet in the bathroom that didn't even yield an aspirin. She knew Marcin had his own bathroom, but she wasn't that bad that she felt she could sneak in and check. If it had been a month ago, yes, she probably would have taken the risk. But it wasn't as bad as usual. Still there. Still gnawing at her, sort of like a mosquito bite that still itched now and then.

"I'm fine now though."

Marcin sat at the table, his plate piled high with scrambled eggs. He shoved a forkful into his mouth, a dab of egg catching in his beard.

"I have to go to town," he said between bites. "Need some things from the store. Moll's food for one."

Upon hearing her name, Moll gave a little wiggle of excitement, assuming that perhaps a bit of egg would come her way.

"Great!" Suddenly, Clara felt awake. A trip out. Away from the cabin, from her thoughts, from her past, her father's past. Just a normal day out.

"You no coming," he mumbled.

"Why not?"

"Because the store is next to my friend's bar and it isn't right. Not yet."

"I can handle it," Clara said. He had no idea what she could and couldn't do. She had gone months at a time of not taking anything, not drinking, and it hadn't bothered her in the slightest.

"It's too much, Clara. I think we should have not spoken too much about things just yet. It is bringing things up for you and I don't know whether you can cope."

"I can. It's helping," she said. "You can't say what I can cope with. You don't really know me, not really. Not anymore."

Marcin swallowed then took a swig of his coffee. "Fair point," he admitted.

"Please. Just let me get out. I just need to do something normal. And besides, I could do with a few things."

"You tell me and I get them for you."

"Ladies' things," she said, even though she hadn't had a period in months.

She watched his face redden and knew she had won.

"Okay, but I watch you the whole time. In, out, then back here, yes? And you must call your mother. I spoke with her this morning. She wants to speak with you."

Clara nodded and agreed she would call her mother. But deep down, she didn't want to hear her mother's voice. She knew it would be laced with worry, with panic, and it would take something from Clara to make her mother feel better, leaving Clara feeling worse. "Later," she said. "After the store."

\* \* \*

The drive to the store took almost an hour. The track from Marcin's house seemed to lead nowhere but into the woods. The car dipped and jolted every few seconds as the tires hit uneven ground, making Clara feel nauseous. She kept her cool by stroking Moll's head, whose tongue lolled out of her mouth, excited at the promise of a walk somewhere new.

"So. Last night." She swallowed down the nausea.

"You want to know more," Marcin said.

"Yes and no. I mean, yes, I do. But it's more I wanted to ask about you, not Dad."

"What you mean?" he asked, side-eyeing her.

"I mean, you know, about the fact you're gay," she blurted, and wished she could fold the words back into her mouth.

"I know."

Marcin reached down to the radio and turned the dial until he found a station where a guest speaker talked about the best places to go fishing in the state.

Embarrassed, Clara stared out of the window. Shit. She could have said it differently. Did he think that she thought it was something to be ashamed of, or that she had some objection to it? The way she'd said it, it sounded like she had some form of problem.

"I didn't mean..." she started over the drone of the man on the radio saying that he once fished for eight hours in the pouring rain to catch one giant trout. "I didn't mean—" she said again, louder.

Marcin flicked the radio off. "I know you didn't mean anything."

"I just, I mean—" She couldn't find the right words again. What the fuck was wrong with her brain, other than the obvious? "It's okay, with me, I mean. I mean, it should be okay for everyone, but some people don't agree. But I'm not like them. I just wondered, you know... if you were with someone. And I suppose I wondered why Dad or Mom didn't say anything."

Marcin placed an elbow on the window ledge as he drove with one hand and chewed at a ragged nail. "No relationships," he grunted.

"Not one?"

He didn't answer.

"So, Mom and Dad, they knew?"

"In a way, I think. I don't know."

"What way?"

"Ah, Clara." He let out a groan. "It's just not something you talk about."

"I have friends who are gay," she said. Then realized that

was a lie. There was the guy at the coffee shop, and a girl who used to visit the library three times a week with her girlfriend, raising eyebrows from the others as they held hands through the stacks. Not friends, but she knew people.

"Is different now. It is getting better. But is still not something you speak about."

"Some people do," Clara said. "Lots of people do."

"I am not lots of people, Clara."

He turned on the radio again, where the guest was now talking about the best reels to buy. Clara rested her head against the glass. Fucking reels.

\* \* \*

When Marcin had said that they were going into town, he had not quite told the entire truth. "Town" was a store at the side of the road; to the left a bar, to the right a diner and a laundromat. All of the signs told the owner—Joe's Bar, Joe's Store, Joe's Diner, and then Connie's Laundromat.

"Joe didn't have the money to get the laundromat then?" Clara joked.

"Connie was his wife," Marcin said. "She died."

Clara, feeling wrongfooted again, was glad to get out of the car and away from Marcin for a few minutes. She got into the store before Marcin and headed for the candy. If she couldn't have alcohol or drugs, candy had proven time and time again to take away some of the cravings.

The store was a treasure trove and she suddenly thought she should tell her dad about it—he would have loved the disorganization of the whole thing. Soup next to toilet paper, homemade jam next to canned meat that had use-by dates a year before. A stand of beef jerky propping up a dilapidated crate of potatoes. She took a stick of jerky, unwrapped it, and chewed on the salted meat as she pursued the aisles. Yes, Dad would have liked this, she thought. He would have made a game of it and challenged Clara to find the oddest thing she could, the oldest or the strangest arrangement of goods.

She decided to play the game herself and found a small garden gnome and a kids' pink feather boa next to each other and decided she would buy both. She picked up a basket and began to fill it with random goods that were giving her a warm glow.

As she trudged to the next aisle, she saw Marcin at the counter talking to a man standing behind it. Joe, she assumed. Then she took another bite of the jerky. She saw Joe—this similarly bear-like man to Marcin, with a beard, checked shirt, and hair that could do with a cut—look at her and give a small smile and a nod.

She smiled back, waved the jerky at him so he didn't think she was going to eat it and not pay, and looked at the array of homemade greeting cards that she was sure had either been made by the very young or the elderly. Squiggles of clouds, a flower that looked like it was dead, all of them painted with watercolors that had run, and were oddly charming. She decided that she would start sending cards, now that she was a little better. Would send them to everyone who had helped her. She'd be that woman, the woman who had a card for every occasion. Even one that said, "Sorry you got canned," with a picture of a trash can underneath. It may come in handy, she thought.

"You didn't answer my call," she heard Joe say a little too loudly.

She looked up to see Marcin turning his head in her direction and quickly looked back at the cards. "I've been busy."

"You still up for fishing tomorrow?" Joe asked.

"No. I cannot leave her. Not yet."

"I get it," Joe said. "Well, how 'bout I drop round anyway tomorrow? See if you are both up for it? I've got some steaks comin' in later too that I can drop by with."

"I don't think so," Marcin said.

"No problem. Just let me know when you're free next."

"Clara, you done?"

Clara whipped her head round. "Almost. You have what you need?"

Marcin crinkled his forehead at her.

"You know. Dog food and supplies. That's why we're here, right?"

"Ah, yes!" Marcin said with too much enthusiasm and scooted down an aisle away from Joe.

So who was this Joe, eh? A strange conversation, she thought. Why was Joe so upset about Marcin not answering his call? Clara went to the counter and plonked down her basket.

"Clara?" he said.

"And if you're not Joe, I'll be surprised," she said and smiled.

"Too much?" He laughed. "The signs. Some folks think I could've come up with some different names, but I'm not the creative type. It does the job."

Joe began to key in numbers on the till and bag her purchases. He didn't comment on the strange array, but did raise an eyebrow at the feather boa.

"So you're Marcin's friend," she said. "You know. Fishing."

Joe grunted. "I fish with a lot of folk. Marcin has a good cabin, right next to the lake. Good spot for trout. You fish?"

"Nope. I didn't know he had a friend. I mean, I haven't seen him in years, so I suppose he does have friends."

"Sure," Joe said.

"Sorry. Rambling, I know. Haven't spoken to many people lately. I'm trying to be normal in society again and all that."

"Marcin mentioned," Joe said. "It's good that you are sober. Took my brother three goes."

"Is he okay now?"

"Sorta. Falls off the wagon now and then. But nothing like it used to be. There's an AA meeting at the church tomorrow night. You could go. Not so many people there, but good cookies."

"I might. I mean, I'd have to get Marcin to bring me."

"Bring you where?" Marcin heaved a giant bag of kibble on the counter.

"To AA. Joe said there's a meeting tomorrow night."

"I bring you," Marcin said.

"Tell you what," Joe said with a grin. "You drop her off. Then I'll bring her back with those steaks I mentioned."

Clara looked to Marcin, who stared blankly at Joe.

"Great!" Clara answered for Marcin. "Sounds like a plan."

\* \* \*

As Clara climbed into the car, she turned to Marcin and said, "Joe, eh?"

"He is a friend," Marcin said.

"Just a friend? It's just that I—"

"Enough, Clara!" Marcin said. "You are seeing things that are not there. He was married."

Marcin's prickliness made her shut her mouth for the drive home, but she was sure he was hiding something. If not Joe, then there was someone. Someone he didn't want to talk about.

Despite Marcin's grumpiness, the trip to the store had light-

ened Clara's spirits and cleared her mind. She felt elated, somewhat, that she was acting normal again. Then, as she went to
her room and laid out the odd greeting cards on her bed, she
realized she knew this feeling. The lightness she felt was false.
It could not be trusted. It came each time she had been sober
for a few days, lulling her into a false sense of security. She
would believe she was fine when really she was borderline
manic. She would clean her room, the apartment, until her
eyes stung from the bleach. She would cook her roommates
dinner, buy them gifts. She would see her mother, take her for
lunch, turn up to work on time, stay late, eat a vegetarian diet,
go to bed at 9 p.m. It was all or nothing with Clara, and she
would go full force into being, or at least acting, sober, doing a
good impression of someone who had it together, until the day
would come when it all fell away again and she realized that
the whole thing had been a show. A charade. A farce.

She sat on the bed, the cards around her. One caught her
eye. A rudimentary angel, its halo slipping off its head. *We go to
a better place*, the platitude read.

She picked up the card. A better place. Better than this, she
hoped, feeling that elation, that "normalness" slowly slip away.

How could she be normal? How could she ever get over
what had happened to her father? She rooted around in the
bag and drew out a candy bar, unwrapped it and stuffed it into
her mouth, willing it to take away the desire for something else.

A better place. Better. That's what one of the therapists had
said to her. "One day you will be in a better place." Had they
meant dead? Or just able to feel happiness, or in control? And
what was that, exactly?

She had asked a young therapist this question when she
was in the state hospital. A young man who she was sure had
only just graduated, so she had decided to test him.

"What is control?" she had asked. "I mean, how do you know you are normal and can control things now without thinking that this is just part of the downward spiral again?"

Downward spiral. She had stolen that phrase from another doctor who had tried to explain to her the cyclical nature of her actions.

The young doctor had smiled at her. "It's when you find enjoyment in the everyday things. And I don't like to use the word 'normal.'" He used air quotes.

"But how do I know what I find enjoyment in?"

"Well, what did you used to find enjoyment in?"

"Last time I felt anywhere near happy it was when I got a new doll for Christmas. Then I became a teenager and there wasn't much to be that happy about."

"And then, after that?"

"There was no after that." She laughed. "Read the file."

The young doctor reddened. "I know you started using drugs and alcohol at a young age."

"So there, you see. How will I know I am in control; not normal, but functioning? How will I know I am happy?"

He had tried to give her answers that he gave to everyone. "When you delight in seeing friends and family, when you find something you are passionate about, when you sit down to eat a meal and enjoy it. You have to try things until you find something you like too," he had suggested.

She had smiled at him and thanked him, but had thought he was a fucking idiot.

Now, though, she thought maybe he had been right. When had she actually tried to do anything but get sober, wait to spiral, get drunk and take drugs? Never, was the answer.

She finished chewing on the candy bar then made her way downstairs.

"Marcin?" she hollered as she descended. "Can you please teach me how to fish?"

* * *

Two hours later, Clara sat on a cold, damp rock, a fishing rod in her hands, worms wriggling in a container at her feet.

Marcin had cheered since she had asked him to teach her to fish and immediately taken her to the garage to show her the rods, the reels, the feathery bits and bobs that fitted on it. "A lure," he had said. She thought they all looked a bit like the feather boa she had bought and decided she would call them fancy lures. Marcin said that wasn't the correct term, so she repeated it until he started to whistle to drown her out.

She started to talk as they fished, then he told her that you had to be quiet so as not to scare the fish away. Great, she thought. Quiet time. That was what normal people found enjoyment in. But as the minutes ticked by, she found she could not sit still. The rock was too hard, her jeans too damp. Her right thumb had an itch, which she scratched and made the rod jump up and down and Marcin sigh at her.

She tried. She really did. Tried to look at the beauty around her, the Chiwaukum Mountains in the distance, the ripples on the lake, Moll paddling in the shallows then backing away and barking at an imaginary foe.

It worked for a little while, but soon it all became a bit boring, and thoughts of her father, her life, and questions about what she was going to do next began to seep in. She would have to live with her mother, take care of her for a while. But later, could she move abroad, go somewhere new? But no, her problems would follow.

She realized if she could not control her thoughts, there was no way she could control her actions. Fuck.

"What you say?" Marcin asked.

"Ah. Sorry. I meant to say that in my head. I said it out loud?"

"You shouldn't curse, Clara."

She sighed, then placed the rod on its stand.

"Do you do this a lot?" she asked, and stood and stretched her back.

"Yes. It's peaceful."

"It is. But it's also boring."

"Because you are thinking too much."

"I'm not," she insisted.

"I see you, Clara. Can't sit still. Looking everywhere. What are you thinking about?"

"Everything."

"Okay. Start with one thing."

"What do you think happens when you die?" Clara asked.

"That is what you are thinking about?"

"Yes. And no. But it was one thing. Earlier I thought about it. I got a greeting card and it said something about going to a better place. Do you think we do? What do you think happens?"

"Your father once asked me the same question."

"When?"

"When he was young."

"And what did you tell him?"

"I told him, yes, we do go to a better place."

"Do you believe that?" she asked.

"I wanted to. For a long time, I wanted to believe that. I had to, in a way. When we came here, to America, and then found out about your father's parents, my friends, I stopped believing it could be possible to have something up high, that would allow that kind of horror to happen. I just thought we switch off like a light, perhaps."

"And now?"

"And now? Who knows. I told your father and the other children many things to keep them calm, to keep them thinking that death wasn't the end, that you could be fine, that there was a God that wanted to take care of you. But it was a fairy tale, I think. Because like I said, what God could allow the killings of millions? What God could allow people to live and die in such a way?"

"So you believe there is evil, but not good in the world?" she asked.

"I believe there is good. I believe there is evil. But that's here, on earth. What happens after that, I don't know."

"But you admit there may be something?" she argued.

"Why this line of questions, Clara?"

"I dunno." She kicked at some dead leaves. Then, "No, yes, I do. I mean, if there is a better place, do you think Dad just wanted to get there as quickly as possible? Because it's pretty shit here."

"Shit for now," Marcin said. "But not forever. Not for you. And don't curse, Clara."

"You think it will get better for me?"

"I do. If you keep trying. Like the talking. The fishing."

"Ah, yes, fishing will solve my problems. Didn't Aristotle mention something like that?" she joked.

Marcin smiled. "When you came here just two days ago, you were like a ghost. Now, you are coming back to life. I see it in you. Joking a little, smiling a little. The real Clara is still in there. Just give her time."

"I'm impatient," she said.

Marcin laughed. "I know."

"So." She plonked herself down on the rock again. "Things got better for you, I suppose, after the war. Got better for Dad; well, you know, until he decided to leave. So maybe things will get better for me."

"Good girl!" Marcin wrapped an arm around her. "See."

"I don't believe it. But I'll keep saying it and hope it comes true."

"It will."

"Marcin." She rested her head on his shoulder, feeling calm, warm, and safe in the moment. "Tell me about what you told Dad when he was younger. About how we all go to a better place. How everything would be okay."

# 15

## MARCIN, SUMMER 1942

*Outskirts of Warsaw, Poland*

On a train heading south of Warsaw, a woman wrapped her arms around her daughter and whispered a prayer. The girl, no more than five years old, did not know why her mother was crying as she prayed. She had never cried before.

The girl clung to her mother as the train sliced its way through the darkness and as the mother wept. The mother had a first name, but the child in her arms did not know it yet. Only knew her by Matka and would only learn of her mother's name years later. The mother was smart, had talked to others before getting on the train and had been told to count the stops. Just after the third stop, the train would pick up speed and would not stop again. This was the moment to let her daughter go.

"Tuck your head," she told the child. "Tuck your head and put your hands over it. Like this, see?"

The mother demonstrated it for her. "Then it's going to be the ground under you. It's going to be hard. It will hurt. Tuck everything together. Think that you are a ball—remember the ball at home we play with? Yes? You are the ball now. Do you understand?"

The little girl nodded at her mother and raised her hands over her head, placing them firmly on her skull. "Like this?"

"Exactly! You are so clever!"

The girl was glad that her mother had called her clever. Glad that she knew how to be a ball.

She watched as her mother went to the door—a sliding door that someone else had jimmied open a few stops before.

"It's time," a voice from the darkness whispered.

The girl felt hands underneath her armpits and she was taken to the door, to the inky night where wind rushed by but she could not see anything.

"Like I said!" her mother shouted over the wind. She kissed her head and let her go.

The girl spun in the air for a moment, trying to do as her mother said, but it was hard, so hard. The wind seemed to drag her and her arms would not come down on top of her head like they were supposed to do. As she flew, she was certain that she did not look like a ball.

She heard screams behind her. Was that Matka, she wondered as she flew? No, not Matka. Other voices. Should she be screaming too?

Suddenly, she stopped flying, and the ground hit hard. She tried to wrap herself into a ball, tried and failed. Her arms smacked against things; her legs dragged behind her. She opened her mouth to scream now, but there was no air in her lungs.

Before she blacked out, all she heard was a voice above her, a voice she had never heard before, telling her it was all right, that she was safe now.

"Are you God?" the girl asked the figure above her.

"No. Not God." The figure picked her up. She felt pain in her stomach as he did. And in her leg. And maybe her arm. She began to cry.

"Hush now," the figure told her. "You're safe now. Everything will be all right."

The girl buried her head in the figure's neck and tried to stay quiet. She could smell the figure. A man. He didn't smell like her *tata*, who had gone to heaven months ago. He smelled like the cold and a wood-burning stove all at the same time.

The man stopped walking and sat her gently down.

"Adam," the man said. "You take care of her. I'll be back with more."

The girl rubbed at her eyes, then looked to see a boy standing over her. She could not see his face properly in the dark. But she knew it was a boy and not a man, not big like that other shadowy figure.

"What's your name?" the boy, Adam, asked.

"Sara," she said. "Where's my *matka*?"

"Sara. That's a good name. My *babcia* was called Sara."

"My *babcia* went on a train last week. Matka said we were going to see her."

"Well. It's better you are here, for now," Adam said.

"Will we go and find them soon?" She started to cry again. "I want my *matka*."

The boy crouched down and held her close. "We'll find them soon. They've just gone to see my *matka* and *tata* too. They will all be fine. And we'll stay together and one day we'll go and find them, all right?"

"My arm hurts!" Sara wailed.

"Shh. But let me see." Adam took her arm and then reached into a bag and started to wrap a bandage around it. "I know it hurts, but you're being so brave, and it will stop soon. We'll get it all fixed up."

The girl nodded, watching as this boy wrapped her arm, sniffling as she did.

Soon the shadowy figure came back with another bundle, then there was another figure, with another bundle in his arms too, then another.

"Adam, how is she?" a man asked.

"Good. But I think she has broken her arm. Her name's Sara."

"Only four tonight," she heard one of the shadows say.

"How many did you expect?" Adam asked the shadow.

"There are more," the shadow replied. "But they are—"

The shadow did not say what they were. He stopped, and no one asked him to finish the sentence.

"We have to hurry now. Time is wasting away," a shadow said.

"Can you manage to carry her?" someone said as Adam helped her onto his back.

"I can do it."

The girl was not really sure what happened next. It was all blurry.

Adam carried her, but he had to keep stopping and resting. But he never stopped trying. As the night gave way to day, she saw the shadows transform into men, each carrying a child. She found out their names were Marcin, Piotr, and Janos.

She found she liked Piotr, who made jokes, and liked Marcin, who tended to their wounds when they stopped in a forest. Janos, she was not sure of. His accent was wrong, and he smoked a lot, and told everyone what to do and looked like he was afraid, or angry. She couldn't tell the difference.

It might have taken a month until they reached a church.

But it could have been days, she was not sure. They stopped in barns, in a house, and walked so much, most of the time Adam carrying her.

He told her stories as they walked. Told her about magicians, about pirates and how he had wanted to be a pirate once, but now he wanted to be a doctor perhaps.

She missed her *matka* but did not cry anymore about her. As Adam had said, she was with his parents and they would see them soon.

One of the other children had a cut on their leg, and one night, perhaps in the barn, maybe in the house, the child was crying and the man called Marcin told the child about heaven and how it was so nice there.

The next day, Marcin carried Sara sometimes. She asked him where the other child had gone, and he told her that they had gone to heaven to be with angels, and that there were puppies to play with, kittens too, and all nice things to eat.

"Can I go there?" she had asked hopefully.

"Not yet. It's not time for you yet, Sara."

The church they reached had priests there. Dressed in robes. She knew they were priests and she wondered why she hadn't been taken to see a rabbi instead.

"You'll stay here, for now," Adam told her as she was given a bed, and a nun came to see her, smiling, telling her she would clean her up, get her some food.

Adam turned to leave, and then the girl cried. "Where are you going?"

He turned back and placed a hand on her head. "I'll come back and see you soon," he said. "You be brave and I'll come back."

"You promise?" she asked.

"I promise."

She nodded. Sniffed and waved goodbye to him, to the man Marcin, and let the nun look at her leg and then her arm.

"What's your name?" the nun asked.

"Sara," she said.

"That's a pretty name. Sara."

"It's the same as Adam's *babcia*," she said, then told the nurse all about pirates, and how one day Adam might be a doctor.

\* \* \*

Marcin and Adam were greeted by Czeslaw when they returned home.

"That took a long time," he said as he made them sit, fetched Marcin a nip of vodka and Adam warm milk.

"Janos says we can't do that trip again. He and Piotr are going to go back and recruit more people in Poland and the Slovak Republic to courier as close to the border here as they can. We'll meet them closer. He says, too, trains are cutting their way through the Slovak Republic now, packed full. He says we'll have our hands full. Too full here to go back to Poland again."

"Well." Czeslaw sat with a glass of vodka in his own hand. "I'm glad to hear it. It aged me ten years, waiting for you both to return. I told Father Aldony that it was a fool's errand, going all that way and mostly on foot. But it was a success, yes?" He raised his glass in celebration.

"One died on the way," Adam said.

Marcin looked to the boy, a boy who looked more like a man now. Maybe it was the way his face was drawn, his skin pale, a tiredness under the eyes that only comes from seeing hurt during the years.

"But Marcin was so good with him," Adam continued, flicking a smile at Marcin. "He told the boy about heaven, about how he will be with angels and puppies and things, and how it would all be all right. He just fell asleep in Marcin's arms and he didn't look scared. Not one bit."

"Well done, Marcin," his uncle said sadly.

"It isn't something to celebrate, nor be commended on," Marcin replied.

"Yes, it is," Adam interjected. "You tried everything you could. You carried him, talked to him, tended to him and then made him feel safe and at peace when he was in pain and scared. You did everything right. I want to be able to do that. I want to be able to be as strong as that."

Marcin, strong? He almost laughed at the thought.

"Adam's right." Czeslaw sat forward and raised his glass. "To all those orphans who have at last gone home. Finally found their family again in heaven. We pray they are not the last orphans we save."

Marcin clinked his glass and sat in the silence that came with the toast to the lost children, even though he wasn't sure he believed they were in a better place, even though he wasn't sure they would ever find family again.

# 16

## MARCIN, SUMMER 1942

*Outskirts of Malé Straciny, The Slovak Republic*

The sun burned the early morning mist away slowly, like a theater curtain, revealing parts of the world bit by bit, as if it knew that Marcin needed the time to process the scene in front of him.

Still bundles lay next to the tracks, and Marcin watched them, wishing they would rise as the sun greeted them, yet he knew they would not.

The children that were alive were not yet awake, and Marcin did not want them to see this view. They should have moved in the night, but the boy with the broken leg and the boy with the slice taken out of his arm were not able to. So now, they were left with this.

As they slept, Marcin made his way to each bundle, placing a hand over the small faces and whispering a prayer. He picked each one up in turn and took them toward the trees, lying them down next to each other.

"Five," he heard Janos say behind him. "We've never lost five before. The train was too fast. We need to change spots."

Marcin swallowed. "They're children."

"I know."

"But you speak of them like a thing, like cargo."

"You can't get too emotional about it, Marcin," Janos said. "Trust me. I see their faces in my dreams every night. I think of them all the time. You may think me cold, but it is the only way to keep doing this."

"Who will come for them?" Marcin asked.

"Piotr will come back tomorrow night and take them to a rabbi we know. They will be buried appropriately," he said. "For now, we need to concentrate on the living."

Marcin was reluctant to leave them alone. But he had to admit that after six weeks, he was starting to understand that death comes with life, that not all of the children could be saved. "The last orphans," he whispered as he walked away.

"What did you say?" Janos asked. "Last orphans?"

Marcin nodded. "It was something my uncle said. After the first time. He meant that one day there will be the last orphans. As in, no more of them. That we have saved them. And these ones, these children that didn't live, are now somehow also last orphans too—they have gone home, gone to a better place."

"You believe that?" Janos asked.

"I don't know what I believe anymore," he said.

"It's hard to believe in anything, really." Janos stopped at the clearing then sat down, reached into his pocket, and drew out some tobacco and started to make himself a cigarette.

"You want one?"

Marcin shook his head.

"Sit for a minute. Let's just sit and take a moment."

Marcin sat down, feeling uneasy. Janos was always moving,

always telling everyone to keep going, look behind you, watch, listen, hide. Now, as he smoked, his eyes squinting against the rising sun, Marcin saw how tired Janos looked. Almost defeated.

"You know, I always wanted to be an actor. Can you believe that?" Janos said. "I mean, me, an actor?" He laughed. "It wasn't what my father wanted though. Off I went to be a teacher, a professor of all things. And now look at me. Covered in dirt. Tired. I often wonder what my father would think of me now, if he could see me."

"He's dead?" Marcin asked.

Janos nodded. "You still have parents?"

As far as Marcin knew, he did. But his mother might be dead now. Maybe even his father.

"I think so."

"You don't write them?"

"No."

"Were they happy when you became who you were... Wait, what is it you do again?" Janos asked.

"A bookkeeper."

"So. Were they happy to have a son that is a bookkeeper? Anything you wanted to be instead?"

Marcin shook his head and looked at his shoes.

"I think I'll be an actor one day still," Janos said, filling Marcin's silence. "Be myself, you know. Maybe live in America. Maybe have friends like me."

Marcin looked at him. "Like you? You mean other actors?"

Janos matched his stare and grinned. "Aren't we all actors, Marcin? Playing a role?"

Marcin blushed, thinking that these were the same words Filip had said. Did Janos know? Had Marcin done something to make him suspect?

"One day we will be who we are." Janos refused to look away from him. "And we will be happy."

Marcin swallowed. "I hope so."

Janos laughed and nudged his arm. "Ah, Marcin. I'm so glad you are here with me. I'm so glad we can be actors together."

Before Marcin could ask any questions, Janos stood, dusted off his trousers, and headed toward Piotr, Adam, and the sleeping children.

\* \* \*

The two children they had managed to rescue were Slovak Jews; neither of them spoke Polish or Hungarian. Janos was the only one who could speak a smattering of Slovak, but whatever he said did not seem to calm them. They cried and fought as they were carried the few miles to the border and then into Hungary.

It was Adam who finally soothed them. He walked ahead, dancing about, being silly. At first, the children, perhaps six and eight years old, looked at him, confused. Soon, though, they began to smile, and then to laugh.

Marcin watched Adam, pride welling in his chest. He was still a boy in age, but his actions were that of a man. A man who was more than anything Marcin could ever expect to be. He was kind, thoughtful, brave. On all of their missions, he never complained, never waned in his desire to help, even though, as Janos had said, he wasn't really needed anymore now they were venturing into the Slovak Republic at night, often only away for a few days at a time. Marcin thought differently. If anything, Adam was still needed; he brought trust with him. The children would connect with him, trust that this ragtag bunch of strangers would help them because Adam was there, smiling, talking gently to them.

That evening, they reached the church and were let in by Father Aldony. Marcin explained that they did not understand the language and Aldony reassured them that he had a nun who would be able to communicate with them.

"Can I go and see Sara?" Adam asked Aldony.

"She's over in the cloisters now," Aldony told him. "Her wounds have healed; her paperwork is coming through any day now."

"So she'll be safe?" Marcin asked.

"As safe as she can be. A Catholic name, a baptism certificate."

"Where will she go next?" Adam asked.

"Either to the orphanage or, if we can, we will house her with members of our church who are sympathetic to the cause."

"Marcin?" Adam had already turned away, ready to leave the basement.

"You go," Marcin insisted. "I'll wait here."

**\* \* \***

Sara sat in the cloistered gardens, wearing a new skirt and shirt. She wasn't sure she liked them. The fabric was stiff and scratchy in the heat, but the nuns had told her it was her new uniform for now.

The waning of the day had brought with it a cool breeze, which Sara enjoyed. It was her favorite part of the day, where she was allowed to sit and watch the bees bumble from flower to flower.

She scratched at her arm where a small wound had

scabbed over. The nuns had told her not to bother it. She couldn't help it, though; the uniform and the itch from the scab was too much.

"You're bleeding." Sara looked up to see Adam walking toward her.

"Don't tell anyone," she said.

He sat beside her and drew out a dirty handkerchief and placed it over her forearm.

"Press down," he told her.

She did as he said and kicked her legs.

"You look like brand new," Adam said. "All fancy in your new clothes. Do you like it here?"

"It's boring," Sara said. "They make us learn the Bible and read and write. Then we have to say prayers. And then we have to remember our new names."

"New names?"

She nodded. "Mine is Sara Kowalski. My old name was Sara Zimmerman. But the nuns say we can't say our old names anymore."

"My name changed too," he said. "My name used to be Adam Abramowicz and now it is Adam Piotrowski."

"Do you like your new name?" she asked.

"It's okay. I'll change it back one day to my old name."

"My *matka* might be upset that I have a new name," she said, looking at her kicking legs. "Has she had to change her name too? I don't know Matka's first name. I know she has the same last name as me and Tata. But I don't know her first name. Do you know your *matka*'s first name?" she asked him.

"I do. It's Cyla."

"That's a pretty name," she said. "I once had a friend and she was called Clara and she was older than me, but she was still nice to me. That starts with the same letter, doesn't it? And they rhyme, don't they, Clara and Sara? I like that they rhyme. My friend Clara, she lived next door but then she moved. She wasn't Jewish; she went to a school like this. All old and lots of nuns. Do you go to school, Adam?"

"I will soon."

"Will you have friends at school?"

"Maybe," he said.

"I don't have friends here. But the nuns said I will be going somewhere else soon. To an orphanage, where there are more children, and they said I'd make friends there."

"You will," he said. "In fact, the same orphanage that you are going to is where one of my friends is now. Her name is Zofia. You should make friends with her."

"Zofia." Sara nodded. "I'll remember that name. But I have to remember my new name too. So many names." She sighed.

Adam laughed.

"Why are you laughing?"

"Nothing," he said.

"Will you come and visit me in the orphanage?"

"I'll try to."

She nodded and stopped kicking her feet.

"I miss my *matka*, Adam," she said. "Will we go and find her soon?"

"Soon."

"How long is soon?"

"It's just a while."

"How long is a while?"

"Ah—I don't know."

"Have you been looking for your *matka* yet?" she asked.

"No. I don't think I can find her."

"Why not?"

"Because I think maybe she has gone to heaven to play with all those puppies that Marcin talked about."

"She has? But Marcin said I couldn't go there yet, so why has your *matka* gone there?"

"It was just her time to go there," he said.

"When is my time?"

"Not for a long, long time."

Sara thought about this for a moment. It seemed that everyone else could go and play with puppies and have sweet treats but her. And she had to learn new names and wait a while, and wait until soon was over and she could find her *matka* again. It didn't seem fair. Not one bit.

"What's wrong?" Adam asked.

"I just want to go home," she said and began to cry.

Adam wrapped his arm around her and Sara sobbed into him.

"I tell you what. How about I go ask the nuns if I can take you for ice cream? How about that? We'll go and fetch Marcin and we'll all go together."

She sniffed. Ice cream sounded nice. "Can I have as much as I like?"

"As much as you like," Adam said.

"All right then." She wiped her eyes and stood, holding out her hand for Adam to take. "Then we'll go find Matka. Because it will have been a while then."

"Maybe," he said.

"Maybe," she repeated.

# 17

## MARCIN, SUMMER 1943

*Eger, Hungary*

It seemed to Marcin that the year had gone too fast, blurred by work, by mundanity, then rescues of children, adults sometimes, on train tracks in the iced nights, in the rain and in thick snow.

Then, the summer heat had come back and Marcin welcomed it at first until it beat down so hard that the thought of sitting for hours, sometimes days, in the dust, sweat dripping from every pore, made him wish once more for the cold of winter.

The days of waiting for children to be thrown from carriages had changed somewhat. The cattle cars now padlocked, some with wire mesh inside, were stopping those from escaping as the train slowed.

Instead, the resistance had grown. Armed themselves and prepared to fight as trains slowed and stopped, where men Marcin did not know ran out from thick trees, cutting at the locks, telling the frightened faces inside to jump as bullets screamed through the air.

Children arrived from ghettos, from homes they had been hiding in, and from other orphanages that were under threat.

Adam was not allowed near the train tracks anymore, and there was no need. The number of children had swelled and couriers came with more from all over Poland and the Slovak Republic. Instead, he waited in a safe house in Eger, where children would arrive with their couriers, hand them to Adam, to priests, to anyone willing to help, where they would then be ferried quickly to churches, cloisters, orphanages and relative safety.

Adam had started school and said that he hated it.

"It's boring," he whined daily. "Just let me help more. Let me do more."

"You can't." Marcin was firm this time. The tide was turning in the country. A bubbling current of tension sat just below the surface. Jews were leaving if they could; talk was turning against the government and there were whispers that soon Hungary would no longer be an ally of Germany and instead would soon be invaded. Czeslaw warned Marcin daily that they had to be careful now of who they trusted; even those who had once helped could turn against them.

"They wouldn't," Marcin told his uncle.

"You'd be surprised what someone will do to save themselves when they are afraid," his uncle had said.

Marcin had felt a cold panic course over him when he heard those words. Yes, he knew all too well what someone might do.

The feeling in Hungary now reminded Marcin of those months leading up to the day that Poznań heard the rumble of trucks, saw the soldiers and knew that all the rumors had come true. He remembered how everyone was convinced that Germany wouldn't do it, they would be talked down—what did they want with Poland anyway?

He heard those same comments now, here in Hungary. People tried to convince themselves that they could stay safe, that Hitler wouldn't come for them—he hadn't yet; why now? But Marcin knew it was coming. It was inevitable; it was just a question of when.

* * *

Agata sat close to her thirteen-year-old brother, Ryszard, as heavy boots disturbed the dust that clung to the floorboards above them.

She watched the motes dance in the air, swirl in the light, and then disappear into the shadows. She could hear her brother breathing heavily, feel the tremble of her mother's arms that were wrapped around them both.

She looked to her father, who stood on the stairs to the basement. In his hand, he held a plank of wood, ready to fight if someone opened the hatch.

Agata knew she should be scared, but this had happened many times before, and the woman and her husband who sheltered them never gave them up, always said the right thing to the soldiers, making them go away.

Although only eleven years old, Agata had seen too much and knew too much. She had seen her neighbors torn from their home, and the father shot in the street as he fought back. She had seen the pale, frightened faces of those hiding in the woods, where she and her family had spent an icy winter before finding sanctuary in a basement on the outskirts of

Katowice, given to them by a kindly couple who had hidden people before.

Gunshots no longer scared her. They were simply a background noise to her everyday life. The threat of being taken, too, did not scare her. In fact, if she had the words to express how she felt, she would say she felt numb and no longer cared what would happen.

At night, she would sometimes whisper a prayer that she would go to heaven in her sleep. That all of them would, just like the old woman in the woods had done. How they had found her, eyes closed and mouth slightly open. Heaven had to be a better place than this damp cellar, watching her father go mad with fear, watching her mother waste away as she told them all they would survive, that they would live a life again, just as they had before.

"Hush!" Her father backed down a step and raised the plank of wood in his hand. Upstairs, there was shouting, a gunshot that made Ryszard jump. Agata, however, stayed still.

More shouting. The footsteps came heavier now. Agata watched as the dust fell from the ceiling.

"You have to be ready to run!" her father said as the cellar door flung open and shiny black boots appeared.

* * *

Now she sat with a man called Marcin and a boy called Adam in a new house. A house that was in Hungary, as she had been told by the man called Piotr who had taken her to safety after a woman had found her hiding in a garden.

"Do you remember what happened next?" Adam asked her.

"Leave her now. Don't ask any more," Marcin said. "We will

rest here a few hours and then we will make our way to Budapest. You can rest now, Agata."

"It was like a dream," she said. "When the boots came. When Tata swung the wood, Ryszard grabbed my hand. I think we ran. We must have. But I don't know how we got past the soldiers. Ryszard said Matka stopped them, but I don't know."

"Hush now," Marcin said. "This is all too much. Rest now."

"No," Agata said. "I don't want to rest. I don't want to. You don't see, do you? I'm not afraid. I've not been afraid for a long time. I knew they would die. I knew it. But I thought I would die too. I'm not dead, am I?" she asked, looking at Marcin and then Adam. "Is this heaven?"

"You are confused. Tired. It has been a shock for you." Marcin tried to soothe her.

She laughed. "No. No, you don't understand," she rambled. "It's everywhere, isn't it? Death. You can't run from it. You can't hide. Just look at my brother and me. We hid, then we ran. And they got him too. Shot him. He was holding my hand, and then his hand wasn't there, and he was on the ground. So I ran alone. I ran and ran. And now I'm here. That man, Piotr. I was handed to him by this woman. I don't know who she was. She gave me to him. And he said "you're safe" and I tried to tell him I'm not. That you can't run and you can't hide!"

Marcin looked at Adam, whose eyes were wide. This was the first time they had seen a child who was not in tears, who was not afraid. It was like, Marcin thought, she had gone mad with the shock, with the grief, and given up hope.

"Agata," Adam said. "You can be safe now. I am. Marcin made sure of it. Piotr too. Everyone you will meet will keep you safe."

Agata looked past him to the whitewashed wall. "They're waiting for me. I can't stay long here."

Marcin went to the kitchen, where he found Ilona, a woman who ran the safe house with her husband. "There is something wrong with her," he said, panicked. "I don't know what to do."

Ilona wiped her floury hands on her apron, leaving the pastry she was rolling on the countertop, and went to look at Agata, who sat talking to a wall, seemingly not hearing Adam as he tried to talk to her.

"Agata?" Ilona said.

The girl refused to look at her. Instead, she spoke to the wall, to her parents she imagined standing there, to her brother, whom she told she was sorry for leaving and running away.

"It's normal that she is like this," Ilona told Marcin.

"I've not seen it before."

"Everyone is different." She shrugged. "You go now. Leave her here with me for a few days. Send one of the nuns back to collect her. I think that will be better for her now."

Marcin and Adam reluctantly left Agata with Ilona and returned to Budapest by bus. Adam stared out of the window, his jaw set.

"Are you all right?" Marcin asked.

Adam shrugged.

"It's not your fault, you know that, don't you?"

"I saw how she wanted to be with her parents, with her family," he said quietly. "I saw it and felt it. I know how that feels. I should have been able to get her to talk to me, just like the others."

"But your parents—" Marcin started.

"Are dead," Adam said.

"We don't know that, Adam."

Adam turned to look at him. "Do you remember when I

asked you never to lie to me, to always tell the truth? Tell me now, Marcin, do you really believe my parents are alive?" he asked once more.

Marcin looked at the bobbing heads of the other passengers as the bus weaved its way toward the city. He wondered for a moment who they were, if that one day he would see a face he knew, perhaps Adam's mother or father. They would turn around and smile, and in amazement, rush to Adam and embrace him, telling him they had been searching for him all this time.

Dreams, Marcin. Stupid dreams, he told himself, then turned to the boy. "I think they are dead, yes."

Adam nodded solemnly. "Thank you," he said, then turned again to the window to watch life outside rush by.

* * *

That evening, Adam refused to eat with Marcin and Czeslaw, and Marcin was glad of it. He had to tell his uncle what he had heard from Piotr and did not want Adam to hear.

"It can't be true." His uncle paced the living room, getting more and more irate with each step. "Janos can't be telling the truth?"

"He said he had heard it from the other couriers."

"Gas? Gassing them?" His uncle stopped pacing and looked at him incredulously.

"That's what he said."

"And did Adam hear this?" Czeslaw asked.

"No. And I don't want him to."

"Oh God!" His uncle raised his hands to the ceiling. "He cannot know. Not yet. Don't say anything to him yet. He has to hold on to hope that his parents will survive this."

"I told him I thought they were dead," Marcin said.

"Why would you do that, Marcin?"

"He wanted me to tell him the truth."

"We don't know the truth! You have to tell him you were wrong, that you believe they could still be alive."

"I can't, Czeslaw. I promised to tell him the truth. He needs to know."

"Needs to know?" Czeslaw's voice cracked. "What he needs is a reason to get up in the morning. You give him the truth, Marcin, and you take that away. You leave him with nothing but the waiting—and the knowing."

Marcin shook his head. "I can't lie to him. Not about this."

"It's not lying," Czeslaw said, stopping his pacing and facing Marcin. "It's mercy. You think truth is always noble? In times like these, truth can kill faster than any bullet."

For a long moment neither spoke. Marcin looked away first. "He asked me straight out, Czeslaw. Looked me in the eyes. I—" He swallowed hard. "I couldn't give him hope I don't believe in."

Czeslaw's hands fell to his sides, his shoulders sagging. "Then God help you, Marcin. Because if you take his hope, you'd better be ready to carry what comes after."

His uncle resumed his pacing, muttering to himself. Marcin did not try to stop him. His mind was full of the thoughts of what Janos had said about gassing. He did not want to imagine it, couldn't believe that it was true. And then, he saw Adam's parents' faces, pleading with him to keep Adam safe, then Adam's face when he wanted to know if his parents were dead. He felt sick.

"Listen to me now, Marcin." Czeslaw came to him and placed his hands on his shoulders. "The talk is getting worse. Soon things will be as they are in Poland and beyond. If it comes to that, you, me, Adam, all of us are not safe for our roles in all of this. So you need to keep your head down. Be vigilant—"

"I am," Marcin said.

"Even more so. No more taking Adam. He needs to blend in with boys at his school. He needs to keep his mouth closed. He needs for everyone to think that you are his father, that he is nothing more than a Catholic boy. That is all."

"He won't agree to it," Marcin said.

"I don't care what he will agree to anymore!" his uncle yelled. "The answer is no. No more. We should never have let him participate in the first instance."

"But he is good with the children. You've seen him. You've seen how they are calmer when he is around."

"I don't care, Marcin." His uncle slumped backwards into his armchair. "And another thing. I think it is time for you and Adam to think about leaving. Go to one of these addresses and they will help you both."

Marcin watched as his uncle fussed about in a journal on the side table and tore a piece of paper away. "Here. I've had these for a while now. I was hoping we wouldn't need them. It seems, however, I am wrong."

Marcin read the names on the paper and places in Romania, in France, in Turkey even. "You want us to go to which one?" he asked.

"I'm forming a plan with Father Aldony. It will be your route out of here. If we can get things in motion now, you will hopefully be gone before the Nazis arrive. The children at the orphanage in Vác-on-the-Danube should be safe, but still, we are trying to get as many sent overseas as we can to new families."

"And where will you go, if Adam and I leave?" Marcin asked. "You won't come with us?"

Czeslaw shook his head. "I don't want to start again in a new country, a new life. If I cannot stay here, then I die here."

"That's defeatist of you. You can't be serious?" Marcin almost laughed. "Surely you want to live?"

"I do, Marcin. But by my own rules. You, you are young, Adam obviously too, and you can build a life somewhere. Collect books, get a house, get friends, family even. Me. I've done that and I don't want to do it again."

"You did it by coming here permanently when we fell out," Marcin said. "How is this any different?"

His uncle smiled. "My life has been rich and full. I've lived half my time in Poland, half here. I've loved every second of it. I don't want to die, Marcin. But I want to fight for my right to exist in a country I call home. I won't let anyone take that from me."

"But you want me to do that?"

"Like I said. You haven't really found your home yet. Your family."

"Mother and Father are in Poland," he said.

"Not them. They are your blood, of course. But you make your family as you go through life. Friends you collect along the way sometimes become more important to you than any sibling or parent could be. You forge bonds with these people, spend happy times together, find common ground, and accept each other for who you are. Who you truly are, to your core. You need to find that for yourself, Marcin. You need to find a way to live after all this and find some joy, some love."

If Marcin did not know any better, he would think that his uncle had drunk too much vodka. His emotional speeches were usually reserved for late nights and early mornings, where you could say these things and then forget that you'd ever said them.

"I wouldn't leave without you," Marcin said. "You are my family."

His uncle grinned. "I am. I always will be. But I am but a small story in your life. Soon, there will be people in your life who fill the pages with their stories, shared with you. I am but a chapter."

# 18

## MARCIN, SUMMER 1943

*Eger, Hungary*

Robert and Jean Gronowski were still learning Polish. The man, Piotr, who had rescued them from the side of the railway line, did not speak French well, though he had tried to communicate with them as they walked each day.

Jean, the brighter and older of the two brothers at fourteen, evidently caught on that Piotr was trying to tell them that they were headed for Hungary, that the train they had been in that had taken them from Belgium toward Poland was headed for a place called Auschwitz. It was a bad place, Piotr tried to explain to them.

Jean later said he'd tried to illustrate this to his twelve-year-old brother Robert, who'd asked if, once they got to Hungary, they would soon go home to Belgium. Jean then asked Piotr, and the third time, Piotr seemed to understand and shook his head. "Stay in Hungary," he told him. "For now."

Robert was not feeling well. He told his brother that his

stomach hurt, that something was very, very wrong. Jean told Piotr, who didn't seem to understand.

It was only when they reached a house where a woman called Ilona tried to give them a drink of water that Piotr seemed to understand the emergency of the situation. Robert fell to the floor, rolling onto his side, clutching at his stomach.

He had fallen from the train, Jean tried to explain. Jean had been agile, jumped off quickly when the train stopped. Robert had wanted to stay with their mother and only jumped as the train started to move again.

He saw Piotr and Ilona look at each other. She wringing her hands, Piotr speaking rapidly to her.

They moved Robert into a bedroom. All the while he screamed in pain.

"Please!" he cried. "Please, a doctor," wishing they would understand him.

He tried to calm his brother. Spoke to him of their family back home. Of how Mother and Father would soon return from that place, Auschwitz, and they would all be together again.

Robert cried for his mother and so did Jean.

"It will be okay," Jean told him. "Please, Robert."

Robert's face had paled, and sweat dripped from his brow. Soon, his sobs became quieter.

"He's all right now," Jean said to Ilona, who stood, her arms by her side. "He'll be all right."

Ilona bit at her bottom lip and looked afraid. Jean tried again to tell her that his brother would be fine, but then, the sobs ceased.

Jean looked at Robert, who had fallen asleep. He crouched down next to him and said things would be fine. Ilona started to cry, filling the silence.

It was then he saw that his brother's chest was no longer rising and falling, his mouth open a little, but no breath coming out.

Jean did not know what happened next. He was sure he cried. Perhaps screamed. His next memory was sitting in Ilona's living room, an older man there who could speak French, telling him that his brother had died. That there had been injuries inside his body that no one would have been able to fix.

His eyes darted around the room. A boy was there, too, someone maybe his own age.

"Tell him, Czeslaw, that he will be kept safe. That he was brave, helping his brother," Adam said.

Czeslaw repeated it to Jean, who looked blankly at them.

"Tell him again," Adam said.

"He's in shock," Czeslaw said. "It won't get through to him just yet."

Marcin shook his head. "Just like Agata," he said. "It's too much."

Marcin watched the boy as he went from speaking rapidly, waving his arms about, to screaming and crying, to racing toward the room that held his brother's body. Piotr blocked him multiple times, taking him back to the sofa, Czeslaw trying to tell him to calm down.

Soon, Jean's cries grew sharper, almost frantic. Czeslaw tried to calm him in halting French, but the boy's voice only rose, raw and broken.

Then came the knock. A hard, impatient rapping.

Ilona froze. Marcin moved first, crossing the room in two strides and peering through the lace curtain at the front window.

"It's a man," he muttered.

Ilona joined him. "It's Kovacs," she said.

"Friend or foe?" Czeslaw asked.

"Neither. He lives two houses away. I know him but he's just a neighbor."

The knock came again, followed by a voice. "Ilona? Is everything all right?"

"What do I do?" Ilona looked to Marcin.

"Just act normally, open the door, just say everything is fine. Say you have family here and one of them is sick."

Ilona nodded but Marcin could see that she had paled.

She opened the door a crack.

Marcin could see through the window that Kovacs was a wiry man with a sour face, his hat clamped low.

"I heard shouting," he said. "Crying."

Ilona forced a smile. "A cousin's boy. Fell ill. Nothing more."

Kovacs's eyes narrowed. "Ill? Is that so? I've seen things, Ilona, people coming and going. You need to be careful. Things aren't what they used to be."

"I understand," Ilona said, slowly trying to inch the door closed.

"You put others in danger. Me included. I don't know you well, but you and your husband seem like good people. It would be a shame if something happened."

"Very well," Ilona said. "Thank you, Kovacs."

She closed the door in his face and looked to Marcin.

"You need to leave. You need to leave now," Ilona said. "I don't think Kovacs will say anything, but I don't know. It's not safe here now, you understand, don't you?" she rambled, all the while worrying at her hands.

"It's all right." Marcin went to Ilona and placed his hands on her shoulders.

"You'll forgive me, Marcin." She began to cry. "I have family too. A mother and father in the next village, cousins, grown children."

"There's nothing to forgive, Ilona," Marcin said. "You have been so brave. You have done so much. Please, do not apologize."

"I will go and see some people. Are you able to get him to Aldony?" Piotr asked.

"We can manage," Marcin said.

"I have to find us a new place, quickly." Piotr kissed Ilona on the cheek as he left, scurrying away without a backward glance.

\* \* \*

They waited until nightfall to leave. Czeslaw had managed to calm Jean by giving him a large glass of vodka, which Marcin had said was the wrong thing to do.

"You want him to be quiet, yes?" Czeslaw had said.

"Quiet. Not drunk."

"Same, same," Czeslaw had grumbled.

By the time they reached Pest, light rain had started to fall, making the cobblestones slick. Pest's trams still ran, their bells echoing faintly, but the streets were quieter now, where voices dropped to whispers after dark.

Marcin kept a firm hand on Jean's shoulder as they walked. The boy stumbled once, his shoes slipping on wet stone. Czeslaw had gone ahead to warn Aldony of the boy's condition.

"Someone is following us," Adam whispered as he walked on the other side of Jean.

Marcin glanced back. A man in a dark overcoat was following at a measured pace, pausing at each corner as if to check his bearings.

"Arrow Cross?" Marcin asked under his breath.

"Or the police," Adam replied.

They turned left, away from the route to the church, and into a narrower street where the rain pooled in the gutters. The man followed.

"Faster," Marcin said, half-dragging Jean now, who whimpered gently.

They wove through back lanes, past shuttered shops, until they reached a building with a chipped green door. Marcin rapped twice in a rhythm, paused, then once more.

The door opened. "It went wrong," Marcin said to a surprised Janos.

"Inside," he said quickly, ushering them in. "And keep quiet."

Upstairs, Jean was settled on a sofa, his wet hair plastered to his forehead. Janos drew the curtains tight.

"You were followed?" he asked.

Adam nodded. "Someone must have seen us leave Ilona's."

Marcin recounted to Janos about Ilona and the neighbor, how Piotr had left to secure somewhere new.

"Dammit!" Janos smacked his fist into a side table. "I heard rumors a week ago that the Arrow Cross were sending out people, trying to seek out any resistance to them. They want to get into power; they want to do what Germany has done and rid the country of Jews. It's just a matter of time before they get in."

"We can't go to the church," Marcin said. "We cannot lead them there."

"No. No, you can't. Stay here. I will go out now and warn Aldony and the others. We need to move the children to Vác and the orphanage as quickly as possible."

Marcin was going to offer to go with Janos, but Janos was

quick, and was already out of the door by the time Marcin had stood up to make his offer.

While Janos was gone, Adam and Marcin tended to Jean, sobered him up as much as they could and tried to tempt him to eat something. The boy just shook his head, then lay down on the couch and fell asleep.

"What are we going to do now, Marcin?" Adam asked. "Without Ilona?"

Marcin sat on a chair by the window and inched the curtains open slightly so he could see if anyone was waiting outside. The streets were clear, quiet. Perhaps too quiet.

"Marcin?" Adam said.

"Sorry. Yes, what are we going to do?" Marcin repeated the question back at Adam.

"Yes."

Marcin tried to think of an answer, but his brain was too jumbled. Ilona, the boy, Jean. They had been followed. They were caught? Or at least known about now. Beneath his damp shirt he could feel his heart pushing too hard against his skin.

"Marcin?" Adam asked again.

"Czeslaw said we should leave. He said it a week or so ago. I ignored him, of course. But I think he's right."

"Leave to go where?" Adam asked.

"He had addresses. People he said could help."

"Are we really in that much danger if we stay?"

"I don't know, Adam, I really don't know."

The door suddenly swung open, and Czeslaw stepped inside, brushing rain from his coat. His face was pale, drawn tight.

"I've just come from the church," he said. "Janos is already moving the children. Tonight. They're going to the orphanage in Vác. Janos says he will take Jean tomorrow."

"They'll be safe there?" Marcin asked.

"We are hoping so. Some haven't got papers yet, baptism certificates and such, but Aldony said they will work quickly on them now."

Marcin saw Czeslaw look at Jean, then Adam, his jaw clenched.

"You two will go as well," Czeslaw said, looking to Marcin. "It's time."

Adam, who had been sitting cross-legged on the floor by Jean's feet, looked up sharply. "No. I'm not leaving."

"Adam," Czeslaw began, "it isn't safe. Not for you. Not for anyone."

"I don't care," Adam said, his voice rising. "I'm not running away. I don't want to give up."

"It's not giving up," Czeslaw said, his tone sharp. "It's surviving."

"Same thing," Adam muttered.

Marcin rubbed his face, feeling the weight of the day pressing down. "Adam—"

"No, Marcin. You said you'd tell me the truth. So tell me this —is trying to leave really going to work? Is it really safer? Where could we go? How could we get there?"

"I have friends," Czeslaw started, but Adam cut him off.

"We have seen how the children have had to hide, we have heard their stories of living in forests, hiding in houses. Even going to people's homes, like Ilona's, who is a friend. We can't trust your friends, we can't run and hide like that. What if there is no one to save us, just as we have tried to save them?"

"That's exactly why you should go," Czeslaw snapped, his composure cracking. "If those rumors keep coming true, there'll be no place left for you to hide, not here, not anywhere. We know the Arrow Cross is watching now. It's just a matter of time before either they are in power and enact German law, or, if not, Germany will come here and do it herself."

Marcin hesitated, torn between the urgency in Czeslaw's voice and the stubborn set of Adam's jaw. "We could... wait," he said slowly. "Until winter. If things get worse, if it really looks like Germany will invade Hungary... then we'll go."

Czeslaw's eyes blazed. "Winter? That's months away. You're gambling with his life, Marcin."

"I'm giving him time," Marcin replied quietly. "I'm giving both of us time. Time to think, plan, and make sure, if we leave, we will be safe. Adam's right; we can't rely on the names of people you gave me. We have to make sure there is someone who will help us no matter what. Look at Ilona; she wants to help, but now she is compromised. I suspect many of the people you thought of as friends may now feel the same way."

For a moment, it seemed Czeslaw might argue again, but instead, he let out a harsh breath, turning away. "Fine. But if the rumors keep coming, if Janos hears even a whisper that we are in danger, you go. No debate. No second chances."

Adam looked between them, the fight still in his eyes, but saying nothing more. Marcin gave him a small nod.

The silence that followed was broken only by Jean's restless turning on the sofa and the rain ticking steadily against the windowpanes.

# 19

## MARCIN, WINTER 1943

### Budapest

The snow had come early, drifting in heavy, wet clumps that muffled Buda's streets and made the gas lamps glow faintly yellow in the dusk.

Czeslaw's words from the summer still echoed in Marcin's head: *Leave. Take Adam and go.*

They had agreed to wait until winter to make a decision. And now winter had come, and they were still here.

Marcin told himself there had been reasons to still be here —there were always reasons. Adam had refused, of course, his stubbornness like a wall Marcin couldn't climb. And Marcin, though he hadn't admitted it aloud, hadn't truly tried to make him. Partly because the work here wasn't finished, partly because moving meant trusting new names, new houses, new dangers. And partly because—though it shamed him to think it—he had grown used to Pest. Its narrow streets and hidden cellars had become a kind of uneasy home.

Ilona and her husband were gone now. No one said where

—they had simply disappeared one morning, shutters drawn, the house looking like it had been abandoned for months rather than hours. Piotr was nowhere to be found either, gone after heading back to Poland on what he called "a short job." He had not returned.

"He's probably dead," Janos told Marcin as they sat not in László's cellar this time, but openly in his bar, drinking a cheap red wine that made Marcin grimace.

"You don't know that," Marcin said.

"It's been a week. He's dead and he was our best." Janos raised a glass to him.

"You going back in?" László pulled out a chair and placed a dusty bottle on the table. "This one is much better. Don't think I don't see you puckering your lips on that one." László nodded at Marcin.

"Someone has to," Janos said, then glanced Marcin's way. "We have someone on the inside, and someone has a house in Gomulin that we are using for now. I just hope it hasn't been compromised."

"The inside, where?" Marcin asked.

"The Łódź ghetto. Piotr and his cousin, along with others, have been getting people out. There are a lot of children there. A lot of orphans. We"—Janos pointed to himself and then at Marcin—"have to go back."

"What? Me?"

Janos shrugged. "No real difference from the trains. Same thing. But there are no trains. Just guards and dogs and guns. But there are ways in and out. And so far, well, as far as we know, whoever followed you in the summer hasn't done anything with the information. You're still under the radar for now."

"What about Piotr's cousin—what was his name?"

"Witold," both Janos and László said at the same time.

"Well, can't he go with you?"

"I don't know whether you have forgotten, but he is deaf. His role is at the safe house. I am assuming he is still there. Protocol is for him to wait there if Piotr does not come back."

Marcin swigged back the glass of red, grimaced, and let László fill it with the good wine.

"So you'll do it. Tonight we set off. It will be a long journey. There are patrols everywhere."

The faces of all the orphans he had helped flashed by. There, Sara, crying for her *matka*. The little boy who died in his arms, seemingly at peace. Then, Agata, who he could not help. Then Jean, broken from losing his brother. More recently, Marcin had done very little compared to Piotr, Janos, and the others. His job had been to ferry them the two hours from Eger to the church or orphanage. Then his job was done.

He told as much to Janos.

"What, so you don't think you are brave enough?" Janos said. "Do you know what could have happened if somebody in the government found out exactly what we and you were doing?"

László dragged a finger across his neck.

"And going to the train tracks. There were guards. If they had seen you..." Janos looked to László to finish.

He obliged, dragging a finger along his neck again.

"I wasn't thinking I wasn't brave enough," Marcin said. "I think I want to do it. I want to do more."

Janos grinned. "I knew you were in there somewhere!" He laughed and clinked his glass against Marcin's.

As László talked about a delivery of wine he was expecting, and how the prices had gone up, and the customers had disappeared, Marcin had one thing on his mind. Adam. He would make up for everything. This would change him, surely. And, well, if he died trying, then that was his penance to bear. A penance Marcin almost welcomed.

* * *

Anna was small for her age. At fourteen, she resembled an eleven-year-old, but she was quick to learn, took in everything around her, and had become a "big sister" to a nine-year-old girl, Irena, who had lost both parents to a sickness that had raged through the ghetto during the summer months.

Anna, too, had lost both of her parents, and her grandparents. The former had died a year before, her father shot for taking potatoes that had been thrown over the fence by local people, her mother from starvation. Her grandparents had disappeared on a train two days after arriving, leaving Anna with the other children who were old enough to work long hours in the factories, stitching clothes, making uniforms for soldiers, clothes for women who Anna imagined would wear them to fancy dinner parties, or to the theater.

She would talk to the other children during the day, each of them making up fairy tales to while the hours away. Their overseer, Leon, somehow found a way for them to train in a vocational school, where during this, they would write poetry and stories, drawing pictures of a prince in a wondrous land, who threw a great bridge over the water and extended his hand to the children, joy bursting from his eyes.

This would take place on a Saturday, after dinner, and they would be given an extra piece of bread and chunk of sausage. It was a day that Anna immensely looked forward to. A day when the world seemed a little brighter.

She was worried, however, because so many of the younger

children who could not work were being sent away. Leon told them that the work in the factory would save them for now, but there was little to be done for the smaller children.

Anna, as an orphan, lived in a cramped room with other girls, in Przemysłowa Street, away from the other side of the ghetto. Here, they had formed their own family, working together, talking together, and hoping that one day they would be free.

She wrote poems for herself, stories too, whenever she could, and at night she would read the stories to the other girls to help them sleep.

"One day, a man arrived at the gates. He was tall and kind and had friends who were kind too. They told us that they were here to take us to a new home, with new parents. We all ran to them, full of joy."

"Where would we go?" one of the girls interrupted.

"To a big house. All of us. There would be lots of food."

"Like *pączki*? And chicken, and fruit?" another girl interrupted.

"Yes, all of that," Anna said, not minding the constant interruptions. "Every food you could think of would be there."

"And we wouldn't be cold," Irena said. "And we wouldn't have to sew anything anymore!"

"Exactly," Anna said and put the paper away. She didn't need to tell this story again; the girls would fill in the gaps with things that they wished for.

She sat and listened to them as they imagined their new lives. They would have new clothes, and in summer they would swim again in the river. They would have a huge bed and could lie in it all day if they so wished. They would never have to be hungry or thirsty and none of them would have to go on a train.

"Do you think it will come true?" Irena said later that night as she lay down beside her. "Do you think someone kind will come for us?"

"I do," Anna told her. "They have to come." Because, Anna thought as her little sister fell asleep, the alternative was too much to think about.

* * *

It was still dark when Anna woke. She thought that it was morning and time for work, but outside, the snow fell quickly on the quietened street below, the shadows still thick. Why had she woken?

She looked to the other girls, all crammed together, seeking each other out for warmth.

Then, she heard it. Footsteps.

She quickly got under her blanket next to Irena, holding her tight.

The footsteps got louder. Two—no, three pairs.

The trains were running again, Anna thought. It was their time.

"Hush," someone said above her. "I'm here to help."

Anna opened her eyes to see a man with a kind face. Another figure was behind him, and another she had seen before in the ghetto, smuggling in medicines and food.

"My name is Marcin. And we must hurry now."

There were seven girls in the room, but the man did not wake them all. He woke Irena next to Anna, and one more near the door, a girl called Jutta who was older than Anna but acted like she was a small child.

"That's enough for now," the smuggler's voice warned. "We've already got someone getting some of the boys."

"We can't leave them here," the man called Marcin said.

"We'll come back."

Within a minute, Marcin and the two others ushered the girls out of the room, Irena and Jutta frightened and listening to Anna as she told them to stay quiet.

Before they left, Anna turned to look at the building where the other girls were still soundly asleep and felt a knot in her stomach. Her fairy tale was coming true and theirs were not.

"Hurry now." Marcin ushered them to the barbed-wire fence where two other men stood on the other side, holding up a piece of the fence for them to climb under.

Anna shepherded Irena and Jutta through first, then on hands and knees, the snow burning cold through her clothes and on her skin, she got to the other side.

"Quickly now!" Marcin told the girls to run. To follow the smuggler and the other man. He would be behind them.

As she ran, the iced air burned her throat. She could feel the soles of her feet were wet, her toes starting to numb. Irena and Jutta tried to say that they wanted to stop, but Anna grabbed their hands tightly and dragged them on. They would not stop. They would not go back.

It seemed as if they ran down every dark alley in Łódź. The houses and shops silent in the snowy night. They came out of one alleyway, their breathing hard, and found a butcher's van waiting.

"Get in!" Marcin opened the rear of the van, ushering them in, where Anna found four boys already sitting, their eyes wide with fear, each of them shaking in the cold.

Marcin climbed in after them. The other man too. The door closed. The van sped off into the night.

"Don't be scared," Marcin told them.

"I'm not." Anna spoke up. The others stayed silent.

"I'm Marcin. And this is Janos. Janos is from Hungary. And that's where we're going too."

"How?" Anna asked.

Marcin looked surprised at the question.

"I'm not stupid, you know. I'm not young either. I know I look it. But I'm fourteen. How are we going to get to Hungary? How did you get in to rescue us? Why didn't you take everyone?"

"Wait, wait. One answer at a time," Marcin said. "We will get to Hungary because Janos here and our friend in the front have friends from Poland all the way to Hungary."

"Fine," Anna said. "But how did you get in?"

Marcin looked to Janos, who sighed. "You ask a lot of questions. Most of the time, you are all too scared to talk."

"Not me," Anna said.

"I see that," Janos replied. "We bribe the guards when we can. We had some luck with you all. There were two new young guards posted near you. Young and frightened and wanted money so they could get out of there too. It's not always that easy."

"And..." Anna started, ready with her next question, when Irena began to cry.

"Hush now." She cradled her friend, then squeezed Jutta's hand. She looked as though at any moment she would cry too.

"Let me tell you a story," Marcin said. "It will keep you calm."

"I like stories," Irena said. "Anna tells good ones about kind people coming to rescue us."

"Is that so?" Marcin asked. "Well then, how about both Anna and I tell you a story? Anna, you start, then I'll add some, then back to you, yes?"

Anna nodded, understanding that she would have to help

these kind, strange men keep this bunch together. Keep them from crying, from running away. She looked at the boys, who must have been no older than ten, and smiled at them.

"So," she started. "One day, these kind men came to the gates to take us home..."

# 20

## MARCIN, WINTER 1943

*Vác Orphanage*

The orphanage in Vác stood at the edge of a frozen field, its red-tiled roof dusted white, the chimneys puffing thin streams of smoke into the pale sky. Once a large family home, it had been used by the nuns now for years, transforming each room into dormitories and classrooms.

The van slowed to a stop and Marcin opened the van's doors, helping the children out one by one. Anna aided Marcin and Janos, talking softly to the children, telling them they were now safe, and not to be afraid of the nun who came out to greet them.

"Ah, Marcin!" Sister Krisztina walked toward him.

He had met the sister a few times before, and both times, she had been harried, wispy gray hairs sneaking out from under her habit, and had barely smiled, let alone engaged in conversation with him. This time, though, her smile was wide, her gray hair neatly tucked away.

"Sister," he said.

"We are overrun, as I am sure you know. But we can find more room," she said, watching as some of the younger sisters took the children inside. "I have been hearing tales about you, Marcin," she said, gesturing toward the open door.

"Tales?"

"Come, come inside. You too, Janos. And your friend in the front seat there."

"He has to get back," Janos said, nodding at the driver, who tipped his hat back, then sped away.

"Tales?" Marcin asked again as he and Janos followed the sister into the building.

"Indeed. Adam is quite a storyteller."

"Adam is here?"

"He came with Czeslaw for a visit. Both of them said that it would cheer the children to hear stories, perhaps play games. He is a lovely boy, I must say."

Inside, the smell of freshly baked bread and cabbage soup hung in the air, making Marcin's stomach rumble.

"You must be cold, tired. Head to the kitchen, you know where. Cook will sort something for you," the sister said. "And I'll tell Adam you are here, your uncle too."

As Marcin and Janos walked through the rooms, littered with small beds, some with children sitting on them, playing with toys or reading, he looked about for familiar faces, hoping to see Sara, or perhaps Agata. But the faces that looked back at him with wide, curious eyes were no one he recognized.

"Marcin!"

He turned to see Adam, bounding down the stairs. Sara was with him—her long hair now brushed and tied with a red ribbon, her cheeks rounder than they'd been months before.

"I hear you have been telling tales," Marcin said.

"Some." Adam grinned.

"Have you brought sweets, Marcin?" Sara asked. "Last time you came you said you would come back with sweets."

"Ah now, I forgot," Marcin said.

Sara's face fell.

"But, wait!" Marcin dug around in his pocket, taking out two boiled sweets, one red, one yellow. "I did remember!"

Sara laughed and took the sweets hungrily. "Thank you, Marcin. I'll have the red one and I'll give one to Zofia."

"You are still friends with Zofia?" Marcin asked.

"Best friends." Sara nodded.

"Marcin, I cannot wait for food much longer," Janos complained.

"Go ahead, I'll be there soon," Marcin said, wanting to spend a little time with Sara and perhaps the others. Every time he had visited in the past, it had been brief, dropping children off, checking on how many beds they had left, a few snatched conversations with some of the children, and that was it.

But with the snow that was falling, the warmth from the fireplaces, the tiredness that weighed on him, he felt it was the perfect time to take a moment, sit, and find some joy in seeing these children, if not happy, at least safe from harm.

"Come see Zofia, Marcin." Sara grabbed his hand. "She's in the main hall. Usually, we only use it for schoolwork and for mealtimes, but because it is so cold, and because it has a big fireplace, we are allowed to play in there. Isn't that nice? To have somewhere to play all together?"

"It is," Marcin agreed.

"Do you know what else is nice?" Sara asked.

"No."

"Agata got a new family. She went to live with them last week. I miss her but it was nice that she got a new family. They have a farm and she said she was going to ride a horse. That's nice, isn't it, Marcin?"

"It is, very," he said, and squeezed her hand.

The main hall, which he supposed was once a large ballroom, had been cleared of any furniture, bar long tables and benches that had been pushed aside to make room on the floor for the children to sit and play, read or draw.

He saw one of the sisters with Anna by her side. Anna waved at Marcin, who walked toward her.

"Anna," Marcin said, "this is Sara. And this is Adam."

Anna smiled.

"You're new," Sara said. "I was new once. But then I made a friend." She waved toward a girl sitting cross-legged on the floor by the fire, carefully sewing the hem of a doll's dress. "That is Zofia. She was the first orphan I met here. She didn't talk at first, but... well, she talks now. She talks all the time now. She doesn't talk as much as me though. Everyone says I talk a lot. Do you like to talk, Anna?"

"I do," Anna said. "I also like to tell stories."

"Ohh! That's wonderful! Adam likes to tell stories too, don't you, Adam?" Sara said.

"I do."

"Maybe you could tell stories together?" Sara suggested, letting go of Marcin's hand and taking Adam's and Anna's instead, taking them to sit in front of the fireplace with Zofia.

"Everyone!" Sara shouted, hands on her hips as if she were one of the sisters, making Marcin hide a laugh behind his hand. "Everyone, Anna and Adam are going to tell us some stories!"

The children did not have to be told twice, and within a minute or so, rows of children sat cross-legged in front of Adam, Anna, Zofia, and Sara, some clutching ratty teddy bears or small grubby blankets that they fussed at with their fingers.

"Should I start?" Anna asked.

"Please, do," Adam said. "I've been telling stories all day!" he said theatrically.

The children laughed and Marcin found himself laughing too.

"All right," Anna began. "Once, there was a little butterfly who lived in a city made of stone. Every day, the butterfly dreamed of flying far away, to a place where the air was warm and the flowers were bright. But there were tall walls all around her, and the air smelled of smoke.

"One day, a strong wind came and lifted her high above the walls. She was afraid, because she didn't know where she was going. But then she saw, far below, a garden full of children. They were laughing and running, and there were flowers everywhere. She wanted to go down to them, but the wind kept carrying her higher and higher.

"Just when she thought she would be lost forever, a hand reached out from the clouds—not to catch her, but to guide her gently down. She landed in the garden, where the children shared their food with her and gave her a warm place to sleep. And from that day on, she flew only when she wanted to—and never because she had to."

The children were silent for a moment, the fire crackling softly. Then Sara whispered, "That was a good story. Now. Adam. Your turn," she added authoritatively.

Adam acquiesced and told a funny story about a mouse that lived in a shoe and his best friends were a dog, a rabbit, and a ladybird.

Marcin sat and listened, letting the stories, the laughter,

and warmth spread over him. He yawned then rubbed at his eyes.

"Marcin?"

He turned to see Czeslaw standing there. "Can we talk?"

"Can it wait?" he asked, quite enjoying feeling this relaxed.

"Just a moment," Czeslaw asked.

Marcin followed him to the kitchen, where Janos was digging into a bowl of soup, tearing bread into chunks and dipping it into the liquid.

"Third bowl!" he said, spitting crumbs all over the wooden table. "Get some. It's good."

Marcin sat, taking a bowl from the cook, who then left the three men alone, saying she had to go to the cellar for more potatoes.

A single oil lamp burned on the table, throwing shadows along the walls. Outside, the snow tapped gently against the glass, and once more, Marcin felt at peace.

Czeslaw stood by the stove, slowly turning a mug in his hands. "They've settled quickly," he said without looking up.

"They are," Marcin replied, spooning the cabbage and carrot soup into his mouth, tasting the rich saltiness. "It's nice to hear about Agata."

Czeslaw set the mug down, rubbing his forehead. "You know what I said to you before, about leaving. The situation here is... uncertain." Czeslaw continued. "I went to see Father Aldony earlier today. He says that there are rumors that the Germans are restless along the border. If they push further—"

"Then nowhere will be safe," Marcin finished for him.

Czeslaw met his eyes. "I know we said we would wait. And I think we have waited long enough. It isn't going to get better, Marcin. I was glad you did this, with Janos, glad you saw the ghettos, because now you can see what it will be like here soon."

Marcin glanced toward the main hall, where the sound of muffled giggles drifted through. "And them? They cannot leave."

"They will be safe here," Czeslaw said quietly.

"Janos?" Marcin looked to his friend.

"Your uncle is right. You should leave. But maybe it can wait another few weeks. Maybe there is a chance we can do one more mission, get a few more out?"

Marcin looked from his uncle to Janos. He knew he had to do what was right for Adam and to keep him safe, but at the same time, he wanted this feeling again. He wanted to rescue as many children as he could, bring them here, and see the light slowly return to their eyes.

"Think on it," Czeslaw said quietly. "You may not get another chance."

Marcin stayed a moment longer, listening to the soft clatter of the stove and the faint breathing of the kitchen. He thought of the butterfly in Anna's story, of hands reaching down from the clouds. He wondered how many hands would be needed for all the children here—and whether they'd arrive before the wind took them somewhere they couldn't return from.

# 21

## MARCIN, WINTER 1943

*Budapest, Hungary*

Marcin and Adam said their goodbyes, and Sara had to be cajoled to leave Adam alone by Anna, who took her hand and said she would put her to bed.

The snowfall made their journey last an hour longer than usual, the buses not turning up or stopping short of their stops.

Tired and yet calm, Marcin walked alongside Janos, who spoke of the next mission, of how so many more could and would be saved. Marcin watched Janos as he spoke and saw that he loved not just rescuing the children, but the adrenaline, the rush at having gotten away enlivened him.

"You will come inside, Janos, and toast to another successful day?" Czeslaw asked.

"I don't see why not." He grinned.

As they turned onto Dárda, the first thing Marcin saw was the black car. A car that should not be in this narrow alleyway, a car that did not fit. Its windows were fogged, engine humming in the cold.

"Keep walking," Janos murmured.

Marcin looked behind him, to his uncle and Adam, and nodded at the car.

"Don't stop walking," Marcin said.

They kept up a steady pace, none of them looking at the car as they passed. A few steps away, Marcin turned.

Behind Czeslaw and Adam, he saw the car door open.

"Stop right there!" the man yelled.

Marcin made to run, but stupidly both Adam and his uncle stopped.

"Run!" Janos yelled at them, already a few feet ahead.

But it was too late; the man was on them now, another behind him. Both wearing long black coats, their red-and-white armbands identifying them as members of the Arrow Cross.

"Czeslaw Wójcik!" One of the Arrow Cross men grabbed Czeslaw by the collar and slammed him against the wall. The other lunged for Adam, but Marcin stepped between them, shoving the man back hard enough to stagger him.

"Go!" Janos shouted again, grabbing Adam by the arm and dragging him forward.

The one holding Czeslaw barked for them to stop, for Czeslaw to tell them to stop, but Czeslaw twisted in his grip just enough to look over his shoulder at Marcin.

"Run!" he shouted at Marcin.

The second Arrow Cross man lunged again, fingers catching the edge of Marcin's coat. Marcin wrenched free and bolted after Janos and Adam, the snow sucking at his boots. Behind him, he heard Czeslaw grunt in pain. He wanted to turn back. He had to turn back. He could not leave his uncle there. Memories surged forward, of leaving those two men that day in Poland, beaten because of Marcin.

"We have to go back!" he yelled to Janos.

"Keep moving!" Janos yelled back. "Keep moving, Marcin! Don't be stupid."

Marcin couldn't leave him, and yet, if he went back, he would be leaving Adam and putting Janos in danger.

He had no choice. He had to keep moving.

They tore down Dárda, past shuttered shops and into a narrow cut between buildings. Adam stumbled in the snow and Janos scooped him up without breaking stride.

The church soon came into view, and Janos was at the main door, pounding on it.

Father Aldony opened it a crack, saw Janos, Adam, and Marcin and opened it wide.

"This way," he said, ushering them in, past the altar with its lit candles, and Christ on his cross, past the knave and down into the crypt.

Once safely inside, Aldony looked at the three of them. "Who was it? Who came? Was it the orphanage?"

Janos shook his head.

"Czeslaw," Marcin said. "Arrow Cross have arrested him."

Aldony crossed himself and whispered something to God, a prayer that Marcin could not quite hear. "I had heard that some arrests were coming. I told your uncle this very morning."

Marcin thought back to his uncle talking in the orphanage's kitchen, how somber he had seemed, how he had tried to warn Marcin. He didn't know it was going to happen so soon, but he knew it was eventually, and he had wanted Marcin and Adam out of harm's way by then.

"They'll be looking for all of us now," Janos panted.

"This is where you'll stay tonight," Father Aldony said. "We'll move you tomorrow, if it's safe."

Adam stood stiffly, his eyes shining in the dim light. "We have to go back for Czeslaw," he said.

Father Aldony's face softened, but his tone stayed firm. "You can't."

"I don't care," Adam said, his voice rising. "He's family. He's—"

"Adam." Janos crouched in front of him, gripping his shoulders. "Listen to me. I'll find out what's happened. Where he is. All right?"

"We're not going without him," Adam said.

Marcin looked to the boy and nodded at Janos, whose upturned face was waiting for Marcin to step in. "He's right. We need to find out where he is, save him if we can. We don't go anywhere without him."

"You're foolish," Father Aldony said. "Czeslaw knew the risks and he had a way out for you. I have it planned. All of it."

"We stay. We wait to see what Janos can find out," Marcin said.

Then, Marcin turned from them and walked to the far wall where a picture of the Virgin Mary sat. For the first time since he was a boy, he kneeled on the cold stone floor and began to pray.

* * *

The next day, Janos was gone before dawn. Marcin paced the crypt, the flicker of a single candle casting restless shadows on the low ceiling. He had prayed most of the night, prayed that his uncle would be set free, that he was not hurt, that he could be saved.

Adam sat on one of the narrow stone benches, fiddling with a piece of string, making loops and knots with quick, angry motions. Marcin tried to talk to him, to give him some hope, but Adam would not talk and fiddled with the string over and over again as if by doing so, he could create a new magic trick —one where Czeslaw was returned to them.

By eleven, Janos returned. Marcin could smell the cold that clung to him like another layer of clothing. He stamped the snow off his boots and leaned against the wall.

"Well?" Marcin asked.

"It's not good," Janos said bluntly. "But he's alive."

Adam's head snapped up. "You saw him?"

"No," Janos said. "I bribed a guard. One who doesn't care about politics as much as he cares about feeding his family. He told me Czeslaw's in the city prison. Interrogations started last night."

Marcin felt the room tilt slightly.

"The guard says he's holding up," Janos continued. "But they'll keep pressing him. If they find out about us—"

"They won't," Adam interrupted fiercely. "He won't tell them."

Marcin wished he could match Adam's certainty, but he knew what fear felt like, and that, along with plenty of pain, could make almost anyone talk.

"I managed to get this." Janos drew out a piece of paper from his pocket. "An extra bit of money got the guard to go to Czeslaw and allow him to write a letter to you."

"Why did you ask him to do that?" Marcin asked as Adam jumped up and grabbed the paper from his hand.

"Because you won't leave, and you have to. You know you do. Czeslaw knows it too. You needed to hear it from him."

"Marcin and Adam," Adam began.

Marcin looked and saw that Adam was reading the letter, his hands trembling as he held it.

*They will not let me go. I know this already. The questions do not stop, but I will give them nothing. They want names, and I give them lies. They want locations, and I send them chasing shadows. I hope that I will not break. I hope I can keep you all safe. But I am old, and I do not know how far they will go and if I will be able to keep my mouth closed.*

*Leave Hungary as soon as you can. Father Aldony will help. Do not stay for me. You must not. If I survive, then I will find you. I promise you that. But please let me have that hope, held deep within my heart, that you will both be safe. That is all I want, all I wish for.*

*I have seen you, Marcin, how you have changed these past years, how you have become brave, braver than I ever could hope to be. You have grown into the man you were always meant to be. Be proud of what you have achieved, and I am sure that your successes will continue in life.*

*And Adam. Although in age you are but a boy, you have shown yourself to be a courageous man, taking on more than any boy should. I am proud of you, my boy. I am proud of both of you. Proud to call you my family.*

*Please do not be afraid for me. I am not afraid. Whatever comes, I have lived my life knowing I fought for something that mattered and that I have loved and been loved. What else could anyone ask for?*

*Czeslaw*

Marcin took the letter from Adam and read it again, then a third time, tracing each word with his eyes until it seemed burned into his memory. Adam sat close, reading over his shoulder, silent until the end.

"He's not afraid," Adam said finally, though his voice cracked. "If he's not afraid, then we shouldn't be either."

## 22

### CLARA, 1982

*Alpine Lakes Wilderness*

"The days after leaving Hungary are still a blur to me," Marcin said as Clara tried to fix a worm onto the hook, and after one week she was getting rather adept at it, but the feel of the slimy skin on her fingers still made her queasy.

She gave up with the worm and looked at Marcin, who had folded the yellowing piece of paper, his uncle's letter, away and placed it in an inside pocket.

"Your uncle. What happened to him?"

Marcin sighed. "After his arrest, he was taken to Auschwitz."

"He didn't survive?"

Marcin shook his head. "I don't know what he experienced. I can only imagine the fear. But I tell myself every time I think of him that when he was there he would have still tried to help others. He still would have fought to do the right thing to his last breath. I try not to think of it. Try not to think that we never said goodbye."

"I'm sorry, Marcin," she said, the words feeling meaning-less. She had heard the same thing over and over again, after her father had died, and she found that soon the words became worthless, yet no one really knew what else to say. "I felt that too, with Dad. That I never got a chance to say goodbye."

"Perhaps it is for the best?" Marcin said.

"Perhaps."

The quiet sat gently between them, until Clara could no longer bear it and had to get him talking again. She had to fill the silence that would eventually deafen her. "How do you know about all of it—like how do you know about Anna and Jean?"

"I listened to their stories," he said. "Adam and I. We listened to them when we would visit them. They told us of what it was like for them. I needed to know. You see, the life we had in Hungary at the time was relatively safe, and word of what the rest of the world was dealing with came in bits and pieces. I needed to know what the truth was for these people. And, too, what we could probably expect to happen."

"And it did," Clara said.

"It did."

"What was it like, escaping with Dad? It must have been hard?"

"It was," he said, looking out at the placid lake. Then, "Come. You will not catch anything today," he said.

"I might," she insisted.

"Too cold. Come now, inside. Enough for today."

Clara did as she was told. He was not going to say anymore, not today anyway. And she knew not to press him.

**\* \* \***

The following day, she watched as Marcin scanned the lake, his forehead creasing as he thought. Why was his journey to America seemingly bothering him more than all the other stories he had told? she wondered.

"It is not easy to leave it all behind," Marcin said quietly. "I was made to leave. At first it was fine, because we needed to get to safety. But I remember being on the boat from England to America. I remember feeling lost as I watched England disappear, knowing that beyond it was Europe and my old home, my old life. It scared me to think of who I would be now. I was not good at English. Adam wasn't either. But we would soon be somewhere foreign, with foreign tongues, a different way of living, and I wasn't sure I was going to be able to adapt to it."

"That's why it's hard to talk about?" Clara said.

"Yes. That's why. And because I felt guilty. Your father did too. Like we were saving ourselves, but there were so many others that could not have what we had. Would die, or would live a terrible life, wishing they were dead."

"Your uncle," she said.

He nodded. "He should have come with us. He was a stubborn— Wait, what you call it? Eee-aww?"

"Mule?" Clara said.

"Yes. Mule. Stubborn as one of them. I thought, after his arrest, he would be set free weeks later. I held on to that for years. Then I found out he had died in Auschwitz and it made me feel guilty all over again."

"You don't have to say any more," Clara said. "I've made you talk about so much. You don't have to tell me any more."

"It's okay." He looked at her and smiled, patted her knee. "There is not much to tell. We followed the instructions my uncle gave us. Went from house to house, person to person, country to country until we reached Istanbul. We went to the

British Consulate. They say to us, you can go to Palestine or a Quaker charity is helping people get to America. I thought America is better, you know. I was not Jewish, only Adam. I was thinking about myself really. How could I, the way I am, you know—"

"Gay," she said for him.

"Yes. That. How could I go to Palestine? Maybe it would be all right, maybe worse. Maybe they would never know. But I thought America is big and maybe it would be better for me."

"Is it?" she asked.

"I don't know," he said.

"Have you been happy here, Marcin?" she asked. "In America?"

"I don't know," he repeated.

"Do you think, if your uncle was alive now, he would be proud of the life you have lived?"

Marcin narrowed his eyes at her. "What are you trying to say?"

Clara took a deep breath. It was now or never. "I just think you have punished yourself enough. You have lived with guilt all this time. But you haven't really done what you wanted to do."

"Like what?"

"Like find someone. Have friends. Family."

"I have family." He grinned at her and nudged her.

"I know." She smiled back. "But aren't you lonely? And don't you think you deserve to have the best life possible?"

"I have a life," he said, then looked away from her and concentrated on his fishing.

The silence sat for an hour, making Clara regret what she had said. She had obviously upset him, been too familiar; or had she? Surely after everything he had been through, the fear, the trauma, he deserved something better. She tried to imagine her father and Marcin, fleeing Europe, coming to America. She wouldn't have been able to do it, that was for sure.

"What you thinking?" Marcin asked.

"Eh?"

"You scrunching up your nose when you think. Like a little rabbit does."

"I was thinking about how afraid you must have been, imagining the danger of it all. I don't think I could have done it."

"You could have. Anyone can. It is about survival. And yes, I was afraid, and yes, it was dangerous. Everywhere there were soldiers. Guns. Planes. Bombs. It was like it was never quiet. That's what I remember the most. It was never quiet. And we had to walk all the time. But we were not alone. There were so many other people too, walking, looking for escape. We had to sleep in ditches, in forests. We had to beg for food. It was not easy."

"And Dad?"

"Your father was braver than me. Always was. When we met other people and walked with them, if there were children, he would make them laugh. He would sing songs to them. He never wanted anyone to be afraid, so he pretended he wasn't.

"There was this one day, though. It was raining hard. I can't remember exactly where we were, not even which country. But I remember the rain. It came down so quick, like sheets, so you couldn't really see in front of you. It was cold too. We were tired. Adam had blisters on the backs of his heels and he limped when he walked. I told him we could stop a while, find somewhere to get out of the rain, and he agreed.

"We sat under some trees. We still got wet but it was less, and the noise, you know, the noise, pitter patter on the leaves, it was nice. Adam, he leaned against me. I could feel he was shivering. So I took my coat off and wrapped it around him and held him close to me. It was the first time, I think, since he was a small boy that he let me hold him like that.

"He asked me what our lives could be like. He asked me to tell him a story about what the picture could be for both of us.

"So I told him that we would live somewhere sunny. Somewhere nice, but not too hot, you know. We would have a house, with a garden, and he would finish school and find friends.

"'Will you get married, do you think?' he had asked me.

"I said maybe. Then I made the story as crazy as I could imagine, you know, telling him that I would become an actor, like Janos had wanted to be; you know, he made it sound nice. I would be famous, and we would be rich and sail about the world and come visit Czeslaw and all the orphans. It made him smile, that story. Made him stop thinking about the pain, the cold."

"Do you think he knew... you know?"

"No. I don't know. He never asked if I would marry again though, so who knows. Maybe he guessed?"

"It's hard to picture you and Dad walking all that way, the danger, the fear you must have felt."

"How can I explain?" Marcin said. "Yes, we were scared, but there was no other option. You have to keep moving, keep walking. You get so used to the soldiers, to the danger, that soon it becomes normal. I can't explain how. It just is. Maybe the best way to understand is how Agata said she felt. Like death wasn't as scary anymore. It was a probability and you start to let it in, let yourself think that this is just a part of it too." He shook his head. "I'm not explaining myself very well."

"No. I think I understand. It's like when I took pills and

things. I went too far all the time. I wasn't trying to kill myself, I just wasn't scared if it happened."

"But you don't feel like that now?" he asked.

"I don't know how I feel. I try not to think too far ahead. I just keep thinking, I'll go fishing and we'll talk and then have dinner. Past that, I try not to think about it."

"Do you think this has helped you? You know, piece your puzzle together?"

"I think so," she said. "I think I understand Dad a bit better now. Like, to me, he was just Dad, you know. A parent. I never really thought of him as his own person who had fears, insecurities, worries. I can see now how his past might have made him feel, how it impacted him."

"But he had a good life, Clara. He loved being in America, found it easy to fit in, got friends, got himself an American accent." He chuckled.

"And he went to school, university, met Mom," she said.

"You know that story. You know what his life was like then. And how he loved you."

"But you were there too. But you stopped talking. What happened there? I still don't know that part of the story."

"AA," he said.

"What?"

"You didn't go last week. You should have gone. I'll take you tonight and wait outside."

"But the rest of the story?" She nudged him.

"Not now, Clara," he said. "I have to think about it for a while. Find the right words for you."

He rubbed at his face. She could see how the past had tired him. His accent had become more pronounced, almost as if he had relived it all as he'd told her the story.

"Don't wait for me," she said. "You're tired. Joe, your friend, said he would fetch me back and bring steaks. Let's do that."

"That offer was last week," he said. "And I called him to say you weren't going. He might not still be offering."

"He will. We'll stop by the store on the way." She stood and patted his arm.

"You have become bossy," he said, packing away the fancy lures.

"I always was. I'm just finding myself again," she said. "Don't you remember how I used to boss you about when you'd come over? Tell you what make-believe game we had to play and what your role was?"

"I believe you made me a king, a prince, and one time, and I don't understand why, you made me a tree."

"It was a magic tree." She sighed. "It was an important role. Dad always got the rubbish roles. Remember I made him be a log once so I could be a frog and sit on him?"

Marcin laughed. "He never complained."

"No, he didn't." She smiled. Then she realized that that had been the first time she had thought of her father, of a good memory, without thinking about the toast, about the day she found him. And instead of feeling anxious and scared, she just felt happy, with a tinge of sadness.

She looked out across the lake and memories began to flash in her mind. There, her dad lifting her up out of the water then throwing her back in to whoops of joy from Clara in a yellow swimsuit. Her father at her piano recital where she cried and messed up the piece, but he stood and applauded anyway then took her out for ice cream and invited Marcin, both of them saying how they loved ice cream and in Poland they had some of the best.

More and more memories toppled one on top of the other, each one making Clara's heart swell with joy.

Her dad on her birthday. He would wake her early, just as the sun was peeking, and tell her to get dressed. They would go out on their little adventure together, to an early-morning bakery where Clara was allowed to choose a sweet pastry or cake. They would take them to the park, sit on a bench and watch the world wake up together. It was simple, but it was something she would miss for the rest of her life.

"You all right?" Marcin placed his hand on her shoulder.

"Yes, just thinking about Dad."

"You're crying," he said.

"Am I?" Clara reached up and felt that her face was wet.

"You're sad?"

"No. And yes. But more thankful than anything. Thankful for Dad, for you, for Mom."

She wrapped her arms around Marcin and felt him stiffen under her embrace. "Thank you for taking such great care of Dad," she said. "Thank you for taking care of me. I love you, Uncle Marcin."

She thought she heard him mumble back an "I love you too," but wasn't sure. He detached himself and gruffly told her to hurry up and get changed and meet him in the truck.

Clara watched him walk toward the cabin, his shoulders slouched. What had she said to upset him? Or was it too much emotion? Too many memories?

She shrugged it off. Marcin was a complicated man and she knew he would say what he needed to, in his own time.

# 23

## CLARA, 1982

*Alpine Lakes Wilderness*

Joe was more than happy to take Clara back to the cabin. It was her opinion, however, that his happiness came from the fact that he would get to spend an evening with his friend and have dinner.

"Not a problem," Joe said three or four times as Marcin bumbled about the store, saying it was fine for him to wait, that he could sit outside the church hall.

"Marcin, take the steaks home now." Joe placed the paper-wrapped bundle in his hands. "You cook them better than I do anyway. So you go back and we'll see you soon."

Clara saw that Joe's hand lingered on Marcin's for a few seconds, and it made Marcin smile. Then he corrected himself and briskly told Joe not to worry if he wanted to change his mind.

The church hall was only a few yards away from Joe's store, but Marcin was adamant that he drive her there and see her safely inside.

"I'm not going to run back to the bar, if that's what you're worried about?" she said as she opened the car door.

"It's not that," he said. "I just want to make sure you are safe."

"I'm fine," she said, realizing that maybe she was.

\* \* \*

The meeting was like any other Clara had attended. Fold-out chairs, a table with a coffee urn, stale donuts, and a plate of cookies.

Only three people came. A large woman in a floral shirt, blue eyeshadow, and a bad perm. An old man who stared at his shoes and clasped his hands when they shook. A young man called Nick, who ran the meeting, who looked not much older than Clara, who smiled at her and told her he was glad to have some fresh blood.

The floral woman went first. She was three months sober but she said she was bored in the evenings and needed to find something to do with her hands.

The old man mumbled something about getting through two days, which Nick made a huge fuss of and told him that two days was something. Then, it was Clara's turn.

"Hi. I'm Clara. I'm an alcoholic and drug addict," she said. The words, normally, were a script she knew she had to follow and they had never meant much to her before. But this time she felt a knot in her chest and a lump in her throat.

"You all right, Clara?" Nick asked.

"Yes, I just..." The words mixed with tears fell out of her so quickly she was sure they didn't make much sense.

"My dad," she started with. "He died. No, he committed suicide. And I saw it. You know, found him. And then there was the toast. I didn't understand the toast. I mean, did he just make that and then, boom, decide to do it? Did he plan it? I don't understand the fucking toast. But it's important to understand. I have to. You know?

"And Marcin, he's my uncle, but not a real uncle." She shook her head. "No, he is. But he has been telling me about my dad, about who he was and what he went through in the war, and I think I understand now. And I think I can see the whole picture at last, you know, like a puzzle. I mean, most of the pieces are there. Some still aren't but maybe they're not meant to be. Maybe I am making a picture of something that doesn't exist—you know, like the picture on the lid of the jigsaw puzzle, how it shows you what it should look like. Maybe I got the wrong lid, the wrong picture." She took a breath.

"I'm not making much sense," she said. "I'm sorry."

"Keep going, Clara," Nick urged.

She looked at floral woman who nodded eagerly and saw that the old man had stopped looking at his shoes.

"When he died, I didn't know what to do. How to be now he wasn't there. Mom, she got sick, cancer, and I tried to help her," she said, realizing how selfish she had truly been. "But I couldn't deal with it. Started drinking, pills, anything to make it all a bit fuzzy round the edges. Less sad.

"Mom, she got better for a while and that made it easier, you know. I felt less guilt. But then, she got sick again recently. She told me, and she told me she was fine. But she's not fine, and I knew she needed me, but I didn't help. I carried on, drinking, pills, having sober months, then going back again, trying to ignore everything.

"Then one day, it all got too much. I say it was too much

because I saw this man in a store that looked like my dad and it made me want to take something or drink something. But that's not the truth. I mean, it was part of it. But earlier that day I'd been fired from my job—the only thing that was sort of keeping me sober. Then, I went to see Mom. I saw how frail she was. I saw that she might die. That she needed me and I had let her down. She tried to cook for me, tried to take care of me." She prodded her chest hard. "Me! And I knew I didn't deserve that from her. I didn't deserve to be alive. So I did what I always did. Drank. Took things. More than usual. And then I just waited. Waited for it to be over."

She sobbed, her head hanging low.

She felt an arm round her shoulders and smelled a lemony perfume.

"You're safe," floral woman said. "You keep going. You weren't meant to go then. There's so much for you to look forward to. So much to do. You keep going."

"Yeah." The old man's voice came from his chair. "You're young. Keep going. Don't get like me."

More and more encouraging words came. A cup of weak coffee was placed in her hand by Nick. The old man brought her the least stale donut. "Only one with icing," he said as he handed it to her. She smiled through her tears at this man, who was struggling just as much as she was, and yet, he found compassion. He wanted to help. He wasn't judging her; he understood. They all did. She wasn't alone.

\* \* \*

"Good meeting?" Joe was outside in a truck not dissimilar to Marcin's, but this one was a burnt orange, the window down.

She climbed into the cab. "It was... a lot." She sighed.

"Good? Bad?" he asked as he turned the key in the ignition.

"Good. Just a lot. Stuff that I should have said ages ago but didn't. It sort of makes me feel lighter, you know, but at the same time, really tired."

"I get it," he said as he swung out of the parking lot. "My brother said something similar. Whenever he had one of those types of meetings, he'd sleep for like two days. Takes it out of you. You can wind the window up if you want," he said.

"I like the cold air. Do you mind?" Clara asked.

"Not a bit. I run hot all the time. Always have a window cranked down, even when it snows. Your uncle says I'll die of pneumonia, but I told him that's not how you get pneumonia. At least, I think that's not how you get it. But whadda I know? I mean, I'm no doctor or nothing."

Clara let Joe ramble on as he drove. Talking about fishing, his store. Why people bought what they did. He couldn't understand why anyone would eat cereal for breakfast when you could have eggs and bacon, but that was what the world was coming to apparently, and he had to stock all this cereal— all different types, taking up too much room on the shelves.

Between his narration of his life, Clara thought back to the meeting, of how everyone had been so kind to her, and had made her reevaluate herself. Yes, she had been selfish, yes, she could have done more for her mother, but she had been dealing with something that no one, least of all a child, should have to see.

She should have listened to the therapists; she should have gone to more meetings. But as floral woman said—Barb, her name was—no point dwelling on the shoulda woulda couldas. Best to leave it where it is in the past and learn from it to move forward.

She decided she would do that now. Yes, the addiction would always be with her. Yes, she would have bad days, but she could be something more, someone more. She could be the Clara she was always meant to be.

As soon as they got home, Clara told Marcin she needed to speak to her mother and dragged the phone into a small cupboard as if she were a child.

"We won't listen, promise!" Joe grinned at her.

"I know. It's not that. I just need to be alone with her. With what I need to say."

"Understood," Joe said and pushed Marcin into the kitchen.

Her mom answered on the third ring, her voice tired and scratchy on the other end.

"Mom?"

"Oh, Clara! I haven't spoken to you in days. But Marcin says you're doing well?"

"I am, Mom," she said, feeling the lump in her throat and an eagerness to cry once more.

"That's good. I'm glad. I told Marcin maybe in a few weeks, when I'm feeling up to it, I'll come and see you. We can go for walks, sit by the lake. That would be nice, wouldn't it?"

Clara coughed to disguise the tears that were now falling; her mother's hope was too much for her. "Mom, don't worry about me. How are you? How's the chemo going?"

"Oh, that. It's all fine, Clara."

"No, Mom, please tell me. How are you? I don't think I've actually asked you that in a long while, and I'm so sorry I haven't been there for you. But I will be from now on. I promise. I really do. I won't let you down this time."

"Oh, Clara." It was her mother's turn to choke on her words and fight back tears. "You've never let me down. Not once. It's understandable what happened. It wasn't your fault. You were just a kid, who had lost her father in the most unimaginable way and then had to deal with me being sick. You were terrified. I knew you were. Terrified that I was going to leave you too."

"I was?" Clara asked. She didn't remember feeling that scared. She didn't remember much of those years from fourteen to eighteen to be honest.

"At night, you would have nightmares. I'd come into your room and you would sob and sob and beg me not to leave you."

Clara listened to her mother as she spoke about those hazy years. She let her mom tell it from her experience, how it had affected her, how she was sorry too and how she felt she had not done enough.

Meanwhile in the kitchen, Marcin and Joe spoke in hushed tones, each of them eyeing the door in case Clara made an appearance.

"You don't have to tell her," Joe said.

"I do," Marcin said. "You know. You are the only person who knows. And she should know. It is the right thing to do."

"Do you think she will be able to cope with it, with the truth?"

Marcin stopped chopping the potatoes he had been working on, placed his hands flat on the counter and stared at them.

He felt Joe stood close behind him, then his arms around his shoulders. "If you think it will help you both, then tell her," Joe said.

"I don't know whether I have the right words for her."

"You could write it down first. Write it down tonight, then tomorrow, we'll look at it together and figure out how best to say it to her."

"You really think?" Marcin turned so Joe and he were close, their faces almost touching. He knew what was going to happen. Wanted it, and yet was scared of it at the same time.

"Marcin." Clara bounded into the kitchen and Joe stepped away from him.

"Erm. Everything okay?" she asked.

"Yes. Fine. You speak with your mother?"

"I did." Clara slumped on a chair. "It was a lot. But we needed to do it and say what we needed to. I think I need to see her in a few days. Maybe she could come here?"

"Of course," Marcin said. "Clara, pass me the salt please."

She picked it up off the table and handed it to him. He stared at the salt pot in his hands. He didn't need salt. Why had he asked for it?

"You all right?" Clara asked.

"Fine. Just fine."

* * *

Joe left at ten. Clara, emotionally drained, had fallen asleep on the sofa next to Moll. Marcin placed a tartan blanket over the pair of them and went to the kitchen with his journal. He would do as Joe suggested. Write it down first. Read it back and see if it was too much. If it was something that she could handle.

He had lied so many times to so many people. Some had learned the truth. Adam, for instance. He had learned what Marcin had done on that day, so many years ago. The day that Marcin had told Clara about—the two men, the German police, the beatings.

But what he hadn't told Clara was what else had happened.

What had sent him spiraling and seeking solace in Filip's bar, in the neck of a vodka bottle.

And he hadn't told Clara why he and her father had fallen out, how the two episodes, one in 1939, the next in 1970, were connected, and why he was part of the reason that Clara now found herself in the mess she was in.

# 24

## MARCIN, 1939

### Poznań, Poland

The beating of the two men seemed to take an eternity. Marcin lay on the ground, heard their screams, wishing for silence.

The silence, when it did come, was worse. He waited to hear the two men grunt perhaps, shuffle away, but there was nothing but the labored breathing of the two Gestapo who now stood over him.

"Get up!" one of them shouted.

Marcin unfurled himself, the pain in his stomach still too much, pulling at each muscle as he rose.

"So," the blond one said, smirking. "You're not one of those *homosexuells*." He said the word as if it tasted of vinegar.

"No, I—" Marcin began.

The blond man held up a hand to silence him. "I don't believe you. But, on this occasion, you have an option to keep me from coming back to find you again. You a Jew?" The same vinegar grimace.

"No." Marcin managed to pant out the word.

"You know any?" the other man asked. It was now that Marcin looked at him properly. Unlike his comrade, he had a crop of dark hair, eyes that almost seemed black, and a scar that reached from his left eyebrow to his hairline.

"I... I mean maybe," he said.

"Where do you live?"

Marcin gave his address.

"Apartment?"

"Yes. One of twelve."

"Any Jews live there?" the scar man said.

Marcin coughed. "I'm not sure."

"Well, you'd better find out then, hadn't you?" the blond man said, stepping forward so that their noses almost touched. "And if there are none there, you'll find some for us, won't you? Or you'll be going in their place. These pigs are clever. Changing their documents, getting forged birth certificates already. They think they are smarter than us, but they're not, are they?"

Marcin was unsure whether to answer.

"Are they?" the blond man hissed.

"No. They're not."

"They're dirty pigs, aren't they?"

"Yes," he mumbled, seeing now where this game was headed.

"Say it."

"They're dirty pigs," he said.

"Even worse than your man friends, eh?"

"Yes, even worse."

"So. You listen here," the blond man said. "You'll report to us tomorrow. We have your address, so don't think we won't come and find you if we have to. You'll report to us and we'll take some more details, and then, all you need to do is keep a list of anyone you know, you see, you work with, and give it to us when we ask. You understand, Pole?"

"I understand," Marcin said.

"Good," the scar man said, then thrust the baton into his stomach again, sending him reeling to the ground.

"And if you think about not complying, we'll do far worse to you than what we did to your friends over there."

* * *

The days became a blur for Marcin as he sought solace in Filip's bar, trying to drown out the deal he had made to save himself. He wanted to tell Filip what he had done, but couldn't bring himself to. All Filip knew was that he had pointed out the two other men and allowed them to be beaten half to death, and that was bad enough. He couldn't bear to think of what Filip would say, or how he would look at him, if he knew the full extent of Marcin's betrayal.

* * *

The knock on the door, when it came, was from Adam's parents. Marcin opened it to see their frightened faces. He had been expecting anger.

"They're coming," Cyla said. "Tonight, they're coming."

Marcin swallowed. "Who?"

"The Gestapo. We had papers and everything to say we were Catholic. We were going to leave in two days. Two days!" Cyla screamed.

"How do you know they are coming?" Marcin asked, waiting for her to say, *Because you told them to.*

"My brother told us he had heard something. Told us to run. But there's nowhere to go. It's too late. We left it too late."

Marcin nodded.

"Take Adam for us," Cyla begged. "Please."

"I... I..."

"Please, Marcin! Take him. Hide him. Get him out of here. Please. You have been such a good friend to us, to Adam. Please. We need you to help us."

Marcin only nodded; no words would come forth.

Cyla hugged him. Abraham patted him on the back then shook his hand. "You're a good man, Marcin. Keep our boy safe, won't you?"

Marcin could not say anything. He watched Adam's parents leave, then closed his door.

The next time someone knocked on his door, it was soft. Adam was hidden. The knock came from the Gestapo, letting Marcin know he was safe. That he had done a good job.

Marcin looked to Adam, who asked him where his parents had gone and why they, he and Marcin, were safe but everyone else had been taken.

Marcin lied. Said he didn't know. His first lie to Adam. A lie that would ruin both of them.

## 25

### MARCIN, DECEMBER 1970

*Greenlake, Washington State*

Marcin watched Adam as he looked through papers on his desk. The fire in the hearth roared, making the room too warm.

"It's here somewhere!" Adam laughed, then stepped back. Marcin saw him furrow his brow, then reach down and knock back the whiskey in one.

"Another?" Adam asked Marcin, who hadn't even touched his yet since arriving two hours ago. "Come on," Adam said as he poured a hefty measure into his own glass. "It's the festive season!"

"Not for a few more weeks," Marcin said.

"Well, I start on the first of the month." Adam sat across from him.

"Should we go and see how Jane is getting on with dinner?" Marcin suggested, wanting to leave the stuffy study and hoping that Jane's presence might calm Adam down a little.

"I'm annoyed about those papers," Adam said. He waved his hand about as he spoke, sloshing a little whiskey onto his jumper. "I wanted to show you what I found. About all those children we saved and the ones we didn't."

"What papers?"

"Newspaper clippings. Some articles. I've been digging, see. To find out more about my parents. To find out more about everything, really."

Marcin felt a tightness in his chest.

"And what have you found?"

"Not much. We knew they died in Auschwitz; Czeslaw too, of course. Filip—did you know that?"

Marcin shook his head and tried not to think of his old friend.

"I've been looking for the survivors too. Like me. All the little orphans you saved." Adam belched.

"Well, I don't think we need to think about the past anymore," Marcin said. "Let's go and see Jane and Clara."

"No. No! They can't hear this. What I need to say to you, Marcin..."

Marcin placed his glass down. "Well, I'm going to see what they are up to," he said.

"When were you going to tell me, Marcin? When were you going to stop lying to me, stop pretending?"

Marcin had not reached the door. He turned and looked at Adam, whose face lit up orange from the glow of the fire. His eyes bored into him, into his very insides, seeing everything that Marcin had done.

"I didn't know how to," Marcin said.

"You know, Marcin. I'm ashamed of you. Of who you have become now." His voice cut through Marcin's skin. "I think of my life, and how I am struggling, drinking and still being a father, being a husband and still trying to be me." He prodded his chest. "And here's you, pretending the whole time, not trusting me with the truth!"

"It wasn't like that." Marcin took a step toward him, seeing Adam's parents' faces in his mind, the Gestapo that beat him, the deal he made that day.

"You think I'm weak, don't you?" Adam slurred.

"I don't think that."

"Yes, you do. You always did. Little Adam tagging along while big brave Marcin rescued all those children. Look at me," he said self-pityingly. "I'm no one, Marcin. Never have been. I kept trying though, trying to be like Marcin. Trying to be brave. But you're not brave, are you? You're just like me." Adam stood and went to his desk, poured more whiskey in his glass, and knocked it back. "Here." He handed Marcin a manila folder. "You take this. You see how brave you used to be," he said.

Marcin took the folder, his hand shaking. "I'm sorry, Adam. Truly, I am. You don't know how sorry I am."

"I'm sorry too." Adam slumped in his office chair. "I've let you down. I've let everyone down. I'm sorry."

"You don't have to be sorry!" Marcin cried. "It was me. All me. You have nothing to be sorry for."

Adam looked at him and for a moment, Marcin thought he was going to forgive him, to be the Adam he had always known, to say that he understood why he had made that decision that day.

"You should go now," Adam said softly. "You should go and think about what I said. And don't come back until you are ready to be who you truly are."

Marcin felt like Adam had slapped him. He opened and closed his mouth, willing the right words to find their way out, but nothing came.

"Go. Please."

Marcin opened the study door, his head swimming.

"Marcin? Where are you going?" Jane stood in the kitchen doorway, drying her hands on a dish towel.

"Uncle Marcin?" He looked upwards, and there at the top of the staircase was twelve-year-old Clara. "Aren't you going to tell me a story? You always tell me a story over dinner."

Marcin turned away. "No more stories, Clara," he said, letting himself out into the cold street, walking away from the family he had built and then destroyed.

## 26

### CLARA, 1982

*Alpine Lakes Wilderness*

She closed the journal. The journal that had been sat on the kitchen table. The journal she had decided Marcin had left out for her to read as she drank her morning coffee while he was walking Moll.

She knew she was breathing, she knew she was alive, but it was almost as though she were not in her body. Clara pinched the thin skin on the back of her hand, hard. Yes. She felt pain. She was definitely alive. But why wasn't her brain working properly? Why couldn't she feel inside herself?

Then the thoughts came, one after another. Vodka, sleeping pills, whiskey, pot. Dad. Marcin.

The last pieces of the puzzle.

It was Marcin who told the Gestapo about Adam's family. He was the one who said where to find the Jews in the building. And it was all to save himself.

Vodka, pot, sleeping pills.

Her grandparents, who she'd never met. Dead because of him. Dead so he could live.

Whiskey, cigarettes, pills. Adam, Adam, Adam.

Dad.

She stood and went to the kitchen, pulling open cupboards, searching their innards for her medicine. Adam. Marcin.

Where was the fucking vodka?

Her dad on that autumnal afternoon, swinging, dust motes dancing in the air around him.

She flung open the pantry door, launched herself onto the shelves in a frenzy, desperate to feel the cool of a glass bottle under her skin.

Fucking Marcin! Not a drop? Not one thing? She needed it, had to have it.

She was back in her body now. She felt everything, too much of everything. Nothing was safe. Plates on the sideboard were dashed to the floor; she ran the faucets under the sink at full power just to hear the rush of water in her ears. The refrigerator was emptied, yogurts, mayonnaise, leftover casserole pitched to the floor where they seeped into one another.

Clara knew that there was nothing to take away this feeling. The house would be empty of anything—unless of course—unless...

She slid to the floor, her legs in the congealing mess of food, and told herself to breathe as calmly as she could.

There was one place that perhaps there would be something. Marcin's bedroom. Aspirin would do; if there was enough, it would knock her out, or at least take her out of all of this.

A small voice way back in her head told her not to do it. Told her that she had come further in these past days than she ever had with any therapist. She had started to laugh again, to smile. She was swimming every day in the cold lake, delighting in the rush it gave her. She walked Moll through the woods and scrunched icy leaves underfoot.

*But that wasn't really me*, she told the voice. *That was Clara who knew no better.*

Then the image came to her—that stupid image of the toast on the plate—the toast that her father had eaten as his last meal.

She scrunched her eyes closed, trying to make it go away. But she could see him, standing at the counter, buttering the toast, knowing that he was going to go into his study and do what needed to be done. She saw him chewing a bite, saw tears slowly dripping down his face, making the bread soggy. He was trying to delay it. Trying to con himself into believing that he would change his mind. Do something normal. Eat toast. And maybe it would draw him away from the thought.

She knew that this was what had happened. How many times had she tried to do the same? When that urge or sadness overwhelmed her, she would clean the house, go to a coffee shop and watch herself act normal, do normal things, telling herself that the other thoughts were to be ignored. But she could only ignore them for so long. Just like Dad, she thought. Two bites into the toast. Two bites into trying to be normal hadn't worked. It had just delayed the inevitable.

She stood up and dragged her forearm under her nose, then rubbed at her cheeks to rid herself of the tears that she hadn't even realized she had been shedding, and went to find her salvation.

Marcin's bedroom was cold, colder than the rest of the house. She switched on a light and saw that the window was open just a crack, the air tickling at the curtains.

She started in his bedside drawer and found little of interest. Next, his bathroom, and there, right there in the cabinet, were two bottles of aspirin, and next to them an orange-brown medicine bottle with the words flurazepam on the label. Prescribed to Marcin over six years ago. She didn't care that they were so old—surely, she thought, sleeping pills never went out of date?

She shook the bottle and heard the comforting rattle of the little white pills all jostling together and felt a calm wash over her.

She went to Marcin's bed, sat on the edge, and shook the pills out onto his green comforter, lining them up like little soldiers. Next, she lined up the larger aspirin tablets and counted her stash out. Fifty-five in total. That should do it.

She lifted one of the sleeping tablets onto her index finger and stared at it. Then, she opened her mouth.

"Clara!"

The tablet fell onto the bed before it could reach its destination.

"What?"

"What are you doing?" Marcin yelled.

"What do you think I'm doing?" she spat. "I saw your journal. You left it for me, didn't you? Just like the first time."

"No!" Marcin said. "I wrote it down, for me, to help me find the words to tell you in person. I wanted to tell you in person. Not for you to read it like this."

"He killed himself because of you. Because of what you did to his parents. My grandparents. How you gave them up. And yet you act like the brave Marcin, saving Dad, those other children, but really it was just because you felt guilty!"

She stood up and stormed past him, into her own bedroom, flinging clothes into the red bag.

"What are you doing?" Marcin was in the doorway.

"Leaving. What the fuck do you think I'm doing? I can't stay here with you. I can't bear to look at you!"

"Clara, please! Just calm down. Just come and sit down and let us talk about this."

"Hello?" Joe's voice sang from downstairs. "You all good up there?"

"Joe!" Clara grabbed her bag, half of her things falling out of it, pushed past Marcin and ran down the stairs. "Joe. Can you take me to the city please?"

"What? Now?" Joe looked to Marcin.

"Don't look at him for approval. I'm asking you. Can you take me?"

"I don't know, Clara, I mean—"

"I'm not going to do anything. Take me home. Take me to my mom. You can walk me inside the damned door to make sure that's where I'm going to be if that makes you feel any better?"

"Marcin?" Joe said.

"Take her, take her home."

Clara did not turn around. She marched to the door, flung it open, and went to Joe's truck, her nerve endings prickling.

Joe tried to talk to her on the drive, but she didn't engage. All she could think about were all the lies, and all the times Marcin could have told why her father killed himself, but once more, his guilt had kept him silent.

She wanted her mom now. No. She needed her. She needed to know what she knew. She needed to feel her warm hug. She needed her to say everything was going to be all right.

*But what will you do, Clara, if she knew all along too?* a small voice said in her head. What will you do? Will you go and see your friend Thomas outside his parents' deli and hand him some money and see where the night takes you? Will you go to the liquor store and buy as much as you can carry? What will you do, Clara, if your mother cannot give you want you want, what you need?

"I won't do anything," she said as they drew up outside her mom's house.

"What?" Joe asked.

"Nothing. Nothing at all."

Joe did walk Clara into the house and tried to make small talk with her shocked mother.

"Can I get you a coffee?" her mom asked Joe.

"No. He's leaving," Clara said.

"Clara! Don't be so rude!"

"No, no, it's fine. Thank you though. I have to get going."

* * *

Clara went to the kitchen, then into the living room, then into her father's study that had not changed since he had died. She felt like she could run a marathon. Every part of her was alive, alive with rage.

"Clara, what on earth is going on?" Her mom came into the study. "Sweetheart, what's happened?"

"Did you know?" Clara blurted.

"Know what?"

"Know why Dad killed himself. How it was Marcin's fault?"

Her mother's mouth made an O in surprise.

"You didn't?"

Her mother walked away from her to the living room and sat in an armchair. Pink rose floral. Clara hated it.

"Would you stop pacing and come and sit with me?" her mother said, low but sternly.

Clara went into the room, tried to sit, but her legs would not rest, and she jittered up and down.

"Clara. Try and calm down. Calm down and tell me what you think you know."

Clara tried to tell her mother the best way she could, but she knew that it was fragmented and sometimes interrupted by the need to angrily rant. It was the only way she could talk, though. She had to let it all out in one big go and hope that her mother understood.

Finally, Clara ran out of steam. "So Dad knew. He found out about what Marcin had done and was ashamed of him. Hated him. And he hated what had happened to his parents and all those years of lies from Marcin."

Her mother smiled gently. "Oh, darling, but that's not what happened."

"It is. I read it. Black and white."

"That's what Marcin thinks happened. I tried to tell him before that he was wrong about what your father was saying, but he wouldn't listen. It was almost like he wanted it to be true. Like he wanted to punish himself. It fit his story."

"So Dad never said those things? Why would Marcin lie?"

"He did say those things." Her mother sighed. "But he wasn't talking about Marcin lying about his parents. He had known for years, Clara. For years. He never held it against Marcin. He kept it to himself."

"But it's still Marcin's fault! He caused it all."

Her mother shook her head. "Your dad blamed him at first but then... but then he knew what Marcin had been facing. He took that into account."

"So why did they stop talking then? Why does Marcin think Dad was ashamed of him?"

"Because when your father was drunk like that and off his

medication, he said awful things. But he was talking about Marcin being gay. He was ashamed, not of Marcin being gay, but that Marcin was lying to himself and not telling the truth about who he was. It came out wrong, I know that. Your father knew that too when he sobered up. But by then it was too late."

Clara shook her head. "I don't understand. Dad was okay that Marcin basically got his parents murdered, but was upset about him not telling him he was gay?"

"Oh, Clara. Don't you remember what your dad was like? What he was really like? I think you have cherry-picked the good memories. And I wanted you to, of course I did. After he died, I wanted you to think well of him. But he was a complicated man, Clara. It wasn't always sunshine and rainbows. Don't you remember that on one birthday of yours, he took you to the bakery and the park then left you there? Don't you remember how the police had to bring you home and your father turned up hours later, drunk out of his head, not understanding what he had done?"

"But it was still Marcin..." Clara started. She didn't want to think about that birthday, about how scared she had been, how she had cried all day and run into her father's arms when he returned, more worried about him than herself.

"I told you, Clara. Your father knew for years what had really happened. He had done research into the war, into his family. He knew. He'd known all along. But he knew that Marcin had been put in an impossible situation. You cannot judge Marcin for that. What would any of us have done in that situation?"

"The drinking though. That was because of it all. That's why he was the way he was," Clara decided.

"I'm not saying that those years did not impact him. He tried to talk about it, wrote about it too and tried to make sense of it all for himself. He said once, though, that wasn't he lucky to be able to write about it? He could be dead. Gassed at Auschwitz along with his parents."

"But his parents could have escaped if it weren't for Marcin," she said.

"Ifs and buts, Clara. You have to think of the reality of the situation. They may have gotten away, but then they might not have. Millions didn't. All we do know is that Marcin, despite what he did, tried to take care of your father the best way he could. He took care of so many others too."

"He didn't do much," Clara spat. "He wasn't like the others, going into the war. He was mostly safe in Hungary, in a safe house. Just moving children from one place to another."

"Please don't say that, Clara. Do you know what a risk that was in itself? Someone had to do it, and that someone was Marcin."

"No!" Clara stood. "No! Dad was a good man. He drank a bit. Not a lot. He was good. And Marcin did this."

"No," her mother interrupted sharply. "You're sounding like Marcin now. Wanting it to fit into your story, your reality, when it simply isn't the case. When will you and Marcin stop punishing yourselves? You want this to be true so you can be angry. So you can leave here and go and do what you usually do. Don't think I don't know you, Clara." Her mother's voice had an edge to it. "I know you, Clara, and all your tricks."

Her mother had never said anything like that to her before. She had always mothered her. Told her everything was going to be fine.

"I'm not doing anything," Clara said, indignantly.

"Clara, when are you going to be honest? When are you going to finally wake up?" her mother suddenly yelled, then started to cough with the exertion.

"Mom?"

"I'm fine." She waved her hand.

"I'm sorry." Guilt suddenly surged through Clara's body. A normal but quicker reaction than usual. Normally, she would drink, wake up, then feel the guilt and apologize. Now, though, she was sober, yet could see how her behavior was still the same. Her mother was sick, very sick, and here Clara was upsetting her, getting ramped up for a big showdown so that she could do what she usually did. Her mother was right. When was she going to be honest? When was she going to wake up and start living in reality?

She sat back down, neither of them speaking for a few minutes, letting the bad air disperse.

"Your father"—her mother broke the silence—"your father had a lot of problems. Things I suppose you don't really know about. He resented being a husband sometimes; he lusted for freedom, he yearned for escape. That was nothing to do with his past. It was who he was. Who that secret part of himself was. And he hated himself for it."

"So that's why he drank sometimes?"

"Sometimes, Clara?" Her mother laughed. "He drank all the time. When I met him, he liked to drink socially, but then when he didn't get into med school and had to take a teaching position, it got worse. I shrugged it off because I loved him and at first, he was a fun drunk. Made every party better. He finally decided to study more but this time to do with Polish history. Got himself his job as professor and the drinking abated for a few years, especially when you came along, and I naively thought that was the end of it, that he was finally happy."

"You said he was on medication?" Clara said. "I didn't know. What for?"

"Mania and depression. Don't you remember that summer

at the lake? What happened and how your dad had to go away for a while?"

Clara said she remembered the lake, remembered her dad going away for work.

"It wasn't work, Clara. He went to a hospital. A mental hospital. He was gone for three months."

She thought back to that summer. She had been perhaps eight. Maybe nine. Either way, she'd known how to swim, how to swim well enough to go onto the dock with the other children, their wet feet slapping down onto the wood, leaving behind footprints that would soon be burned away by the heat. She'd run along the dock, to the deep end of a lake, and waited her turn to jump in. An older girl behind her had told her not to be scared. She hadn't been scared, not of anything. When it had been her turn, she'd jumped in and sunk down, watching the surface above her, a blur of sun, of bubbles popping the surface. She'd known she should break the water, but for some reason, she hadn't. She'd liked it down there, where laughter and voices had been muffled. She'd liked the glimmer of sunlight as it kissed the water. Down there, everything had been perfect.

Then she'd felt arms around her, her dad pulling her to the surface, telling her not to do it again.

She'd said she wouldn't, promised him. But he'd been so angry, so angry that by the time they'd reached the shore, he was yelling at her so much, she was crying. Her mother had tried to hug her. Her father had pushed her mother away. People had started to stare.

"He didn't mean it," she said quietly.

"I know he didn't. He felt so guilty about it that evening, he drank more than usual, then went manic. Decided he was going to go and yell at the lifeguards, beat them up, even though they were teenagers. He then decided to go down to the lake on his own. I let him. I shouldn't have. That's when we found him an hour later, on the shore, barely breathing, a passerby with their dog trying to wake him up, telling us how he had tried to drown himself. You clung to my leg; you didn't cry. Didn't speak for one week after that."

Clara tried to remember the scene her mother was describing, but it would only come to her in flashes.

There were other flashes of memories now, too, though. How her father would get it into his head to go on vacation at three in the morning. How he would wake Clara and make her pack and get in the car, ready to set off, then all of a sudden, the mania would subside and he would lean his head on the steering wheel and start crying.

How he'd twice turned up at her school to pick her up wearing pajamas, how he would sometimes disappear for days and come back smelling of someone else's perfume.

"I loved him," her mother said. "I knew what he did when he got drunk, or when he didn't take his medication."

"He cheated on you," Clara said as the realization hit her.

"Yes. He did. I loved him anyway. I knew that wasn't the real him. He would yell and scream at me too. Then apologize the next day and I would forgive him. God knows how many times I forgave him."

"I—" Clara didn't have the words. More puzzle pieces were all falling into place and it was certainly not the image Clara had wanted to see.

"It doesn't mean he wasn't a good man, Clara. He just struggled. Then one day, he didn't want to struggle anymore. Didn't want to put us through it."

"But his past," Clara said. "That was part of it. Part of him. It ruined him."

"Yes and no, Clara. It affected him, yes. I don't really know how much. But he told me once how his father had drunk too much, too. How he, too, had had depressive episodes. He wondered if it was something that ran through the family."

"Maybe it does," Clara said. "Look at me."

"Oh, Clara, darling." Her mother stood and sat next to her on the sofa, pulling her close.

She could smell her mother, her perfume, and something else, something sterile. She could feel her mother's bony body underneath her, and Clara wondered where she had disappeared to.

"I just wish I had been more honest with you," her mother said. "I blame myself for that. I saw you were struggling, putting your father on a pedestal, much like Marcin has done all these years too. I should have reminded you of who your father was as a person, and I should have insisted that Marcin listen to me and try and believe me when I tried to tell him what your father really meant. It would have stopped a lot of hurt."

"It's not your fault, Mom."

She heard her mother sigh. "Your father, he tried to apologize to Marcin. Went to his house, then found out he had gone to the cabin. He was certain he would go and see him, straighten it all out. Then, he was asked to take leave from work. The shock of it made him spiral. He started to drink more and more. Refused to take his meds. Then, you broke your arm and he blamed himself, saying that you had fallen down the stairs, trying to get to him as he stumbled through the front door. The guilt just kept wearing at him, making him angry, sad, remorseful."

"But he was at work, he went back? He was. That day I came home, he had come home from work early?"

"No, Clara. He wasn't. You're remembering it differently to how it was. Your dad never went back to work. He went out during the day, sometimes to AA, sometimes to his therapist on the good days. But on the bad days, he went to the bar."

As Clara sat with her head against her mother's chest, listening to her heartbeat, she started to piece together her father's life, from what Marcin had said, from her own, newly found memories, and started to appreciate that even though she had been scared to see this image, it still held some beauty within.

## 27

### MARCIN, 1982

*Alpine Lakes Wilderness*

He had no other photographs of Adam, Clara, and Jane other than the one in the silver frame. Not even one of his uncle. He closed his eyes and tried to remember what he looked like, but there was nothing there but a generic old man. He scrunched his eyes tighter and thought of his features—surely there was something, a mole on his face, his eyes wide perhaps, but nothing came to him.

Where were the photographs now, he wondered, of his family. There were few, that was certain—his parents with him and his grandmother at some moment in time, another posed photograph of them again some years later. That was all that they had ever been able to afford. But where were they? Who had them now that they were gone?

Suddenly, he heard his mother's voice, heard a laugh. There she was, wearing a summer dress, blue perhaps, all of them at the banks of the Warta River. She sat beside him and stroked his hair and told him to always live near water, that it was the lifeblood of the world, that the flow of it would always soothe his soul.

His father's voice broke through, and he told his mother that she was a dreamer. She laughed. But Marcin had been angry with his father for saying that and he promised his mother he would always live near water.

He held on to that memory of his mother for a moment, wondering if there were more memories, happier ones, before it all went so wrong, before they started to despise who he had become.

He opened his eyes and looked out to the lake, where Moll paddled in the shallows. Her nose dipped in and out of the water, then barked at something hidden beneath.

He had kept one promise, he supposed. Just one. He was still near the water, although he wasn't sure that it was soothing his soul.

All his other promises had been tarnished by his lies and selfishness.

Jane had tried, over the years, to tell him that Adam had not meant what he'd said. That he didn't blame him for his decision in 1939. She claimed he had just been angry that Marcin had not been honest about his sexuality. This explanation seemed absurd to Marcin. Why would Adam be more angry with him for being gay than for sending his parents to certain death? He loved Jane, he really did, but he had seen how she had tried to make excuses for Adam over the years, how she had tried to think the best of him. God, even Marcin had been guilty of that too. Always telling himself that Adam wasn't as bad as he was, believing anything Adam told him, that he could stop anytime, that he wasn't a drunk, that there was nothing wrong with him. He had believed him because he wanted to and couldn't bear the thought that somehow Adam was the way he was because of him.

He was glad, in a strange way, that Clara had been so angry. He deserved to be yelled at, he deserved to be alone, deserved for her to trash his kitchen. Although he only lived with the mess for an hour or so before he could not stop himself from cleaning it up.

Then, he thought of Joe. Joe, who hadn't judged him when he had told him the truth two years ago, when they had had too many drinks after a fishing trip and each had been honest with themselves.

"Had Connie known?" Marcin had asked him.

"I think she knew, yes," Joe had said. "We got married young, straight outta high school. I was this big jock and she was a cheerleader. It was what everyone wanted, and what they told me I should want. It was only years into our marriage that the difficulties came. Connie wanted children but we were not, you know... I slept a lot of the time in a separate room. But I truly loved her. She was a good woman and deserved better than me. I told her that, but she wanted to stay with me, kids or no kids. So, I was selfish. Led this life of the perfect couple, each of us pretending we were happy. Then, she got sick and, well, we were friends, you know, the best of friends, and I cared for her, held her until she died. I wanted to do that for her."

Marcin had nodded, understanding how Joe had felt trapped, and yet there was no real way out. It was all about keeping up appearances and hoping that the feelings went away.

Joe and Marcin had been careful with each other. Careful around prying eyes and simply fished, ate steak, sometimes drank at Joe's bar after hours. There was no staying over at each other's houses, no declarations. They both were still pretending, he supposed, or waiting for one of them to make a move, or ask the question—were they a couple? Was this a relationship or a friendship?

He decided that he had to see Joe. Now. He had to cut ties with him once and for all. Joe thought he knew Marcin, but he didn't, not really. Marcin's past was not something Joe should forgive and he wanted to make sure Joe knew that he was not worthy of whatever it was between them.

\* \* \*

Marcin knew that Joe would be working in the bar that evening. He walked into the bar and saw Joe pouring a Scotch for Old Tom who Marcin knew would have been in the bar since it opened at midday.

"Marcin," Joe said.

He sat next to Old Tom, who started to tell him about the problems he was having at home with a wife who had put up with his drinking for years, and how she was threatening to leave again.

"She's an ungrateful bitch," Old Tom spat. "After all these years!"

"Calm down, Tom," Joe said. "She ain't left you yet and she says this every week to you. Maybe you oughta try not coming in here so much?"

"What else have I got?" Old Tom snarled. "What else am I supposed to do?"

Marcin looked at the old man, his thick skin indented with deep wrinkles from hard labor in the wood mill, followed by hard drinking in the leftover hours. Was this how Clara and Adam had felt? he wondered. Had they not seen any other point to life?

No, Clara wasn't like Tom, he told himself. Clara was young and she had seen something awful that had changed her, made her want to escape. But then, he realized that maybe something once had happened to Tom too. Maybe he had seen something or done something that had made him this way. Surely it just didn't happen by itself.

"Marcin?" Joe was talking to him. How long had he been talking?

Marcin wiped a hand over his face. "Whiskey please."

"What's going on? You rarely drink," Joe asked. "You heard from Clara?"

"No."

"Jane?"

"No," Marcin said.

"You should call them. Find out what's happening."

"What happened is what's happening," Marcin said and sipped at the whiskey. "She was right to be mad."

"She'll cool off," Joe reassured him.

"She won't. And she shouldn't either. What I did is unforgivable."

"Now, come on," Joe said.

"Unforgivable?" Old Tom asked. "Whaddya do? I cheated on my wife and she forgave me. Can't be that bad, can it?"

"I let everyone down," Marcin said, not willing to share with Tom the truth, that he, Marcin, had let Adam's parents die and had caused Adam's own death to boot.

"Ah, come on now." Tom belched. "Excuse me. It ain't that bad."

Marcin looked at Tom, then at Joe, realizing he suddenly did not want to be here listening to their platitudes.

"I'm off." Marcin stood, placing ten bucks on the counter.

"You know you don't have to pay," Joe said. "Look, now, I'll come by tomorrow. We'll fish and talk, it will all be fine."

"I don't fish anymore," Marcin said, seeing the surprise in Joe's eyes. "No more fishing."

Joe gave an uncertain nod.

Marcin left the bar, opened his truck door, and sat inside for a moment, wishing he could drive off and disappear. Then he thought of Moll, who was waiting for him at home. Good old Moll. It would just be the two of them from now on.

# 28

## CLARA, 1982

*Greenlake, Washington State*

She thought she could ignore the grief. She thought she could ignore the pain that held on to her like a ship's anchor. She was always treading water, gasping for puffs of air, for respite, while the weight tugged at her.

She thought of her father as a boy; his weight was twofold, maybe even three. He had also—like her—kept treading water, kept trying to breathe, until he no longer could.

The grief of losing his parents the way he had was not what killed him, she now knew. Nor was it Marcin's compliance and lies. It was more than that. It was the trauma and simply who he was, what he wanted in life. He had thought if he became a parent, got married, lived a life his parents would be proud of, then he too would be proud.

But there was always something that he wanted, just out of reach. Who was to say that the trauma of his early life had not impacted this? Or if he had sought help, maybe he would have found balance. But he didn't. And so, he went through life, much like Marcin, acting a role, scared of who he might truly be.

Clara made herself sit with these uncomfortable emotions in her room for two days. All day and night she noted things down, her feelings, those memories that she could no longer deny, hoping to see something by morning that would bring her peace.

"I have an idea." Her mother sat across from her at the breakfast table, cupping her mug of coffee in her frail hands. "You're not sleeping, hardly eating and I'm worried about you. You need to see something else of your father, of Marcin too. You're too focused now on the negatives."

"You said two days ago I had been living in a dream world, focused on only the positives. I can't win!" Clara said.

"I know I said that. But you have to see both things. People are good and bad. People are one thing to you, and another in private. Your father was a father, a husband, a friend and he was his own person when he was alone too. Same goes for Marcin. Same goes for all of us. You're not telling me you're everything all at once with everybody? You go to work and put on one side of you, then when you get home, you discard that and be your private self."

"So. Your idea?" Clara yawned. She really wasn't in the mood to get into deep philosophical discussions right now, as right at the edge, always there, was that feeling to race out of the house and find something to smother all of what she was feeling.

"You should go and see Sara," her mother said.

"Sara who?"

"Sara Zimmerman, the girl Marcin rescued. Sara, whom your father took a shine to."

"What, in Poland?"

"No. Don't be dense. She lives here now. Came here a couple of years ago to live closer to her son and was doing some research into her past, and she came across your father's name. She called round, but your father had already passed away. She said she'd come back, I think, or maybe I said I'd call her or go see her. I can't remember." Her mother looked past Clara as if seeking out the memory. "Regardless. I got sick again, and I think I forgot. And maybe she forgot too. Or maybe she moved. But I have her address. You could go and see if she's still there, and she can maybe tell you some happy things, or at least some positive things about Marcin and your dad. You keep saying you need pieces to fit together; well, maybe this is a piece you are missing—hearing about them not from me, but from someone else. Go see her, hear what Marcin and your father did for her. It might help you."

"But you don't look well," Clara said. Her mother had dark rings under her eyes, was paler than usual.

"It's just the chemo," she said. "I had a dose three days ago. I'll be fine. You go. Go and make it all make sense in your head." She wafted her hand. "Besides, I could do with some peace and quiet."

Clara took the address from her mother and watched as she eased herself into the pink rose armchair that was oddly growing on Clara now.

"Are you sure you're all right?" Clara asked.

"Honestly, stop fussing. I'm fine." She smiled.

Clara bent down and kissed her mother's papery cheek. "When I get back, I'll cook something for us, okay?"

"Sounds lovely, darling. Really lovely."

Clara left her mother, wanting to stay but also feeling the tug to go and see Sara. Perhaps her mother was right, she thought as she closed the front door. Perhaps once she had spoken with Sara, that would be it. The final piece of her puzzle, and she would be able to understand her father, even understand Marcin, and forgive them both.

* * *

Sara lived on Mercer Island, taking Clara over an hour to reach her. She walked up the garden path, each side littered with dormant rose bushes awaiting the return of spring.

The porch held a small white wicker table and one white chair, which Clara found sad. Where was the other chair?

Composing herself, she knocked on the red door. There was no answer. She tried again, harder this time, and soon heard feet approaching and a singsong, "I'm coming!"

The door opened and in front of Clara stood a woman in her mid-forties, her long brown hair scraped back messily into a ponytail, a streak of yellow paint on her cheek. She wore a long blue shirt covering her clothes, spattered with old paint.

"Yes?" she asked.

"Sara? Sara Zimmerman?"

"Yes?" The woman narrowed her eyes. "Do I know you?"

"I'm Clara. Clara Abramowicz. Adam Abramowicz's daughter. I think you once knew him as Adam Piotrowski?"

Sara opened her mouth into a big O, then slapped her hand against it.

"I just thought," Clara said, then realized she wasn't sure what she should say.

"Clara!" Sara found her voice and rushed at her, flinging her arms around her. "Oh my goodness! Clara. He named you Clara!" She laughed. "After that friend I had. I told him about that!"

Clara stiffened a little under the unexpected force of the embrace, but Sara either didn't notice or didn't care.

"Come in, come in." She disengaged and led Clara inside. "You'll have to forgive me, I'm working on something at the moment for my new exhibition. It's fortuitous you coming right now, actually!"

She grabbed Clara's hand and dragged her into a rear sunroom where easels displaying bumblebees sat on each. Some realistic, some blurred as they took off from a flower, some staring straight at you.

"These are amazing!" Clara said. "I mean, they look so real. All of them. Like a photograph. And this one, looking at me. I wonder what he's thinking."

"I was hoping I'd got that right!" Sara beamed. "Come, sit, sit." She indicated a white wicker chair, splattered with dried paint.

So that's where the other chair went, Clara thought.

Sara pulled up a small wooden milking stool and perched on it.

"No, please, you sit here," Clara said, ready to vacate the chair.

"Pish posh. You're a guest. I won't have it. Sit. Sit. Oh goodness, you look just like your father. Has anyone ever said that to you before?"

Clara squirmed.

"Ah, come now. Your father was a handsome man and he made a beautiful daughter. I'm sorry to hear about him, by the way." Sara's tone dropped, and she looked through the large bay windows that faced out into the bay. "When my son, Patrick, went off to college, I found I had too much time on my hands and started to look about for things that happened back then and then started to search for people I knew. I found your father, but too late it seems."

Clara nodded.

"So sad. All of it. Your mother was lovely when I asked about him, but she was poorly and I said I'd come back another time, as she said she'd get me Marcin's address. But then I got busy with exhibitions, and Patrick finishing college then moving back in for a spell. I'm sorry. I should have gotten back to your mom. How is she? Better?"

"No. Not really. She's still fighting it," Clara said.

"Seems like a tough cookie, your mom. I'm sure she'll be fine."

"Thank you."

"So, tell me. Tell me about you." Sara reached out and patted Clara's knee. "Tell me about your life."

"I was really wondering if you could tell me something," Clara said. "I know Dad helped you. Marcin too. It's just I found something out about Marcin recently, and, well, I'm confused." Clara gave a nervous laugh then shook her head. "Sorry. This isn't making much sense."

"Not at all!" Sara said. "I tell you what. I'll go get us a coffee and you start from the beginning. Tell me as much or as little as you want and I'll try to fill in any gaps for you."

Sara quickly disappeared into the kitchen and Clara wondered how much she should actually tell this stranger. Normally, she wouldn't tell anyone what had happened with her dad, with her over the years, even what Marcin had done to make her father an orphan. But Sara was so full of life, so welcoming, she felt she could trust her.

She looked at the paintings of the bees, and just as Sara re-entered the room, it clicked. "The bees!" she said. "Dad told

Marcin that you liked to sit outside and look at the bees. At the cloisters."

Sara grinned. "I told you. Your arrival was fortuitous."

She placed the coffee next to Clara on a small table filled with silver tubes of oil paint.

"So, tell me, Clara, tell me why you're really here."

The day wore on, passing noon and reaching two by the time Clara had finished. She had told her about her father's suicide, how she, Clara, had gone off the rails, how her mother was sick, how she went to Marcin who told her about her father, then about how she had finally come to know the truth of what really happened and perhaps who her father really was.

"But you still blame him, Marcin?" Sara asked.

"I do. I don't want to. I understand why Dad might have done what he did. It wasn't because of Marcin—he had a problem too with depression, with alcohol—but I think it still would've played a part in it all. I mean, to go through all that and have it not affect you?"

Sara sighed heavily. "I'm not saying it didn't affect him. I'm sure it did. But he knew, like he said. He had known for a long time and he understood the position that Marcin was in. Marcin is a good man, you know? A very good man. If that was his sin, then he surely made up for it with all of us poor souls he rescued."

"I know," Clara said. "I just need to get my head around it all."

"You look tired. Worn out. Have you been to a meeting since it all?"

"No." Clara felt guilt gnaw at her.

"You should, you know. It will help, then you get some rest and the next day, things will feel a little lighter. I should know.

My husband—well, ex-husband—had a problem with it for years."

"Is he okay now?"

"Oh yeah, sure. He's fine. His new wife keeps him on the straight and narrow."

"So you're here alone?"

"Indeed! Alone but not lonely. There's a difference, you know."

"Tell me about you, Sara. What happened after you went to the orphanage?"

Sara gave a sad smile. "I missed my mother still. Of course. But I missed Adam too. And Marcin. Did you know that Adam wasn't the only one to keep visiting us at the church? Marcin would come at lunchtime from his job across the river and bring us treats. He would tell us stories, too, ones about princes and princesses, you know, all the stuff kids like to hear. He was a good storyteller."

"Still is," Clara said.

"Well. I was sad to go to the orphanage, but I did find a friend. Zofia was her name. A girl your father told me to befriend. We did become the bestest of friends, you know. And when the war ramped up in Hungary, we were sent away together. First to England, then on to America. California to be exact, to a couple who raised us as their daughters."

"Where is Zofia now?"

"Ah, she went back to Poland! Became a historian. Wanted to document what happened. She's at Poznań University. Quite high up in the ranks. She visits from time to time, but she's busy with her work and five children, would you believe it!"

"Five?"

"She says she'd have more but her husband Bartek says no. She loves it, having kids around all the time. Me. I like 'em, but not that many. I think of it like eating candy, sometimes too much is just too much!" She laughed.

"But you have a son?"

"Yep. Patrick. My one and only. He's enough for anyone. He's the reason I ended up here too. He got work after college at some fancy-pants law firm. I came to visit a few times and ended up getting a commission from a gallery. Of course, I could have stayed in Cali and brought them for the exhibition, but I sorta like it here. Cooler, calmer. It suits me."

"You've done amazingly well then, with your art."

"It has its ups and downs. Didn't really get noticed until I was thirty-five. Had Patrick when I was young, too young really, twenty, just as I was working at this art collective and getting into my stride. His dad, my ex, was a proper hippy. But when he found out I was pregnant, he turned into a corporate bore overnight. Insisted we get married, big wedding, house, picket fence, the whole shebang. So painting was put on the back burner for a while. What about you? Plans? College?"

"Just getting through each day for now."

"But what do you like? What brings you joy? What makes your heart sing?"

Clara suddenly felt like she was back in her therapist's office, trying to understand what happiness really was and whether she had felt it. "I like books," she tried. "I liked working in the library. It was quiet and I could read what I wanted."

"Ever tried writing?"

"A little. In a journal. Nothing of note."

"Everything is of note. Maybe give it a go. See where it takes you. Take a college course or something. Your world will open up, I promise you. You just have to try. I mean, look at me." She spread her arms wide. "When your father and Marcin met me,

I was this terrified little girl. I wanted my mother so badly. I was shipped here and there. All the time not knowing what had happened to my family. Then I found out. All of them gassed at Auschwitz. The knowing didn't make it easier; in fact, it made it harder. I sank into a depression for years. Didn't pick up a paintbrush until Patrick was nine. Then, I tried. You know. Putting one foot in front of the other, trying to find some joy again."

"It worked," Clara said.

"It did." She smiled. "And it will for you too. Now, are you staying for dinner or shall I drop you home? I know you came by boat, but it's not far on the bridge with the car, especially at this time of day."

"I have to get back, sadly," Clara said, noticing that it had gone four. "I told Mom I'd make dinner. You could come in, stay for dinner with us? Mom would like it."

"Are you sure? Because I'd love to!" Sara sprang up. "Let me get changed. I can't go out like this. I mean, I do. But not when I'm going for such an important dinner!"

On the ride back, Sara amused Clara with the same tales Marcin had told her, adding in more color, more joy. Her father carrying Sara, telling her stories, making her smile. How Marcin had brought her a postcard with a bumblebee on it before she left for the orphanage and told her to keep it safe.

"I did, you know, still have it!" she said as she weaved in and out of traffic.

Clara already loved Sara. Her energy was uplifting. Like a cool breeze on a summer's day. She wanted to stay in her orbit as much as possible and was glad she had invited her for dinner.

"Marcin, I'm sure, would love to see you," Clara said.

"And me him! He'll probably ask where the sweet little girl has gone, leaving this madwoman in her place!"

* * *

As Clara opened the front door, and as Sara blabbed on behind her, she felt that the house was too still.

The lamp in the hallway was normally on at this hour, but it sat cold on the polished table. Usually, the TV would be on too, her mother either watching something or at least having it on for background noise and company, as she called it.

"Mom?" Clara's voice rang out. "Mom?"

"Everything okay?" Sara asked.

"I just... Mom!" Clara saw her arm first. Drooping over the side of the pink rose armchair.

She took a few steps closer and saw her mother looking at her, seeing and yet unseeing. Her mouth was open a little, as if she were about to ask Clara what they were having for dinner.

"Oh God." Sara pushed Clara aside and checked for a pulse.

Clara saw Sara shake her head slowly. "She's gone, Clara, I'm so sorry."

"No. But, try CPR. Call the paramedics! She can't be! We were going to have dinner. We were going to be okay now. I'm okay now!" she screamed.

Sara tried to hug her, but Clara pushed her away. "She's cold, Clara. There's nothing to be done. I'll call the paramedics but it looks like she simply slipped away."

"No one slips away!" Clara yelled. "Wake her up. Wake her up now!"

"Clara. Please. Calm down. Come and sit in another room."

"No! No! Leave me alone!"

Clara sprinted from the room. Within seconds she was on the street, her sight blurred by tears. She could hear Sara yelling at her, but Clara would not stop.

She knew where she was going this time. It wasn't her subconscious driving her. She knew. She needed a fix. Something. Anything. And she knew her friend Thomas would oblige.

*　*　*

There they were. All lined up.

A small blue pill, an orange one, a red one. Not her medication. Someone else's, or something else. She couldn't remember what Thomas had said.

He was in the kitchen, smoking pot, telling her to take it easy.

She liked Thomas's place. Small, with posters on the wall of bands he liked. But clean. She told him she expected worse from a drug dealer.

"I'm offended by that," he had said and grinned. "But I'm only selling to put myself through school. So I'm not your usual type."

Thomas wasn't. And she was glad she had gone to him and not tried to buy off anyone else. She knew a few who frequented dive bars and sidled around alleyways, but she needed a safe space to do what she needed to do.

"Don't drink any more with them," Thomas warned.

She didn't listen and downed each pill with a gulp of vodka.

"No, Clara!" Thomas yelled. "I mean it. You'll be fucking sick. I can't have you dying here."

"I don't care."

"Throw them up now, Clara. Put your finger down your throat."

Clara pushed him away, picked up the vodka bottle, and downed more.

"Fuck, Clara, man. I thought you needed a buzz. What the fuck is this?"

Clara started to laugh, then cry. Then laugh again, watching Thomas pace the small apartment, wondering what to do.

Then it all kicked in. It was soft. Welcoming. Like that moment you are just about to fall asleep at bedtime but you are still half awake so you enjoy that moment of slipping away. She liked this feeling. This is what she had been looking for. But suddenly, the softness disappeared. It wasn't like falling asleep. Now she was falling, drowning. It was black, all black, and she tried to breathe to reach the surface but she couldn't. The weight pulled at her. She remembered screaming. And then. Nothing.

# 29

## MARCIN, 1982

### *Alpine Lakes Wilderness*

Marcin woke to the sound of the telephone. It was a shrill cry that made Moll, the yellow lab, bark.

He rubbed his eyes.

"It's okay, Moll," he said, then stumbled to the living room, the floorboards of the log cabin creaking under his weight.

"Hello," he said.

For a moment, there was nothing. Then a squeak.

"Hello," he tried again.

"Marcin?" The voice cracked.

"Jane?" he said.

"No. It's Sara."

"Sara who?"

"Sara Zimmerman," she said. "But I was once Sara Kowalski."

It took a moment for the pieces to fall into place. "Sara?" he asked. "It's little Sara? From Hungary?"

"It is," she said. "And I'm so sorry to call like this."

"No. Not at all," Marcin said.

"I would have called you before. But I didn't know you were here. It's a twist of fate that I am. But look, Marcin. I'm calling about Clara. About Jane too."

He felt the drop of fear in his stomach.

"Jane's died. Clara and I found her, but Clara was in shock and in a state and ran off. I couldn't catch her—"

"Where is she now?" he butted in.

"Her friend, Thomas, he called the house. She's okay. Well, as okay as she can be. She's in hospital, Marcin. You need to come and see her. She's at Harborview."

Marcin dropped the phone, hurried to his bedroom, and threw on his clothes. Moll barked at him and he quickly put a leash on her and took her to the truck.

This time, he did not take Moll with him and dropped her at Joe's, trying to explain that it was all his fault and that it was all happening again. Joe did not press for more information and let Marcin go, taking Moll and patting her head.

"Call me," he said to Marcin's back. "Call me and let me know."

Marcin waved randomly and said he would and then drove through the night to get to Clara. He had to save her. He had to save her.

# 30

## CLARA, 1982

*Seattle City Hospital*

When Clara first tried to wake, it was gone 2 a.m., but the hospital was just as alive as it was during the day. Shoes squeaked on linoleum floors, sirens from the ambulance bay below her room waxed and waned, and fluorescent strip lights flickered every now and then as their tubes wore out.

There was a scent of disinfectant in the room, along with something sweet that she was sure did not belong. She wanted to open her eyes, but the lids were too heavy, and she was sure someone must have taped them shut. She wondered about the time of day and whether she had been there for days, perhaps weeks.

It was then that the sense of déjà vu hit her. She had been here before. She had been in a room just like this and could not open her eyes. She waited; she knew what would happen next. She would try to open her eyes again and a nurse would bash into things, then she would be left alone with just the rain pitter-pattering on the glass. Then, she knew, she would hear her mother's voice. It would break through the fog in her brain and she would wake and tell her it was an accident.

"Clara?" The voice. Oh, thank God! Clara wanted to weep. It meant she had been wrong. Her mother wasn't dead in the floral armchair with her eyes open, her skin shrunk to her bones.

"Mom," she managed to croak.

"Clara. No. It's me. It's Sara."

The thud of dread hit her in the chest. She opened her eyes and then flailed about, trying to rip the tubes from her arms. "Mom!" she screamed, causing a doctor to rush into the room and tell Sara that they had to sedate her.

"No!" A voice cut through Clara's screams for help. Marcin. "No more drugs. She is an addict. She is just upset," he said firmly.

"I know that and that's why she needs to be sedated," the doctor pushed.

"Clara." Marcin appeared before her, his shirt buttoned up wrong.

She fell into his embrace and sobbed. Trying to tell him she was sorry. That her father had always known. That none of it was his fault. That her mother was dead. That she had gone too far this time.

Marcin did not speak. He held Clara as she cried and tried to explain herself until she wore herself out and her cries became whimpers, her eyes slowly closing.

\* \* \*

Over the next few days, Clara told Marcin what her mother had said. That Adam had known for years, from the very beginning, that it had been Marcin who had given the Gestapo his parents' names. He had heard Marcin talking in his sleep and for years had put it down to nightmares, but as he became an adult, as the war ebbed away, he had found out that Marcin had been telling the truth all along.

"He didn't hate you," she said.

"But the argument we had." He shook his head. "He said to me after I told him, after I was honest and said that's why he was drinking, that's why he was struggling with life, to blame me, and he said he did. He blamed me. He was ashamed of what I had become, and was angry that I had not been honest with him and hadn't trusted him."

"Mom said he didn't mean that. He meant that you had denied who you were. Denied things to him—that you didn't trust him. Mom said that the day after it happened, he wanted to apologize, to make some form of amends, and went to your apartment but you weren't there."

"I went to the cabin," Marcin admitted.

"She said he tried again and again. But then the months wore on and he soon stopped trying. Not because he didn't want to, but because he couldn't, Marcin. Remember how I was? I mean, was; look at me still. The drinking became his everything. That's what mattered to him in the end. His days were melded into it."

"I should have been there for him. For you. For your mother. I should have listened to her when she tried to tell me the truth. It was just easier for me to believe my version. I wanted to. I wanted to be punished."

"It wouldn't have made much of a difference, Marcin. Mom said she reached out to you a year before he did what he did, and that you said you would come to see him. Dad overheard and said no. He didn't want you to see him like that. He said he wanted you to think of him as the brave boy you once knew.

Mom said she had to do what he wanted and called you when she could."

"Still. I should have done more."

"Shoulda, woulda, coulda," Clara said.

"What?"

"It's what Barb at AA said. You can't think about what you should or would or could have done. You're punishing yourself and not allowing yourself to move forward."

"Wise woman. Wise words. You think you will listen to them now?" he asked hopefully.

"I hope so, Marcin. I really want to. I don't want to be like this anymore."

"Sara, she is helping you, yes?" he asked, noting that whenever he went to visit Clara, Sara was always there.

"She is. She told me about how she loved Dad and you. About her life and how much she has lost. I keep trying to think that if she can do it, so can I."

"You can," he said.

"With your help too, if that's not too much to ask?"

"Of course." He reached out and held her hand.

"I guess you're saving the last orphan now," she said.

"What?"

"Me. I'm the last orphan." She yawned and closed her eyes, whatever drugs they were giving her kicking in with force.

* * *

When Clara woke next, she found herself alone. Alone and lonely.

She looked to the chair where she wished her mother was sitting. She sat up and tested bringing her legs to the side of the bed. She could move, albeit stiffly.

Her chest hurt. Not from the pills and the booze, but from the loss. It reverberated throughout her body, making her feel nauseous.

Her mother was gone. Her father was gone. She was alone. The last orphan.

She reached over to the bedside table and took the small plastic cup someone had filled with tepid water and drank it down. Then something caught her eye. Her journal. Marcin's too. And another journal too. One she had seen her mother, just a few weeks ago, put into her bag. But that Clara had completely forgotten about it.

She picked it up. It was blue leatherbound, with gold-edged pages. Her father's, she knew.

She opened it. On the first page were doodles of flowers, of a balloon, of a dog. The next page yielded a little more. Thoughts about his life. Snippets of times he felt utter remorse for his actions, where he promised he would do better.

There was a section, though, a section that ran for four pages of him trying to remember those days with Marcin. Clara supposed it was his way of making sense of things too.

She started to read the first orphan's story, delighting in hearing her father's voice talk to her once more.

*October 1968*
  *The doc told me to write more things down. He said my scribbles and doodles were not enough. I'm not sure I need to do this. But he said it would help me talk about the past in some way, because I won't open up properly to him, nor to Jane either.*
  *I told him I won't drink again, won't get mad like I did at poor Clara, won't run off into the lake. But he says I have to do this, so here I go.*

*Where do I start though? In the present, in this mad house with people screaming and yelling? With the doctors and nurses who make you take medication even though it makes your reality all skewed? Do I start here and then delve back into what brought me here, or do I start chronologically? If I were telling my students what to do, I would tell them to get all the facts first, place them in front of them and then begin where it matters, depending on what story you're trying to tell. And I think that's what my problem is. I don't know what story I am telling.*

*I could start with my early years, the years spent at school, going to the synagogue, my mother cooking all the time, friends coming over. I could write about my father, who loved me, but loved to drink more. But back then, all I could see were a lot of people drinking. Men mostly. In bars, at home. It just seemed to be normal. Maybe that's where it started?*

*The doc thinks I should write what happened to my parents, but as I told him, I don't really know their experience. I know they were taken. I know they ended up in a ghetto in Warsaw and then were sent to Auschwitz, where they died. I don't know the horror of it, the trauma, the terror, so I don't think I can write what happened to them. I honestly struggle to imagine it.*

*I could try and write about Hungary, about the orphans, I told him. But then he said that I too was an orphan. Why would I begin with the experiences of others and not my own?*

*Because, I told him, I don't think of myself as an orphan, not really. I had Marcin, and Czeslaw. I wasn't entirely alone.*

*Still, you could try, he said.*

*So here I am. Trying and failing. I just want to go home. I want to see my daughter, my wife. I want to show them that I have changed and can be better than this.*

*I want to go home.*

*I said those words to Marcin, I think, when I was first left with him. I remember hiding under a bed. There was yelling. Sometimes I think I can hear gunshots, but I don't know whether that happened or whether I have added it in.*

*I remember a bar. A man, Filip. He was kind to me and let me in his apartment. I looked at his books, and I remember creeping down the stairs to listen to their conversation. Filip talked about Marcin and me. How we had to leave. But I don't know when we did. It might have been a day or two later, maybe a week. Either way I remember being on a train, and Marcin fell asleep. I heard him talking, mumbling about how he was sorry. How he shouldn't have given some man my parents' names.*

*I didn't think too much of it then. Why would I? It was a dream and we all dream strange dreams from time to time.*

*But he did it often. Often enough for Czeslaw, his uncle, to go into his room at night and wake him. He would then find me on the landing, listening, and place a hand on my head and tell me that Marcin was a good man.*

*Maybe he thought I knew then. But I didn't. Not really. It was only a few years ago that I found out. People document things. Neighbors who survived. People talked. Zygmunt, the man in the apartment below, who was taken along with the rest of the building, had survived. I had written to the council, looking for information, and then his name came up.*

*He told me in no uncertain terms that it had been Marcin who had given their names to the Gestapo and he wondered what I was going to do about it.*

*I wondered, too, for a time. Was I angry? No. I was sad. I was sad because I knew that Marcin would never have done it, if not for a good reason. And I was good, as a child, at listening at doorways. I heard him and his uncle talk a few times of the guilt Marcin felt when two policemen beat some men to death. He told his uncle he had made a deal with them, but he never elaborated what it was. It was as though, I think, his uncle just knew, probably from his nighttime ramblings. It was just something that did not need to be said.*

*The more I dug about in the past, the more I saw that everyone was simply trying to survive and sometimes that meant doing something you would later regret. I understood that, and I understood Marcin.*

*There are some that would have been revengeful. But how could I be? He had tried to make amends, saving me, the others. This big, brave man, hiding his sexuality, never finding love for himself, but carrying on regardless—carrying on for me.*

*I just wish he would tell me and trust in me that I would understand. I wish he would tell me he is homosexual, which I have also known for a long time, and really show me who he is, scars and all. I mean, we're all complex human beings, flaws, hopes, dreams. Me included. And I know it would be hard for him to say it; it's only just become legal. But still, I wish he would say it.*

*There are days, of course, I picture my parents and I feel a well of sadness and wonder what life could have been like if we had all gotten away before they came for them. I wonder if I would be different, better somehow.*

*I shared this once, only once, with Jane. She said that if I were any different, perhaps she would not have fallen in love*

*with me, and we would not have Clara. And would I really
want that alternate reality with them not in it?*

*I told her no, of course not. But sometimes I wish I
hadn't fallen in love with Jane, and vice versa. I feel I have
let her down too many times to come back from it. How
many times can one person be forgiven until the other
person simply runs out of sympathy?*

*That's how I feel about Marcin. I forgave him. Quickly. I
had to. Because I have things I am not proud of and all of
my family forgive me almost daily. Maybe that's what forgiveness is? Not doing it time and time again. You do it once,
then repeat every day, an ongoing forgiveness because you
love the person, every part of them.*

# 31

## CLARA, 1982

### *Seattle*

The funeral for her mother took place two months later on a spring day, when the yellow bobbed heads of daffodils danced in the breeze. Clara was flanked by Marcin and Sara, her son, the same age as Clara, behind her. Patrick. A man who had, for some reason, decided to befriend Clara in the hospital, being there when his mother could not, making her laugh and bringing her books.

They watched the coffin being lowered into the ground. A prayer was said and the mourners moved on, leaving Clara and Marcin alone for a moment.

"The prayer," Clara said.

"What about it?"

"It said she would go to a better place."

"You don't think so?"

"Do you?" she asked.

"I don't know. I want to believe. But I don't know."

"I know." Clara sighed.

Marcin felt awkward. She needed words of comfort, just like all those orphans before her. He needed to tell her that her mother was fine.

"Butterflies," he blurted.

"What?" Clara turned away from staring at the open wound in the soil.

"Butterflies."

"What, like the story Anna told about butterflies?" she asked.

"No. It's my story. I told Anna this myself in the van with the other children. I remember now. That's why she told a story about butterflies too. I had a grandmother. My mother's mother. She died when I was six, maybe seven. She came to live with us when she was sick and I liked her a lot. She would tell me stories and would shout at my father if he yelled at me. She understood me, I think.

"I remember being sad, telling her that I was upset that she would die and leave me. She told me not to be sad. That she would always be with me. She said that soon after she died, when caterpillars turned into butterflies, she would be a part of them. And that one day, she would visit me, land on my hand, kiss my skin."

"Kiss your skin?" Clara asked.

Marcin flushed with embarrassment. "That's what she said."

"So you believe that Mom and Dad are butterflies?"

He shrugged. "I just tell you, Clara, what she say to me. And one day, two, maybe three weeks after she died, a blue butterfly landed on my hand. It stayed a while. Just sat there, tickling my skin. I knew it was her."

"A butterfly," Clara mused.

"Like I said. I'm just telling you what happened. It is just a story. For children. I thought it might help."

"No! It does. Don't be embarrassed. I just wasn't expecting you to say something like that." She smiled at him, then linked her arm through his.

"Who knew that my uncle Marcin was so thoughtful?"

"I have thoughts," he said gruffly as they walked away from the grave.

"You should say more of what you think. Be who you are, Marcin. There's no need to hide."

"I don't know what you mean. I am who I am."

"Joe," she said.

"It's not right," he replied, wishing she would stop.

"It is. It's legal now, you know. And he likes you too. I can see it."

"I know he does. But he had a wife and people in town talk."

"Let them talk, Marcin. Do you never wonder what your life could be like, if you could stop denying who you are?"

"I wonder," he said.

"So, don't wonder anymore, Marcin. I have to start thinking of the future and not of the past. You should do the same."

"I am old!" He laughed. "You have many years left. I am too old now."

Clara stopped walking and made him face her. "Your story isn't over yet, Marcin."

# EPILOGUE
## SUMMER 1991

*Alpine Lakes Wilderness*

That Sunday evening, the bitter smoke of a bonfire hung heavy in the humid air, mixing with the sweet jasmine that climbed up one side of the cabin. Marcin sat on the porch and wiped the sweat off the back of his neck with a blue-and-white hand-kerchief.

He picked up the glass next to him, the ice rattling as he lifted it, the vodka burning his throat.

"Got them!" a voice sang out as an engine was killed.

Marcin smiled and watched as Joe bumbled up toward the cabin, a paper bag under his arm.

"I got seven steaks," Joe said, dumping the bag on the table.

"Seven? Jesus wept. I can't see us eating all that."

Joe laughed. "Since I told you that expression, you use it all the time," he said.

"It's fitting," Marcin said, then took a drink.

"When are they arriving?" Joe asked.

"Tomorrow, around midday."

"Hope the heat doesn't bother them."

Marcin shrugged. "She loved it as a child. Came here with her parents a few times. Couldn't keep her out of the lake."

"It's nice that you can remember the good times now," Joe said. "Nice that you are happy."

"Who says I am?" Marcin grinned.

"Right," Joe said, grabbing the paper bag and kissing the top of Marcin's head. "I'll put these away and get started on dinner. Don't have too many." He nodded toward Marcin's glass.

"I won't," he said.

As he sat and drank, he thought back to those days at Filip's bar. How he had knocked back the drink without tasting it, simply wanting to forget. For years afterwards, he had drunk moderately, always scared that he would spiral again. But he hadn't, not yet at least. Besides, tomorrow, there would be no alcohol about, locked away in his and Joe's bedroom. Just in case.

He looked to the bonfire he had made earlier in the day, dead leaves, pieces of wood that were of no use, and some other things he had placed on there when Joe had left for the store.

He thought of them burning now, all those newspaper articles, all that research Adam had done over the years to find out what had happened to everyone. And all of it kept safe under his bed. He would draw it out now and then to read of the horror in black and white, reminding himself, punishing himself of those who he did not save, or perhaps could not.

He wanted now to focus on what he had done. Of those who he had brought back to life. To that girl, Anna, who'd found her way to England and lived in London. He had never written to her after he had found her, instead wanting to imagine the life that she was leading was a happy one.

There was Jean and one of the boys from the Łódź ghetto, too, who had made a home in France, not far from each other, and he wondered if they were friends, if they shared their stories with each other.

Of course, too, there was Sara. Sara, who had come to the hospital daily to visit Clara. Sara, who had insisted on coming to the cabin afterwards with Clara, staying until Clara was settled to help her through it all, and Sara too, who had provided a home for Clara when she wanted to return to the city and start college. She gave Clara a part of her father back, a part of Marcin too, he supposed, allowing her to flourish into the woman she was always meant to be.

* * *

The next day, Marcin paced on the porch, a very elderly Moll trying to keep up, panting in the heat.

"You'll wear the wood away," Joe said. "Why so nervous?"

"What if they don't like me?" he asked.

Joe laughed. "Not long to find out. I hear them now."

Marcin cocked an ear and heard the sound of tires crunching on the dry ground. He wiped his sweaty hands on his trousers, then folded and unfolded his arms.

Soon, the car came into view, a waving and smiling Sara leaning out of the front passenger window, a man in the driving seat.

"We're here!" Sara jumped out of the car before the brake had properly been applied and gave both Joe and Marcin a kiss. "My favorite boys," she said.

"What about me?" The driver got out.

"Patrick, you're still my son! Stop being such a baby. You have babies of your own now for goodness' sake!"

Patrick opened the rear doors and Clara got out wearing a yellow sundress, a smile on her face. "One sec!" she yelled and delved back into the car.

Patrick went to the other side and Marcin felt himself holding his breath.

Then, Clara and Patrick reappeared, a bundle in each of their arms, and walked carefully toward him.

"Marcin, meet Adam and Jane," she said.

Marcin looked down at the tiny faces, scrunched up from sleep, their eyes barely open.

"Adam and Jane," he said.

"After Mom and Dad. Patrick didn't mind, did you, hon?" Clara said.

"Not one bit," Patrick replied, handing baby Adam to Marcin.

Marcin took the child in his arms, then looked at Clara and Patrick.

"Why so scared?" Clara asked.

"He's worried they won't like him!" Joe guffawed.

"They'll love you! Their great-uncle Marcin and great-uncle Joe."

"And grandma Sara," Sara yelled from a seat she had taken at the table, fanning herself with a newspaper. "Although I'm not sure I like Grandma. Maybe just Sara."

Marcin rocked Adam in his arms, imagining that this was his Adam. Imagining that this was what he would have looked like as a baby. "You'll learn magic tricks," he told the baby. "You'll learn them and try to teach me and I won't get annoyed with you, not ever. And we'll go out for ice cream, you, me, and your sister. And you can eat as much as you like."

"I told you your story wasn't over yet." Clara reached up and kissed him on the cheek.

\* \* \*

That evening, as the sun started to dip, as the birds sang before bed, they sat round the table, with Patrick insisting that Joe had not grilled too many steaks and that he could manage them.

"You'll get sick," Sara warned.

Marcin sat and watched as Patrick challenged Joe to eat as much as he did; as Clara looked at her daughter and son; as Sara tried to fan herself to keep cool, and he felt a calmness in him that he had never felt in his entire life.

"Not an orphan anymore," he heard Sara say, breaking him out of his reverie.

"What?"

"I was saying. Clara. Remember. She said she was the last orphan. Said she had no family."

"To be fair, I wasn't in my right mind." She laughed.

"But look now. A mother." Sara pointed at herself.

"In-law," Patrick added.

She elbowed her son, then turned to look at Clara. "Mother. Not just in-law. You have a husband. Two uncles and now two children. Not bad for an orphan, eh?"

Clara grinned. "If you had told me back then that this is where I'd be now, I wouldn't have believed you."

"I believed," Marcin said.

"No, you didn't!" Clara laughed. "You told me once you weren't sure what you believed in."

"I wasn't. I am now," he said.

"Yeah, right," Clara started.

But before she could say anything more, a butterfly landed

on the side of the stroller. It fluttered its wings, and Joe made to shoo it away.

"No! Leave it!" both Marcin and Clara yelled.

Together, they watched as the butterfly lifted up and landed first on Adam, then on Jane, then came to land for the briefest of moments on Clara's hand and then Marcin's.

\* \* \*

## MORE FROM CARLY SCHABOWSKI

Another book from Carly Schabowski, is available to order now here:

https://mybook.to/NewCarlyBackAd

# AUTHOR'S LETTER

Dear Readers,

Dr. Gabor Maté, a prominent expert on trauma and its effects, was quoted as saying: "Trauma is not what happens to you, but what happens inside you as a result of what happens to you. It can be passed to future generations."

And with that in mind, this book's main theme is that of trauma, of familial and generational trauma, and for me, it was painful to write. In so many ways.

It wasn't like the book, *The Rainbow*, when I was writing about my family, my grandfather and his trauma and grief. When I did that, I was writing *about it*. I wasn't writing *with it*.

The idea for this book came from my own family history, a very personal one, that of addiction, that of dealing with trauma and loss that weaves itself through each generation, manifesting in different ways. I wanted to try to understand my grandfather again, then his fathering of my father, and again my father's parenting of me and my brother. That was my goal. To try to see what trauma can do through generations. It does not stop. It does not ease.

When I began this book, my father was alive. As I end this book, he has sadly passed away.

That's where the pain came in. At first, I was writing about grief, imagining it, trying to replicate it as I saw it thread itself into my family (addiction is a trait). And I thought I was doing a good job of it. I thought, naively, that I knew what I was talking about.

Then, one Wednesday morning in March, came a knock on my door. The police stood there and told me that Dad had died. At sixty-six. Unexpectedly.

I remember standing there at 4.30 a.m., my dogs wondering what on earth was going on, me in pajamas, wondering what the police were on about. My dad couldn't be dead, could he? I actually asked them if I was dreaming. It was all so surreal.

The weeks that passed were consumed with the admin of death, and soon, I had to get back to writing this book. Yet, this time, I was no longer writing about grief; I was now writing *with* it.

It was painful. Not only to write about Clara and her loss, about Adam and his, but all the characters held within. Each of them had lost something, and each of them had a story to tell. And I found that my narrative changed. I had to include as many stories of loss. I had to make myself understand Marcin, his loss, his guilt, his fallibility, and his shame. I had to try to ask my readers for some understanding, some care, some love, some sort of humanity in this story.

As I wrote this, the world has gone mad. There is genocide. There's starvation, war, political nonsense, hatred, pointing the finger, blaming the other. But surely, we need to grasp that we are all the "other." Not one of us is the same; we all have our insecurities, our secrets, our guilt. We are all human.

That's, I suppose, what I want to say in this book. There

were orphans of war. There were those who felt guilt and shame. There were those who had suffered the effects of their parents' trauma. There was so much to unravel that I have tried my best to do it, in among feeling and writing with grief, and in among wondering if I could ever possibly do it justice.

I hope too that Marcin's experience as a homosexual man in Poland adds another layer to the narrative. While my novel primarily centers on the lives of these orphans (all based on real stories of orphans in ghettos, in hiding and thrown to safety from trains), Marcin's story emphasizes the multifaceted persecution faced by marginalized groups during this time. Many homosexuals were imprisoned or sent to concentration camps in a brutal campaign against anyone deemed "different." Marcin's journey of self-discovery and acceptance unfolds against the harsh realities of a society that struggled to understand him, echoing the lives of countless individuals who fought to be true to themselves amid growing hatred and discrimination.

As these characters navigate their respective challenges, I hope to impart a deeper understanding of the resilience that blossoms even in the darkest times. The stories of Sara, Agata, Clara, and Anna, alongside Marcin, illustrate the enduring power of hope, connection, and the human spirit's ability to persevere despite the overwhelming weight of loss and fear.

Thank you for joining me on this journey through the lives of these characters. Their stories serve as a reminder of the past, evoking empathy, reflection, and the urgent need to honor the lessons learned from history.

# ACKNOWLEDGMENTS

I'd like to thank my wonderful agent, Jo Bell, and just as equally wonderful editor, Isobel Akenhead. They have both been so supportive and patient with me on the writing of this novel and I am truly grateful to them.

I want, too, to acknowledge my father here. To say that I would not be who I am, warts and all, without him. And I hope I have done him proud.

# BIBLIOGRAPHY

Anderson, Mark, *The Forgotten Holocaust: The Destruction of Polish Jewry During World War II* (New York: HarperCollins, 1992)

Berenbaum, Michael, *The World Must Know: The History of the Holocaust as Told in the United States Holocaust Memorial Museum* (Boston: Little, Brown and Company, 1993)

Braham, Randolph L, *The Politics of Genocide: The Holocaust in Hungary* (Detroit: Wayne State University Press, 1994)

Feldblum, Vadim, *Orphans of the Holocaust: A Study of Jewish Orphanages in Post-World War II Europe* (Jerusalem: Hebrew University Press, 2000)

Friedman, Philip, *Their Brothers' Keepers: The Jewish Orphanages of Europe During the Holocaust* (New York: Yeshiva University Press, 1989)

Karsai, László, "The Hungarian Resistance and the Rescue of Jews in Budapest" *Journal of Hungarian Studies*, vol. 25, no. 1, 2021, pp. 67–89

Meyer, Jean, *The Jews of Hungary: History, Culture, and Society*, tr. Judith R. Dym (New York: Columbia University Press, 1994)

Stolberg, Katherine, "The Children of the Holocaust: A New Perspective" *History Today*, vol. 67, no. 4, April 2017, pp. 36–41

Woods, David, *Resistance and Complicity: The Holocaust in Hungary* (Cambridge: Cambridge University Press, 2015)

"Historical Background: The Jews of Hungary During the Holocaust", https://www.yadvashem.org/articles/general/jews-of-hungary-during-the-holocaust.html

"Jews Who Saved Jews in Hungary During the Holocaust", https://www.yadvashem.org/exhibitions/human-spirit-during-the-holocaust/jews-who-saved-jews/hungary.html

"The Legend of the Lodz Ghetto Children", https://www.yadvashem.org/articles/general/the-legend-of-the-lodz-ghetto-children.html

"The Race Against the Clock: Rescue by Jews in Budapest", https://www.yadvashem.org/blog/the-race-against-the-clock.html

Zsuzsanna, G., *Budapest's Orphanages During the Holocaust: A Historical Perspective* (Budapest: Central European University Press, 2008)

# ABOUT THE AUTHOR

**Carly Schabowski** is a lecturer and the USA Today bestselling author of historical fiction, including *The Rainbow*, with translations in over ten countries. She is a former journalist, and is currently an associate lecturer at Oxford Brookes University, where she completed both her MA and PhD.

Download your exclusive bonus content from Carly Schabowski here:

Follow Carly Schabowski on social media:

facebook.com/carly.schabowski

instagram.com/carlyschabowskiauthor

## ALSO BY CARLY SCHABOWSKI

The Girl with the Red Ribbon

The Last Orphan

# Letters from
## *the past*

Discover page-turning
historical novels from
your favourite authors
and be transported
back in time

*Join our book club
Facebook group*

https://bit.ly/SixpenceGroup

*Sign up to our
newsletter*

https://bit.ly/LettersFrom
PastNews

# Boldw∞d

Boldwood Books is an award-winning fiction
publishing company seeking out the best
stories from around the world.

**Find out more at www.boldwoodbooks.com**

Join our reader community for brilliant books,
competitions and offers!

**Follow us
@BoldwoodBooks
@TheBoldBookClub**

**Sign up to our weekly
deals newsletter**

https://bit.ly/BoldwoodBNewsletter